THE WAITING GAME

Pat Mo~~~~~~

A Quill Publishing Book

Published by Quill Publishing in 2008
www.quillpublishing.co.uk

ISBN 978-0-9545914-5-8

08112008-2

Photography by Dominique Shaw of York Place Studios
www.yorkplacestudios.co.uk

First published in 2008 in the United Kingdom by
Quill Publishing
The Haven
Eskdaleside,
Grosmont,
Whitby, North Yorkshire YO22 5PS.

Also by Pat Monteath

Who Pays the Ferryman?
Operation Orpheus
Codename Beggarman
The Waiting Game

Beware! The man who makes
powerful friends makes powerful
enemies.

Pat Monteath

A contender for 'book at
bedtime'?!
Love from
Sarah
xx

Acknowledgements

This would not have been possible without the unwavering support of Anne who has had to put up with my many late nights and lack of time spent with her and has for many years been my critic and inspiration.

The Prologue

Sir James Johnstone opened the door of the exclusive Civil Service Club in Knightsbridge, removed his leather gloves, took off his Savile Row overcoat and white silk scarf, handed them to Jones the club steward to place in the cloakroom and made his way into the lounge. The lounge was expensively furnished with button leather upholstered chairs and top of the range carpet. Off from the lounge was the club dining room for members to entertain their guests to luncheon. Over by the open fire sat an old friend of Sir James, a retired Brigadier and great friend of the Prime Minister.

"Hello James, and what do you make of this carry on out in the Canary Islands?"

"Which carry on are you referring to in particular?"

"This one." He jabbed his finger at the headlines in the morning paper that led with 'Hirst-Bergan dies at sea. Did he fall…Did he jump? Media tycoon in yacht tragedy'. "What do you reckon, what do you think happened?"

"He was removed. He was pushed," Sir James answered in a matter-of-fact way.

"By whom?" queried the Brigadier. "Was it by us, the Americans or the Russians? Who did it James?"

"Ahh I see, let me tell you exactly what happened and why. The story really starts back in Moscow some years ago…"

The Brigadier settled back into his chair and listened intently as his friend recounted what he knew lay behind the mysterious death of Hirst-Bergan media mogul, whose body had been discovered on the 5th November 1991 floating in the Atlantic Ocean.

Chapter 1

The attractive young woman glanced up from the book she was reading "I'm sorry…"

"Do you mind if I join you?"

She smiled casually and nodded. "Err, no. I mean… of course not, please do." She smiled again and signalled to him to sit down. She looked about the café and made a mental note that there were a few empty tables scattered here and there and wondered why he had chosen to ask to sit with her.

Yes you look just like your photograph, in fact very attractive indeed. He smiled as he sat down opposite her. *Your name is Svetlana Zaslavsky and you are of Jewish parents.* He recalled the notes that he had committed to memory from her father's file. *Yes Svetlana I know all about you. The bureau was right about one thing, your beauty, but I wonder if you are ready to join us?* His thoughts were rudely interrupted by the arrival of the waitress with the coffee he had ordered. He gave a slight cough as if to clear his throat. "Excuse me, but do you mind if I smoke?" he addressed the blonde girl sitting opposite. She glanced up from her book and gave a slight shake of the head. "No not really," she said.

"Do you smoke?"

Once more she again looked up from her reading irritated by this new interruption. "No thank you," she replied curtly. Even if he had noticed the note of exasperation in her voice, he chose to ignore it.

"It's Svetlana isn't it?" Although it was a question, his tone was soft and unchallenging. At the sound of her name a puzzled look crossed her face, and she once again looked up, closed the book she had been reading and placed it on the table in front of her.

"Yes, but…but how do you know? Do I …I mean should I know you?" she asked somewhat taken aback. He smiled at her and she was immediately on her guard. Who was he, this mild-mannered stranger and how did he know her name? *Suddenly it was 1960 and she was a very frightened ten year old girl. Screaming and sobbing as she saw her father clubbed and kicked to the ground by a gang of thugs. People were oblivious to her mother's screams as one of them grabbed hold of her, threw her to the ground and proceeded to tear open her blouse exposing the whiteness of her breasts. He pushed up her skirt and forced himself between her thighs and in minutes had overpowered her.*

On that day she avowed vengeance for her mother's savage rape and her father's brutal attack. Every detail of that evening and especially the face of the perpetrator would remain with her until her dying day. She was determined to find those involved and even the score.

"I believe you and I may have a mutual interest..." she heard him say.

"In what way?" she enquired feeling somewhat uneasy. *But what could happen to me here?* "I mean, I don't know you so how can we have a mutual interest? Who are you?" she asked, but the question went unanswered as he continued with his gentle probing.

"This man," he said indicating the picture he dropped on the table in front of her, "I want you to take a good look and tell me whether or not you have you seen him before?" Svetlana picked up the picture and studied it closely. The face staring back at her was that of a man in his late fifties.

It looks like him! He's older, but I'm sure it's him. The same half-closed eyes. The black curly hair although it's receding. Yes I'm sure it's him! But be careful, play it cool as you don't know this person opposite.

"I'm not sure, why do you ask? Anyway who are you?" She repeated her earlier question, her anxiety at his interest showed. Instinctively she took hold of her bag pulling it tightly

2

to her in case he made a grab for it. She threw the stranger a quick glance as she went to get up. In a flash he grabbed her hand.

"OK, my name is Mikhail and I know your father. Please listen to me." His eyes stared at her imploring her to stay and not to run. *If only I could convince you Svetlana that I am on your side.* She paused just long enough for him to sense that she might just stay. "Please Svetlana, I mean you no harm. Now come, sit down. I promise I can help you." Gradually he felt the tension in her subside and she slowly sat back down.

"OK, you say you know my papa, how?"

"He used to work with me…no I used to work for him. Actually he trained me at my job." He paused and took a long draw on his cigarette, his eyes watching her for the slightest reaction. Slowly he released his grip on her hand and for a moment they both sat in silence.

Funny that papa never mentioned about working with anyone. Come to think of it, he never said much about his work or where he worked.

It was Svetlana who spoke first.

"So did he work in the city right here in Moscow?" she asked.

"Sometimes he worked here but he also worked in other places."

*So papa what **did** you do?*

Svetlana suddenly realised how little she really knew about her father. It had taken this chance meeting with a stranger to arouse her curiosity and now she wanted to know more. "So what did he actually do?" she asked the quiet-mannered stranger sitting opposite her, but the stranger, not too sure how to answer, remained silent. Svetlana shook her head. "So Mikhail, or should I say Mr… whatever your name is…"

"Trepashkin, My name is Mikhail Trepashkin…"

"So Mr Trepashkin, give me one good reason, just one good reason, as to why we should continue with this…this…farce. Either you know my papa or you don't. Now if you know him, and you did say you worked with him, then tell me what he did?" Her frustration at not getting any real answers began to show, "and another thing, why do you think I would know him?" she said angrily stabbing her finger at the picture on the table in front of her.

"Look Miss Zaslavsky," he said in a calm matter of fact way, "Svetlana Zaslavsky, I know an awful lot about you. I know what happened over ten years ago. I know about your father's beating and your mother's rape so trust me. Let me help you." This last statement about her father being beaten and her mother being raped shocked Svetlana.

How do you know about my papa being beaten and the ordeal my mamma suffered?

"Please Mr Trepashkin," her voice a mere whisper, "just tell me what you want."

"Look Svetlana, I am on your side. I need your help as much as you need mine. I can't say too much here…" He gave a cursory look about him to check who was listening and watching, then he leaned forward and in a low voice said, "your father worked for the state and was highly thought of…" He beckoned to her to lean forward towards him and in a low whisper so that only she should hear he said, "he was a KGB man." Svetlana was taken aback by this latest piece of information.

How come my mamma didn't know this and I didn't know this?

"Are you also a KGB man?" she asked in a low whisper. Mikhail gave a slight nod of the head. "Bah, how do I know that what you are telling me is the truth and not something you've just made up on the spur of the moment?"

"Unfortunately," he whispered, "you will have to take my word for it unless you wish me to get you arrested." The very thought of being arrested by the Secret Police and being dragged off by the KGB was enough to put the fear of God into anyone and Svetlana was no different. "Is that what you want?" She shook her head.

"Definitely not," Svetlana answered in a whisper, "but I still need some sort of proof." Mikhail thought about how else he could prove it to her, then a thought struck him, *of course, why didn't I think of it before, her father, yes that was it, get her to ask her father.*

"Listen, I've got an idea and I hope it works. Go from here and ask your father, tell him you met Mikhail Trepashkin today and ask him if he remembers me?" Again Mikhail looked around the café just to make sure no-one was close enough to hear the next thing he was about to say. Having reassured himself that it was safe to speak he beckoned her to lean closer. Svetlana did as she was asked, and cupping his hands to her proffered ear he whispered a codename to her.

"Will my papa know that?"

"Yes, he should definitely remember that. It was used by Yevgeni who your father trained with. Then a lot later he trained me and my codename was..." He leaned forward and whispered ARDOV. "So there you are. You now have a means by which to check my credentials. Hurry now, go home and check all you will and we will meet here at the same time tomorrow."

"But..."

"No buts, go and don't look back." Svetlana frowned then nodded her head.

"Bye, and..."

"Go..." She smiled at the quietly spoken Trepashkin, and once again collected her belongings and headed for the door.

The statue of Felix Dzerzhinsky, the founder of the KGB, stood in the square outside the imposing yellow stone nine storey building in Central Moscow. The KGB's headquarters was known as Lubyanka because of the name of the pre-revolutionary street on which it stood. Just after 4 pm Svetlana Zaslavsky, a blonde, green-eyed Russian Jew, accompanied by a young fair haired Mikhail Trepashkin, entered through the doors of Lubyanka into the inner sanctum of the KGB. Once inside Svetlana was immediately overcome by awe at the magnificent marble and granite surroundings. The parquet floors were buffed to a rich, golden brown, with spotless long red runners; the elevators ran silently and smoothly as they whispered up and down in an endless dance from ground floor to the top and back again. On entering Lubyanka Svetlana felt as if she was standing at the very seat of Russia's power. To offset this awesome opulence Lubyanka hides a murky past; for beneath the spotless red runners, the granite and marble facades and the highly polished parquet flooring is a labyrinth of cells and torture chambers where many prisoners of the Stalinist era had been tortured and scores had perished, but this dark secret was unknown to Svetlana on her first visit.

"Come Svetlana, we take the elevator to my office and I will explain." With that they entered one of the whispering elevators which whisked them silently up to where Mikhail worked in the recruitment section. It was here that she first met the man who was to become not only the head of the KGB, but in future years one of the most powerful leaders in Eastern Europe, Yuri Andropov.

Again Mikhail showed her the photograph of the man that he had shown her in the café yesterday, only this time he offered her more in the way of information. The man in question was a very powerful and wealthy businessman; a man not unknown in the 'old school'. But times were changing and whereas before he had been a great friend of the 'old school' he had since fallen out of favour. He was an arms dealer and had contacts in the West. His crime was that he had upset 'certain seniors within the inner sanctum', so he needed to be brought to task. It was now up to Mikhail Trepashkin to try and recruit the beautiful Svetlana into the KGB with a view to her being the bait to lure this man home.

"So Svetlana do you now recognise the man?"

"I'm not sure." She was still not fully trusting of Mikhail's motives even though her father had vouched for him and what is more she was still unsure of what he really wanted.

"Maybe this will help your memory." With that he pushed a manila folder across the desk to Svetlana, inside which she found photographs of her father as well as detailed reports written and signed by him. There were also a number of photographs of her mother on her own and with her father. There was even one of them both sitting with another woman in Karlovy Vary, in Czechoslovakia. She was referred to as a friend of the family. She had fond memories of the trip to Karlovy Vary, but she did not remember or recognise the woman in the photograph. Then to her horror she saw pictures of herself taken over a number of years and culminating in a series of photographs taken right here in Moscow as recently as the day before yesterday, as she walked along Volkhonka Street near the Pushkin Museum.

"What are these doing here?" she asked pointing at her photographs in the manila folder.

"You must understand, because your father was a senior official here, we have to keep a comprehensive file on the whole family and his contacts. It is for the family's own security."

I don't believe you!

"But why have you been taking photographs of me especially as my papa is now an old man and no longer works for the KGB's state department" She was annoyed at this latest infringement of her privacy and wondered what other information they had on her.

"We have kept the file up to date. I promise there is nothing sinister going on, it's just that…we hoped that…that is… the bureau hoped that the daughter of such an eminent KGB official would consider following in her father's footsteps. That's all." Svetlana looked back at the photographs and the documents laid out on the desk before her.

So this explains a lot of things, she thought to herself, *like the times when you went away on trips, the secret meetings and why you never talked about your work. All this time I thought you worked in the city, in an office. Well I suppose you did in a way. Damn you, damn you papa, why couldn't you trust me enough to tell me? All this time I thought you were like all my friends' fathers but you weren't. You were a spy, a KGB spy!*

She read and re-read the information. Trying hard to take it in, but all she could think of was that her father was a spy. Now it was obvious how Mikhail Trepashkin had recognised her, why he had spoken to her in the café and why he had asked if he may sit at her table when there were others free. Suddenly it all made sense, except for one minor thing. "Why are you interested in this man, why do you insist that I should know him?" She pointed to the photograph of the curly haired fifty year old man that Trepashkin had asked her about.

"Because he has attacked one of our people…"

"I don't believe you Mikhail…"

"It's true, he has attacked one of our people and we want to bring him to justice," he added lamely.

"Who is he? your department must know him," she said as she picked up the photograph of her mother's attacker and stared at the face again.

Be truthful Mikhail and then I'll try to help.

"OK Svetlana, his codename is Oleg. He is a mole, buried deep within the Bulgarian KGB. He is a very powerful and shrewd individual with animal-like cunning who, up until now, has successfully covered his tracks. All we have to go on is a name - Mike Weatherall, possibly American and a CIA operator, so now you know the scale of it. We need Oleg and you need Oleg. You want Oleg because you know that it was him who beat your father and raped your mother." A heavy silence descended over the two of them. Mikhail took out a NETPI (Peter 1) cigarette and lit it and watched as the blue smoke curled its way upwards towards the ceiling, whilst Svetlana wrestled with, and thought about, the information she had just been made privy to. Mikhail took a long draw on his cigarette and exhaled, blowing the smoke towards the ceiling. Then he decided to drop another little bombshell.

"Svetlana," he paused, she looked up from the desk with a dazed look in her eyes, "Svetlana, I need to ask you this. First of all we need your help…we would value your help…"

"Mik…" she started to interrupt, but he was having none of it.

"No, please listen to me. It is a serious question I need to ask and I ask it on behalf of our fatherland, (my country and yours) Russia. Svetlana Zaslavsky," he looked deadly serious as he spoke, "are you willing to join the bureau, or to put it another way, when will you join us?" Svetlana was rocked by his proposal and her voice faltered as she replied. "You…you are asking me to join the KGB. I don't understand…why me?"

"Because I was honoured to work with your father and I think his daughter would make a really good…no, I mean, a top flight KGB Officer. I can see you rising through the ranks in the bureau up to Director level in a very short time. Think how proud your father would be to see his beautiful daughter as a top KGB Officer. How proud your mother will be when she knows it was her daughter who brought Oleg home to face justice. If you cannot do it for yourself, then at least think of your parents and your country. Also remember this, Oleg knows you and he knows that you were a witness to his deeds so at any time he could come looking for you and your aged parents, so think carefully about that and at least consider my proposal." Svetlana was now on the horns of a dilemma, torn between joining the KGB and tracking this Oleg down, or doing nothing and yet risking everything. Either way she could die!

What do I do? If I say no to the KGB then this, this Oleg, as he is known, may kill me, or may well trace my parents through me and kill them. They don't deserve that. My papa is no longer a young man and no longer can he defend himself against such odds. I know what I have to do.

"So if I agree to join the bureau then what?"

"Well, first of all you will meet my boss, Yuri Andropov. Then subject to his agreement you will be sent to the KGB nine-month school just outside the city."

"And what will they teach me?"

"Many different things, such as psychology, instruction in the latest spy technology, whether it be long-range listening devices, miniature cameras, or sophisticated transmitters. You'll be taught about recent advances in coding and decoding; all this and more besides. You'll analyze the CIA operations, MI6 and other spy organisations, see how we at the KGB can improve. So on and so forth, so are you interested? Not only will you get revenge by tracking down Oleg," *now, I'll play the patriotic card and that may just push her in the right direction,* "but you'll also be working for your fatherland."

Svetlana thought long and hard about Mikhail's proposition before making her decision. She again read through the documents; again she looked at all the pictures taken of both her and her parents. She looked straight into Mikhail's eyes and now for the first time she felt he was telling the truth. She knew he was hiding nothing and slowly she nodded her head, "OK I will do it."

Chapter 2

Jan Andrej Berkowitz was an orphaned Czech refugee, but his lifestyle today was completely different from those humble beginnings. Born of Jewish parents, he had escaped the German invasion and arrived in Britain at the tender age of five. In March 1945, he received the disturbing news that his mother and his sister had been executed as 'hostages' by the Nazis. Unlike many ten year olds who would undoubtedly have been beside themselves upon receiving such devastating news, young Berkowitz put on a brave face and vowed to himself that whatever else happened he would make something of himself. *Mamma, for you and my sister, I take this vow. I will succeed, I will make you proud of me and I will always remember you and you will always be in my heart.*

Although he has changed his name to Andrew Hirst-Bergan, and his lifestyle is now a far cry from those shaky beginnings, he still holds dear the vow he made to himself as that orphaned ten year old.

Outside the comfort of Hirst-Bergan's office, the weather had deteriorated to a grey, wet and dismal day. The weather summed up the mood of Hirst-Bergan as he talked to one of his merchant bankers on the telephone.

"But of course there's no problem. I just need to, how shall I put it, redistribute some of the capital…Umm for business reasons…of course John, I understand exactly where you are coming from but you must also appreciate my position in this matter." *Idiot,* he thought to himself as he flipped open the lid of his cigar case and took out a half-corona. "As I said John, I need thirty million transferred across to my account in Tel Aviv…yes of course I'll hold." *Damn fool, just get on with it.* He heaved a sigh of exasperation and started to drum on the desk with his free hand. Hirst-Bergan stopped drumming on the desk, took a long draw on his cigar and then proceeded to amuse himself by blowing smoke rings. He watched each of the smoke rings increase in diameter as they slowly spiralled upwards towards the ceiling to eventually disappear into a thickening blue haze above his desk. Suddenly the phone clicked and he was pulled back to reality. "Yes…oh that's all right, will that be done today?" he asked the person at the other end. "You say it definitely will, so when can I expect the funds to be there? Next week! No, that's no good." *Dimwit! Idiot!* "Then telegraph them through," he added in exasperation. "Thank you and goodbye." He slammed down the phone in frustration. *Fool, so why couldn't you have done that straightaway?* "Why do I have to put up with such fools?" he muttered to himself as he looked across his desk to Ian his son.

Ian looked just like his father only thirty years younger and a lot slimmer. He had inherited his father's looks and his nose for business, but was far less aggressive in his dealings with others. That was not to say he was weak or a soft touch; far from it. He was far more diplomatic and less brusque than the old man; more like his mother in temperament and personality, all in all a shrewd businessman.

"This is the plan," announced Hirst-Bergan to his son, "once the money is in place in the Israeli account then we'll arrange to get our friends in Israel to start buying shares in the publishing arm. If I'm right we should then be able to prove to our American friend what a good deal he is getting, especially when he sees my figures on the reference books side."

"But what if he smells a rat?"

"Don't worry he won't, well not when I've finished."

"So do you think he will buy?"

"Of course he will. Don't you worry son. By the time I've finished, he'll be snatching our hands off."

Hirst-Bergan's idea was to inflate the value of the reference book side of the publishing business by using his friends in

Israel and the family companies to carry out a number of transactions. Once the money was in place he had a variety of tools at his disposal, and a number of deals between his family companies and the publishing business were, through creative accounting, not disclosed. Of course all of this was highly irregular and served no purpose other than to embellish the value of the reference book side of his publishing business indicating on paper that the business was worth a lot more than it actually was. In theory this should have worked, but he had met his match.

Although at first he managed to fool his American counterpart, and negotiations lasted for several months, Hirst-Bergan overplayed his hand. His buyer began to suspect all was not as it should be and withdrew his offer so the deal collapsed. Hirst-Bergan was caught out and ultimately faced court proceedings in the USA. He had to avoid a court battle at all cost otherwise his reputation in the business world would be damaged beyond repair, and he already had his sights set on bigger fish. In the end with a bit of shrewd negotiation and fast talking he managed to stave off the court proceedings by agreeing to pay damages of around 4.3 million pounds. Having managed to extricate himself from, what could have been a major disaster in his eyes, Hirst-Bergan decided to take a well-earned break in Tunisia.

Chapter 3

Port El Kantaoui on the Tunisian coast is a chic, purpose built resort with a modern marina accommodating in excess of three hundred vessels, the majority of their owners being millionaires. With its complex of hotels on cobblestone streets – a perfect reproduction of a typical medieval medina - and its excellent restaurants, it made an ideal stopping off place for jet-setters and high-flying business tycoons who wished to take a nice relaxing break away from the cut and thrust of everyday politics, and high powered business. Yes, Tunisia had a lot to offer and Andrew Hirst-Bergan was no stranger to its shores.

He had first visited Tunisia as early as 1966 and whilst staying in one of the top hotels in Tunis he found out that an old business acquaintance, Mike Weatherall whom he had previously met whilst in America, was also staying in the same hotel. Mike, a quietly spoken American from Cranford New Jersey, had helped him enormously in one of his earlier acquisitions and introduced him to a number of influential contacts, so it was not unusual for Andrew to arrange to meet up with him. That evening he made his way to the hotel bar to renew his acquaintance with Mike and to talk to him about a new venture that he had recently acquired and at 7:30, dead on the dot, Mike Weatherall appeared, accompanied by another man. It was the same old Mike, nothing had changed, well maybe his hair was thinning a little but basically he was the same as ever.

"Hello Andrew, how are you doing?" he said as he pumped Andrew's arm up and down. "It's been a long time."

"I know, how are you keeping?"

"Good and how's business?"

"Doing well and you, what are you doing now?"

"You know, this and that nothing very special."

"Who's your friend?" Andrew asked nodding in the direction of the man hovering in the background. Mike glanced casually at the stranger.

"Kim, come and meet my very good friend Andrew Hirst-Bergan." The stranger, a short stocky man with dark curly hair and a swarthy complexion stepped forward. "Andrew this is Kim Kristoff a business associate of mine. Kim, this is Andrew Hirst-Bergan a very good friend of mine who I've known for quite some time now."

"Pleased to meet you Kim, where are you from?"

"Pleased to make your acquaintance Andrew. Mike was telling me about your business interests. Scientific and electronics I believe. Is that correct?"

Huh, so you think I didn't notice that you avoided my question. So why the big secret, have you something to hide? One thing is for sure, you're not from Western Europe. In fact I wouldn't mind betting you are not a million miles from my homeland Mr Kristoff.

"Sorry Kim. Did you say you were interested in scientific and electronic products?"

"Could be, my firm is always interested in new and innovative products, especially leading-edge technology..." Mike cut him short.

"Hey guys, come on let's grab a chair and get a drink, how about over there?" Mike pointed to a table tucked away in a corner close to the swimming pool. "Walls have ears you know so don't be giving any trade secrets away!" he said giving Andrew an exaggerated wink as he set off through the patio doors towards the table he had just indicated. It only took a moment or two for the three men to reach the table, but it was far enough from the main lounge to afford them an element of privacy. "Right guys now we are settled what can I get everyone, beers all round?" The general consensus was that cold beers were the order of the day. "Good." He beckoned to a waiter as he emerged from the lounge onto the patio not far from where they were sitting and ordered three ice cold beers.

"So Kim what's this about your firm always being interested in leading-edge technology?" Andrew asked in his usual brusque manner.

"Oh, we look at all types of interesting things, from sophisticated electronics to scientific instruments, so we may well be in the market for some of your products."

Hmm, I wonder who you work for Mr Kristoff.

"I see... have you got a card and I'll make an appointment to come and see you?" Kristoff immediately produced a business card and passed it to Hirst-Bergan. He gave it a cursory look and raised a quizzical eye, "Armament Dealers and Brokers! What have guns got to do with electronics Mr Kristoff?"

"As I said, we deal in everything and I certainly think it would be in our mutual interest if we did meet up again. Perhaps we could meet before you leave Tunisia?"

Then we can really get down to business can't we Jan Andrej Berkowitz.

"I'm sorry but that's going to be really difficult this trip."

What I really mean is that I need to find out a little more about you Mr Kristoff before we meet again, after all I may be interested in your company, but only if it serves my purpose and only when I know who I'm dealing with!

"I know it's really short notice but are you sure you can't fit it in this trip?"

Hirst-Bergan grimaced. "Sorry but you know how it is, meetings and things. I really am on a tight schedule this trip. I know it's a pain, but can I give you a call next week when I'm back in London?" he asked.

"Well..." Kim said hesitantly.

That's good at least it will give me time to advise the head of Scientific and Technical KGB Directorate T and to bring in my head of Section.

"Of course you can," Kristoff agreed.

Of course Andrew Hirst-Bergan, being of shrewd mind and an entrepreneur to boot, had only one thing to do on his return to London and that was to use his network of contacts, including those faceless ones in Israel, to ascertain exactly who this man Kristoff really was and above all else, what exactly was his business. After making a number of telephone calls, it soon became apparent that his gut feeling about the man Kristoff had been correct. He was no more Western European than Hirst-Bergan was himself. In fact from what he had managed to ascertain from his friends in Israel Kristoff had close connections with Russia. As Andrew pondered over the Kristoff enigma the red telephone on his desk rang.

"Hello Hirst-Bergan speaking..." a Jewish voice at the other end spoke rapidly. "What!" Andrew's tone sounded incredulous at what he was hearing. "Are you saying that Kristoff isn't his real name but a cover name...yes, yes of course...I understand....Thank you and one day I will return the favour. Shalom.

Thank you my friend, I thought as much.

He replaced the handset and for a moment or two he reflected on what his Israeli contact had just told him.

*So Mr Kristoff, you work for the KGB. Now **that** is very interesting indeed.*

A myriad of thoughts tumbled through his head, as he once more went over the brief meeting in the hotel in Tunis.

Hmm, I may just take you up on your offer of a meeting.

The telephone call he had just taken from his friends in Mossad gave him an idea and armed with this latest information Hirst-Bergan knew exactly what to do.

"Excusee, excusee Mr Hirst-Bergan…" the Tunisian waiter hovered tentatively but Hirst-Bergan just stared at the thin line of blue smoke as it curled upwards from his unfinished half corona cigar. "Excusee Mr Hirst-Bergan…" once more the waiter tried to get his attention.

Damn it what do you want man?
Hirst-Bergan struggled as he tried to get his champagne-soaked thoughts back to his present situation in Port El Kantaoui.

Ah, I know I'll get another bottle of champagne that should keep the little swine happy.

"More champagne, bring another bottle and another glass…"

"Pleeese Mr Hirst-Bergan, no champagne."

"Well what do you want then?" Hirst-Bergan answered, slurring his words as he did.

"Pleeese Mr Hirst-Bergan it eez the telephone. You have a call from your office in London." Immediately he became alert. His head, although befuddled by champagne, cleared and his brain went into overdrive.

Now what the hell? They know I'm away damn them, damn them all.

"I'm sorry Mr Hirst-Bergan to disturb you but they say it eez important…I try to put them off…but they insist on talking to you…"

"OK, OK." Hirst-Bergan's manner was abrupt to the point of being rude. "Where's the phone?" he asked, irritated by the Tunisian's interruption.

"Pleeese to follow me." With that the man led Andrew across the dining room and into a small office. "Pleeese, you sit at desk. Give me two minute I will transfer call from my phone to you. Pleeese and thank you Mr Hirst-Bergan."
With that he disappeared back out through the office door as Andrew picked up the phone and waited to be put through.

"Hello, hello." It was Ian on the line.

"Hello Ian. I told you not to call me. Don't you ever listen….I'm here taking a complete break and once again…"

"Dad, listen…"

"No. You listen to me," Hirst-Bergan responded brusquely. "I left explicit instructions that I was not to be disturbed unless it was a matter of life and death, so why have you ignored my instructions? Well, come on then, I'm waiting…" he said raising his voice, the annoyance at having been disturbed showing through. "Well speak. Is it a matter that couldn't wait, or one that you couldn't deal with eh… tell me then is it?"

"Dad listen, the DTI are in…"

"So deal with it. Deal with it, damn you why do I have to do everything?"

"But dad you're not listening…"

"How dare you…"

"Dad listen I said the DTI are in. We are under investigation by the DTI. This is bad…I mean BAD." Hirst-Bergan was silent for a moment or two, and then the penny dropped.

Shit, that's all I need. What's wrong with them? Come on Andrew think man think…what's the answer?

"Hello… hello…dad… dad, are you there?"

"Yes Ian, I'm still here," he answered in a quiet voice.

"Well what do you…no I mean…what should I do?" he asked in an agitated tone.

"Keep calm Ian and I'll think of something."

"Such as?" His stressed state came across in the tone of his voice.

"Look, calm down Ian. It will be all right trust me. Just leave it for now; I can't talk here so I'll call you from the yacht in a couple of hours time."

"OK. Speak to you soon." The phone clicked then went dead. Slowly the shock of what Ian had said sank in as Andrew replaced the handset. All trace of the champagne-induced euphoria melted away as he snatched up his jacket, tossed a handful of notes on the desk and rushed from the little office.

"Pleeese Mr Hirst-Bergan, the bill. Was everything OK?" the Tunisian waiter called after the figure of Hirst-Bergan as he headed towards the exit.

"Money on your desk should cover what I owe," he called back over his shoulder as he rushed from the restaurant and headed for his boat.

Chapter 4

Shortly after his return from Tunisia, the DTI formalised their report showing how he had, under the 'Takeover Code' used transactions between his private family companies and his publishing company to inflate the latter's share price. However, although the DTI Inspectors' report was a most damaging setback to Hirst-Bergan's plans, he had managed to escape prosecution. He now had to re-evaluate his current situation. He considered his options, and then it occurred to him. *Perhaps the answer to my prayers lies in Mr Kristoff and his contacts!* In all the flurry of possible court proceedings and the DTI investigation he had forgotten about the contact he had met on his trip to Tunis, the trip before that ill-fated visit to Port El Kantaoui. *Perhaps a call to my friends in Israel would be helpful at this stage,* he mused.

Of course since meeting Kristoff in Tunis, there had been a substantial revolution in the field of electronic communications. Satellite and microcircuit technology had changed the face of intelligence gathering. Computers were now much smaller and the emergence of fibre-optic technology meant that the gathering and correlation of data by far exceeded anything that had gone before. These factors were the building blocks used by the USA to develop a new system that enabled the user to electronically probe into the lives of people in such a way that had never been possible before. The new system - the Professional Organisation and Management Information System -showed promise and overnight it would revolutionize the fight against terrorism, the Drug Enforcement Agency's fight against the drug barons and, to the Central Intelligence Agency, it could be a weapon every bit as effective as a spy satellite. The project, developed by a small American company, became known by the acronym PROMIS.

It was a sunny day, one of those balmy afternoons when Israelis like to tell each other that this is why God chose their country as the Promised Land. In a drab nondescript high-rise office situated on the city's King Saul Boulevard in Tel Aviv, a telephone rang.

"Shalom, Uri speaking. Who is calling? Ah Andrew, just a minute I will put you through."

"Hello, is that Amir?" an English-sounding voice enquired.

"It is Amir. Who is calling?"

"Hello Amir, Andrew Hirst-Bergan here…"

Amir greeted Hirst-Bergan like a friend, no it was more like a long lost brother. "Shalom, Shalom Andrew. It is good to hear from you my friend, and how can I help?"

"I need to find out some information…"

"Yes, and about who or what?"

"A man call Kristoff. I was introduced to him by another contact from the USA. I know you have already told me he works for the KGB, no sorry, that he had connections with the KGB. I think the time has come for me to meet with him, but before I do, can you get more details about how well-connected he is and where he comes from?" The line went silent for a moment whilst Amir input the name into a computer terminal.

"OK, Kristoff is KGB and is also known by the name Kaluchin. He is Bulgarian and works closely with a man called Kryuchev. This man is very powerful in Bulgaria." There was a moment's silence. "Andrew I have been thinking…"

"What about Amir?"

"I have a proposition for you, which I think will be of great interest in our common cause. It will serve us both well…"

"In what way Amir?"

"Listen Andrew this…err…this project is a little delicate for us to discuss right now on the phone, perhaps you ought to arrange a flying visit to your interests out here in Israel. My brother, I need to meet with you to discuss certain things, so why not arrange to come out to Tel Aviv later this week?" Andrew thought about Amir's suggestion and very quickly realised that it wasn't so much a suggestion but more of a gentle command; besides he owed his brothers in Mossad a favour.

"All right Amir, I'll come but hold a moment while I check my appointments diary." Hirst-Bergan quickly flicked through his diary. He had only one appointment pencilled in and his son, Ian, could take care of that one. *If I can arrange for the jet to be made ready and a car to drop me at the airport first thing then I can be in Tel Aviv tomorrow.* "Amir, I should be with you tomorrow provided my jet is made ready in time," he paused then had second thoughts. "Damn it Amir, it will be ready and of course I'll be there."

"Let me know when you expect to arrive in Tel Aviv and I'll arrange for a car to pick you up."

"Of course, I'll put a call in to you as soon as we are airborne and give you an ETA."

"Very good. So we will speak tomorrow when I should have more information on Mr Kristoff or Kaluchin or any other name he uses, so until then Shalom."

"Until tomorrow Amir. Shalom and God be with you." *Huh, I wonder why he wants me over there,* but the more he tried to unravel the mystery the more intriguing it seemed.

Andrew Hirst-Bergan wiped his hand across his profusely sweating brow as he waited outside Tel Aviv airport terminal. His eyes, hidden by a pair of very expensive sun glasses, scrutinized every passing car and its occupants, hoping that in each instance it would be for him. *God, this heat is intolerable. I'm sweating like a pig here!* This analogy brought a faint smile to his lips. He pulled out a white 'kerchief and wiped the beads of sweat from his brow. *Come on Amir, where is this damn car, I'm melting here.* The question was immediately answered as a black Mercedes pulled into the kerb not twenty yards from where he stood. Before it had finally stopped the front passenger door swung open and its occupant alighted onto the pavement. The man was in his mid to late forties, slightly less than average height but of average build and he had a receding hairline. The man was none other than Amir himself an important official in Mossad. He walked quickly to where Andrew Hirst-Bergan was standing and with outstretched arms greeted the Englishman as his brother and equal.

"Shalom Andrew, Shalom." He placed a kiss on each cheek as a sign of greeting, and Hirst-Bergan did likewise. "Welcome to my land, our land, welcome to Israel. I am Amir we have spoken many times on the telephone and at last we now meet. Come on we go to your hotel." He immediately grabbed Hirst-Bergan's bags and set off toward the parked car with Andrew in close pursuit.

"So what's the hotel like?"

"The King David!" Amir said as he opened the boot of the car and put the bags in, "Don't tell me you have never heard of it?" But before Hirst-Bergan could answer Amir continued. "The King David is a big hotel, a top class hotel, right in the centre of our lovely city of Jerusalem." He slammed the boot lid shut. "Please Andrew, get in the car." Andrew slid into the back seat as Amir got into the front passenger seat and with a quiet thud they shut the doors. "We have a drive about forty or so minutes before we get there and then you will see it, you will marvel at its splendour and then we will dine." With a quick check in his rear view mirror the driver indicated and with a low purr the car pulled away from where they had been parked and headed along the terminal road to the exit where they would eventually join Highway 1, the main route to Jerusalem.

The King David hotel, a tall pink bricked hotel is set right in the heart of the city and is found on the David ha-Malekeh, not far from Gaozlan Garden. It is purported to be Israel's most famous and luxurious hotel used by many world leaders and celebrities and is a landmark in Jerusalem. The swimming pool is set in beautiful gardens and the hotel boasts having a Royal and a Presidential Suite along with a further thirty-two Special rooms and Suites, that's over and above the two hundred and thirty-seven ordinary guest rooms, so Amir was right when he said it was a big top class hotel.

Upon arriving at the King David hotel Amir made sure that his guest from England had everything he wanted. He then excused himself and withdrew to the hotel foyer whereupon he made a quick telephone call to none other than Uzi Goldstein, the Head of Mossad.

"Shalom Uzi, yes he is here. I have had the hotel put him in one of the Old City Rooms…in thirty minutes you say…no, I haven't mentioned anything about how he can help us, nor have I said anything about the project 'PROMIS'. I thought it better to wait until we are all together then we can discuss it in detail…yes Uzi, he has a number of companies throughout Europe and here…yes most of them are private businesses…yes there is one in particular AHB Computers…no its main products are software based that's why I thought we could use that as a vehicle, what do you think?" Amir listened carefully to what Uzi had to say on the subject. Thankfully from Amir's point of view, Uzi – the boss – agreed with him. "So you think you will be here within the hour…all right then we will meet you here in the lobby in an hour." Having made the necessary arrangements Amir then telephoned Hirst-Bergan's room and arranged for them to meet in the bar within the hour. He then made his way to one of the vacant leather chairs situated in a discreet corner, where he could have an uninterrupted view of reception and the lobby area without him being in full view of the world at large.

Uzi - a man of average build, oval face, with receding light brown hair - was wearing a white open-necked short sleeved shirt and a dark jacket when he took the lift to the basement car park in Hadar Davna Building, the Mossad HQ in King Saul Boulevard. He casually walked to his silver Mercedes parked nearby, unlocked the car, removed his jacket and tossed it onto the back seat before settling into the driving seat.

Outside on King Saul Boulevard not far from the car park exit was parked a black nondescript Ford car with its windows open and its male occupant leaning against the driver's door. The man, who appeared to be waiting for somebody was engrossed in a crossword puzzle, looked up as Uzi's silver Mercedes emerged from the basement car park and started up the ramp towards the Boulevard. Unhurriedly the observer carefully folded up the newspaper, opened the driver's door and settled into the driving seat. With a quick turn of the ignition key the car's engine along with the air conditioning leapt into life. As the silver Mercedes pulled out into King Saul Boulevard the black Ford eased out into the main stream of traffic and keeping a couple of cars back the driver followed Uzi at a leisurely pace. The driver of the Ford flicked a small switch on and spoke.

"Overlord, Charlie 1 over."

"Charlie 1 go ahead," the small vhf set crackled in reply.

"We are moving. Heading Highway 1. Over."

"Roger Charlie 1…Bravo 1… come in."

"Overlord this is Bravo 1 go ahead over…"

It wasn't long before the Silver Mercedes turned onto Highway 1 and headed towards Jerusalem and a couple of cars to the rear a black Ford did likewise. The traffic on Highway 1 was heavy as usual so speed was limited. Uzi glanced up at his rear view mirror and gave a slight smile. *Ah, just as I thought...I suppose you thought I hadn't seen you. Huh amateur!* Of course he had seen the black car tailing him, but what he hadn't noticed was the sleek white Mercedes sports sat behind the black Ford that all the time had been nothing more than a decoy.

As Uzi indicated to turn off Highway 1 into the centre of Jerusalem he noted that the black Ford did likewise. *Just as I thought, my faithful friend, you're still there.* Once again he gave a slight smile at the thought of the tail thinking he was unnoticed. Uzi had played this game many times before and he would not be where he was today if he didn't notice these little things. Unperturbed he continued on his way to meet Amir and Hirst-Bergan at the King David Hotel.

The journey had been uneventful save for his tail and had taken precisely fifty minutes to complete as he swung his car into the dropping off point at the hotel's front entrance. He retrieved his jacket and handed his key to the concierge for him to arrange car parking. He glanced toward the road and smiled inwardly as he saw his faithful tail drive slowly past the vehicular entrance. *Now what my friend?* he thought to himself as he swung his jacket over his shoulder and walked jauntily into the foyer.

The white Mercedes radio crackled into life, "Bravo 1, target entered hotel. Your bag over."

"Roger Charlie 1, see you back at embassy. Out." The driver of the white Mercedes parked close to the entrance to the King David Hotel and nonchalantly made his way to the entrance. He entered the main foyer just as Uzi and another man, whom he recognised as Amir, made their way towards the bar. *Now I wonder what those two are doing here.* He thought to himself as he followed at a discreet distance. As he entered the bar he was just in time to see Amir carrying a tray with three drinks over to a table at the far side of the room. He could see the back of Uzi, but a second chair was obscured from view by an ornate pillar that supported the ceiling. The third chair opposite Uzi was vacant. He observed Amir place the drinks on the table and hand one to somebody obscured from his line of vision, pass one to Uzi and take one himself and place it in front of the vacant seat whilst he returned the tray to the bar. It was obvious that Amir had arranged some form of meeting with a third party, but who was the third party?

"Shalom and what may I get you sir?" The barman addressed him in English.

"Oh I'm sorry. Shalom…I'll have a gin and tonic please." He looked around for somewhere to sit where he could keep a discreet eye on the Mossad party and hopefully learn what they were up to.

Just the place.

He had seen a table tucked away near the corner of the bar where he could sit partially concealed by one of the palms growing in a large plant pot and yet quite discreetly keep an eye on things. Unfortunately the third person was still out of view. *Damnation. Still they will have to move at sometime.* Peter Hinds, the MI6 observer attached to the Trade Commission of the British Embassy, was intrigued to know who the third man was, so he settled himself in the chair with his Gin and Tonic, prepared for a long wait. However he did not have to wait too long as the third person suddenly appeared from behind the pillar and made his way to the Gents. Not to let the opportunity slip by, Peter took a large mouthful of his drink before following his quarry at a discreet distance. He waited a moment or two before entering the toilet, checking that he had not been noticed then pushed open the door. He made his way over to the urinal noting that all the cubicles bar one were open and that apart from himself there was one other person at the urinal. *Was he the third man, or is it whoever is in the cubicle?*

At that moment his question was answered as he heard the flush of a toilet cistern and the click as the lock on the cubicle door was unlocked. He noted out of the corner of his eyes the large profile of the man as he emerged from what had been the locked cubicle. To his surprise he immediately recognised him as none other than the media tycoon Hirst-Bergan, who had been in the news regarding the DTI investigation.

Now what could you be doing out here in Jerusalem Mr Hirst-Bergan, are you the mystery guest of Mossad?
Peter waited patiently for him to finish drying his hands, before rinsing his under the tap. Without bothering to dry his own hands he departed from the toilets hot on the tail of Andrew Hirst-Bergan, following him back to the bar where he rejoined his two hosts Amir and Uzi. Hinds, although he was keen to find out more, knew that this meeting was too important not to report it back to his superiors, so without a moment's hesitation he decided to call it a day and headed back to his car and once there he would call in on the radio's secure link and report his findings.

"Did you have a good journey Andrew?" asked Uzi.

"Oh reasonable my friend, reasonable." He took a mouthful of his drink, turned to Amir and asked, "did you manage to find out more about Kristoff and his connections?"

"Of course we did, but first of all we have a proposition to make to you...Uzi, please you explain." Hirst-Bergan raised a quizzical eyebrow.

"Explain about what?" he asked.

"Well, it's like this Andrew...we have had a problem with certain brothers of ours...what I'm trying to say is that there are a number of Jews still living abroad who dearly need..."

"Not need Uzi, wish is perhaps nearer the mark," stated Amir smiling benignly as he interrupted his boss.

"Yes, yes Amir, you're right...wishing to come home to their promised land, but some Governments are blocking this right. Now we thought that with your companies and your help we could encourage and help our brethren."

"But how do you know where these Jews are?" asked Andrew.

"Ah, well we have developed a program, a software program which can track down misplaced persons."

"And where do I fit into all of this?"

"Well we thought your company AHB Computers could supply the hardware and the software. In fact we could even arrange additional funding from our sources to expand your business interests especially into the Eastern European countries. So would you be interested in such a business deal?" Andrew Hirst-Bergan didn't need too much time to think. All he needed to know was three things; how much investment, what was the software package and when would this start.

Uzi and Amir explained to Andrew about the project, how Mossad had originally *borrowed from America* the most important piece of software in the United States arsenal. How their software experts had since reconstructed the original package called PROMIS and inserted it into a device which enabled them to track the use that any purchaser made of it. How they, sitting in Israel, would know exactly what was going on inside any intelligence services that bought it.

"I'm not too sure that I follow you."

"In what way Andrew?" Uzi asked.

"Well, you have this, this piece of software which you say can track the use that any purchaser makes of it, so how does that help you?"

"First of all with the right person selling this we stand to make money from the sale and..."

"Yes I can see that, but I still don't really understand how, by knowing what use the purchaser makes of it, is this going to help Mossad?"

"Andrew, Andrew, Andrew," Uzi shook his head in disbelief. "I don't believe I'm hearing this. Let me explain once again. For example let's take our present situation with the PLO. Arafat was causing us big trouble even though we have been hitting him hard; he always seemed to be one jump ahead and he even had world sympathy on his side. Now with PROMIS we have reversed the trend...

"How?"

"Well we, or should I say another third party, sold it on our behalf to the Jordanian Military Intelligence and we found that they were collecting data on the Palestinians. Their Intelligence Service found out that the Palestinians were threatening the King; you know Hussein, as well as causing us problems. At the same time as they input their information – dates, time, places and contacts - on to their computers, we were able to share that same information with them."

"Without them knowing?"

"Of course. We had, through our American friends, been able to access their files just as if we were sitting in the same room sharing the same computer, as did our American friends the CIA."

"But what about the CIA, were they in on this?"

"Sort of, but not totally aware of everything."

"So how did you manage that?"

"You know Andrew that is not for you to worry about; the main thing is that the system works. Just imagine how useful such a system would be to the West if we could sell it to Eastern Europe and the Far East. First of all we would know exactly what was going on in Russia; we would be able to find out anything we wanted, whether it be in Russia, China or wherever, so what do you say Andrew, are you good enough to sell this to the Russians?"

I bet that's hit home, now let's see your reaction.

"Of course I am good enough!" Andrew replied angrily. Amir smiled at the instant reaction that Uzi's remark had achieved. "You do realize that I have many contacts the world over, don't you?" *Damn cheek. Who the hell do you think you're dealing with here?*

"Of course Andrew," Uzi calmly replied.

Ignoring Uzi, Andrew continued, his agitation becoming more apparent.

"In the UK alone I know a lot of people in the Government, after all I was a Member of Parliament and at one time I even worked in the Foreign Office; that was before I turned to business. So you see you are not dealing with one of your minions, you are dealing with me - Hirst-Bergan owner of over four hundred companies some of which are here in Tel Aviv."

"I know Andrew, I know," Uzi spoke in a low, calm voice. He turned to his friend and colleague, "Amir would you get some more drinks, I could certainly do with one, how about you Andrew, another beer maybe?" Andrew gave a slight nod of his head, drank the last of his drink and then apologised to his hosts for his sudden outburst.

Hmm, I can see we may have to be careful with you Mr Hirst-Bergan, you're certainly a little volatile to say the least.

"So how does Mossad profit financially from this operation?" he asked in a much calmer voice.

"Well as I stated earlier, there are a number of our brothers living abroad, displaced Jews, who wish to return home but are being blocked by different Governments and we would dearly like to help them. But more to the point, we feel there are a number of our brothers who have been a little less than honest about their individual wealth. These we feel, have been circumventing Israeli financial controls by making large deposits into Credit Suisse in Switzerland. Now, if we can find these people then of course we will suggest that they make a donation to Israel. We shall," a flicker of a smile touched his lips then was gone, "make them an offer that they can't refuse. If you see what I mean." Andrew Hirst-Bergan could see what he meant all right and knew exactly the sort of offer Mossad would propose.

"Of course we also benefit from knowing what is going on in other intelligence organisations around the world, and we can, with your assistance, very quickly assess Russia's capability. This information, or some of it, we would share with our allies. So Andrew are you interested in our proposition? If you are then we all gain financially. You make money through your computer business, we make money, Israel makes money. In fact nobody loses except our enemies and that's the truth!" Uzi looked straight into Hirst-Bergan's eyes and waited patiently for an answer. Andrew Hirst-Bergan, from his time as a Member of Parliament and working in the Foreign Office, had learned enough about various intelligence agencies and how they worked to realise that the truth was always an acquired taste and dependent on whose point of view it was. He sat in silence for a moment or two whilst he considered the enormity of what PROMIS would offer. He could immediately see the benefits afforded to any country that had such a cunning plan as this and that appealed to his greedy nature. He could visualise the amount of wealth he alone would generate by selling such a brilliant system and of course Mossad would know everything they needed to know about a foreign power without them suspecting a thing.

What a brilliant concept, a trapdoor impossible to find unless you're the designer. A program that has thousands of uses such as money laundering, intelligence gathering and information on bank accounts. In fact the list is endless!

He had made up his mind. "OK my brothers," he looked from Uzi to Amir then back to Uzi, "on one condition; that I become part of the organisation, I become part of Mossad." A momentary silence ensued whilst the two Mossad delegates thought about what he was asking for. Amir looked at his boss. Uzi rubbed his chin as he thought carefully about what Andrew had asked of them, and then he slowly nodded his head.

"OK Andrew, but always remember this about us. Our work is to create history and then hide it. On the whole we are honourable, respect constitutional government, free speech and human rights. But in the end you must also understand that nothing must stand in the way of what we do. Also for the record your contact with Mossad will always be through Amir. Amir will be your handler" A smile flitted across Hirst-Bergan's lips then it was gone but his eyes held a look of excitement as he thought about the doors that this would ultimately open.

At last I will rub shoulders with Kings and Queens, Hollywood stars and foreign Ambassadors.

His private thoughts were rudely interrupted by Amir.

"As to Kristoff my friend…"

Kristoff, yes Kristoff I had forgotten about him!

"…I would suggest you encourage that possible relationship as he is known to be a Bulgarian KGB agent and he still has influence there." At this piece of information Andrew gave a sharp intake of breath. After all he thought he was Eastern European but he had not realised the implication of this until just now when Amir told him.

I wonder how Mike Weatherall knows him.

"One question Amir?"

"And that is?"

"If Kristoff is KGB, then can you find out a bit more information about another contact of mine, his name is Mike Weatherall. He comes from Cranford New Jersey." Amir's face broke into a broad grin. "Amir, what's so amusing?" Hirst-Bergan asked somewhat annoyed at Amir's response.

"Sorry my friend, but Mike Weatherall is an old contact of ours. It was through him we obtained the software PROMIS and it was his computer company that was instrumental in selling it to the Jordanian Intelligence Service. He has powerful connections within the CIA so is a very useful contact to have and through him we know exactly the state of play."

Chapter 5

The message received by Hanslope Park Communications Centre was from the British Embassy in Tel Aviv and was headed UK EYES ALPHA. This immediately warned the recipients that the contents were not to be shown to any foreigners, and was intended only for the home intelligence and security services, armed forces and Whitehall recipients. The bulk of the message was just routine information from the Embassy in Tel Aviv, but there was one particular section which was of great interest to certain parties: -

JBAFXYLPPEFOPQYBODXKJBBQFKDJLPPXAQLAXV
MOBPBKQXJFOXKARWF

On the face of it, it looked just like a list of jumbled letters, but to the trained eye it meant something. As soon as the full report had finished spewing out from the terminal, the young communications clerk tore off the sheet and photocopied it for the 'Message Incoming' file then took the original along to the Codes and Ciphers department H. Once in the Cipher section the message would be deciphered into plain language and passed to the Middle East Section P4(DP2) where it would be read and then forwarded with any comments to the Coordinator of Intelligence and Security who is responsible for coordinating the work of the Secret Intelligence Service (MI6) the Security Service (MI5) and GCHQ. Within the hour the list of jumbled letters had been solved. It was a Caesar cipher with a shift of three, in other words the alphabet was moved by three letters. For example instead of following ABCDE….. etc A=X B=Y and C=Z. Thereafter each letter follows the normal alphabet i.e. D=A; E=B and F=C…etc. In this instance the Embassy in Tel Aviv report read as follows:-

Media boss Hirst-Bergan meeting Mossad today present Amir and Uzi.

It was this small section of the routine report that was of great interest to one person in particular, Sir James Johnstone.

In London the weather had started to brighten as Sir James headed through the traffic towards Downing Street for his weekly meeting with the Prime Minister and other members of the Joint Intelligence Council. The main topic, as always, would be the perceived threat from the Soviet bloc and the latest information coming out of Eastern Europe. Another item on the agenda was the recent Middle East situation between Israel and Palestine; in particular the situation with Yasser Arafat and the Palestine Liberation Organisation (PLO). A minor concern for Sir James was the rumour that the media mogul Andrew Hirst-Bergan was courting Israel's Mossad agents. This had now been confirmed by the Middle East Section. The Operator in Tel Aviv, according to the section report, had a positive sighting of him in the company of two of the top Mossad agents, this he found a little disconcerting. *So what's your game Mr Hirst-Bergan?*

Built back in the 17th century by Sir George Downing, 10 Downing Street is an elegant town house tucked away down a side street off Whitehall and is widely judged by those who work inside it to be too cramped for modern government. Over the years it has seen many different Prime Ministers and Heads of State pass through its famous black front door and into the entrance hall. Unlike the White House or the Kremlin, 10 Downing Street was never purpose built as a headquarters of state so its layout tends to be somewhat haphazard by comparison.

After the meeting Sir James and his opposite number from MI5 left Downing Street for Thames House, MI5's HQ, in order to discuss further the recent developments with reference to Hirst-Bergan and the Middle East connection.

"Of course Sir James you are aware of the investigation that the DTI undertook in fairly recent time? I know that there was no prosecution, but that does not mean to say there wasn't a case to answer." Stella, the head of MI5, peered at Sir James over the rim of her spectacles as if she was admonishing a naughty schoolboy. "In fact we at Five felt it better that the DTI dropped any charges that they may well have been considering."

"And why was that may I ask Stella?" Sir James raised a quizzical eyebrow.

"Well…" she paused, and again looked over the rim of her glasses, "because Sir James, we felt that he may well be worth keeping an eye on. After all he has quite a following, not only here but abroad especially in America I do believe, and as you are no doubt aware, he could well be useful to us one way or another, would you not agree?" "Absolutely, I couldn't agree with you more. However I am somewhat concerned about this latest development that our man in Tel Aviv reported."

"Well, what do you want of Five?"

"I think it may well be pertinent just to keep tabs on him whilst at home and to keep me posted of any other connections…in fact how about me seconding one of our operators to your staff?"

"A true secondment…or do you mean to work alongside?"

"I thought along the lines of a combined effort, Five and Six working together on this one."

"Hmm, I'm not sure. Who foots the bill?" Sir James thought about this for a moment or two.

"If Six is to fund the project then we take the lead. In other words the 'Circus' runs the show on this one and I have just the man for the job. However he may need some help from your department from time to time. So what do you say?" The head of Five thought about the proposition.

After all Sir James it all comes down to money and if you are prepared to fund this in total then why not, it gives me funding for other areas.

"How many operators will you want?"

"One maybe two. The most important aspect is that Five is aware of our operation and there are no crossed lines on this. We don't want any cock ups."

"I agree Sir James, the last thing I want is Hirst-Bergan causing waves in the press. So I will hold a briefing with our people and allocate some man-hours just in case."

"Thank you." Sir James stood up and shook his counterpart's hand, "should you ever require a favour give me a call."

"Don't worry I will Sir James," she said and a brief smile touched her lips then it was gone. *No Sir James don't you worry I certainly will* thought Stella.

Outside Hirst-Bergan's office a yellow BT van pulled up. Its occupants, two BT engineers, placed a barrier around the manhole situated on the pavement and proceeded to lift the cover. One of the men lowered himself into the manhole ready to start work on the cable that ran parallel to the front of the building. The other engineer erected a small yellow tent over the hole in order to shield them from the weather. Once the tent was erected, and they knew they were safe from nosy people with prying eyes, they laid out a plan of the offices immediately adjacent to where they were working. The document showed the position of the main service ducts, colour coded in order to indicate which service ran where. From this it was easy for the men to identify the BT feeds that ran to the main PABX board housed in the main reception area. A second plan showed the BT cable runs which were also colour coded indicating to them different pairs as they snaked through the building to their ultimate destination. The cable run coloured

red was the one they were interested in because it was Hirst-Bergan's private line. It ran from his office, bypassed the PABX system then disappeared into a maze of cables that fed into a junction box (JB) not fifty feet from where they were working.

"According to this we should be able to pick up on terminal 108 at the JB...so if you look it up in the tables Nick then we should be able to locate the correct pair here." Nick removed a ring binder from his toolbox and flicked over the pages. "What's the JB number Alan?" he asked his mate.

"FT504W" his mate replied pointing to the JB number on the plan.

"Got it. Fleet Street West, JB FT504W. Terminal 108 you say?" Alan grunted. "OK it's green stripe white pair."

"Right, so if we can find that pair then we are in business..." Alan pushed aside the plan and peered into the hole where Nick, his mate, was standing. Nick had already removed the repeater cover and laid bare a bundle of coloured conductors. With experienced fingers he quickly sifted through each pair, his eyes carefully watching for a white pair with a green stripe.

"Bingo."

"You've found them then?"

"Of course. Pass me the cutters and the two links and we are almost there." He took out a small knife from his pocket and pulled the pair of leads away from the main bundle. Then he started to carefully scrape away the insulation on one of the pair, exposing about an inch of the wire conductors. Having placed insulating tape around the bare metal as a precaution against possible shorting, he then repeated the process approximately three to four inches further along. Once he had removed the insulation at the two points Nick took one of the links – a short length of wire with a crocodile clip at either end – and removed the insulating tape he had used as a temporary cover and connected the link in circuit. Next he cut out the wire adjacent to the two points where he had bared the conductor. At all times the circuit had remained unbroken. Alan now passed him a crimping tool and two connectors, these he crimped on the ends of the two bare terminals.

"Pass me the TX," Nick said. Alan passed him a small black box with six flying leads emanating from it. One pair he connected to two crimped connectors and then carefully removed the link from the telephone lead. "Stage one completed," he muttered to himself. He then repeated the process for the other half of the pair and within thirty minutes the small black box was connected into circuit.

"All done?" enquired Alan.

"Yeah, but we now need to pickup on our system, have you found where we run our secure lines?"

"Give me a couple of minutes." Alan emerged from the tent and went to the van from which he retrieved a plain black ring binder and returned with it to the tent. "Right, here we are," he said as he looked down the index for Fleet Street. "Ah yes, there we are," he said as if talking to himself. "According to this, there is a transponder situated on the roof of the building." He passed the directory to Nick at the same time pointing out the reference Tx – shorthand for transmitter – shown on the HB Media Building.

That's lucky!

"So, hopefully, all we need to do now is to wire this into a Pa2 and then bingo we should be in business. Can you get me a Pa2 from the van Alan?"

"Sure." Once again Alan scrabbled out of the tent and went to the rear of the van to search for the Pa2 that Nick wanted to finish the job. Within a few minutes he returned to the tent clutching another small box with HMG – Pa2 stamped on its top cover. This he passed to his colleague for him to connect. A few minutes later the job was completed and Nick was busy manoeuvring the bundle of coloured wires back into the truncking from whence they had come. Thirty seconds later, the two BT engineers were stowing the tent back into their van, the manhole cover was replaced and everything was back to normal. There was only one more job to do and that was for them to pay a visit to HB Media to clear a fault that had been reported on Mr Hirst-Bergan's direct line.

"Good morning can I help you?" the young lady on reception greeted Nick.

"Good morning. We're from BT and are here to check your line 608 4556," Alan said in his best BT sounding voice.

"Oh, I don't know anything about a fault. Besides that's Mr Hirst-Bergan's private line and I'm sure he would have said something if..."

"Ah, well you see," Alan interrupted, "he wouldn't have realised about the fault as it was reported by another subscriber who had tried to contact him."

"Well, I'm not sure...you see Mr Hirst-Bergan would certainly have said if something was wrong..."

Oh come on lady don't give me a hard time!

"Well I hear what you are saying madam," Nick interjected, "but he wouldn't necessarily have realized there was a fault."

"You say it was reported by someone else?"

"Yes, that's right. Someone was having trouble getting through..."

"But Mr Hirst-Bergan uses his direct line quite regularly to receive calls and I'm sure he would have said something if suddenly there were no calls going to him..."

"Ah, it's not quite as straightforward as that madam. You see it appears as if it could be an intermittent fault..."

"Well...couldn't that be at the exchange?"

Jesus! For God's sake stop being so awkward and let us in

"I take your point madam. Didn't they check the exchange end Alan?"

"Yeah, said it was fine. They checked the line as well and the job was put out to us to sort out." He flashed the receptionist a disarming smile. "It showed up on the test as a possible handset fault or master junction box fault."

"Oh...well...I suppose it must be all right. Unfortunately I can't check as Mr Hirst-Bergan is away at the moment..."

"On holiday?" Nick asked innocently.

"No, on business...but he is expected back quite soon."

Yeah we know exactly where he is. He's been chatting with our friends in Israel has our Mr Hirst-Bergan, that's why we are here.

"Would you direct us to his office please?"

"Of course. Haven't you been here before?"

"No madam. This is our first time. Big place isn't it?"

"I thought I hadn't seen either of you before. What's happened to the engineers who normally come out?"

"Oh, they have too many jobs on today so we're covering some of their work. Now Mr Hirst-Bergan's office..."

"Yes of course sorry. Take the lift to the tenth floor and Sophie his secretary will let you through. I'll just give her a ring to let her know you are on your way up," she said and smiled sweetly.

It didn't take long for the lift to reach the tenth floor. Both men made their way to the polished desk where Hirst-Bergan's secretary Sophie sat typing up a report that her boss had left for her to complete. As the men approached she looked up and smiled.

"Good morning, reception told me that you were on your way. I believe you are here to check Mr Hirst-Bergan's phone."

"That's correct; I believe there is an intermittent fault."

"I'll show you in then," she answered as she pushed back her chair and stood up smoothing her skirt as she did so. From her drawer she took out a key and led the way along the plush carpeted corridor to a heavy oak door situated at the end. "There you are," she said as she unlocked the door and let them in. "Will you be long?" she enquired, "it's just that I have to go out soon and I can't leave the door unlocked."

"We shouldn't be too long, but we could always lock it and leave the key with reception," suggested Alan.

Sophie thought about this for a moment.

"Hmm, I'm not sure. Tell you what if I have gone would you mind locking it up and dropping the key in my top drawer?"

"No not at all." *That's an unexpected bonus.* They waited patiently until Sophie had retraced her footsteps then quietly shut the heavy oak door and as a precaution locked it from inside. Alan opened the tool case he was carrying and immediately took out a small disk microphone. He then unscrewed the mouthpiece of the handset, removed the circular, carbon filled microphone and replaced it with the one from his tool case. Whilst Alan was working on the telephone handset, Nick was busy with skeleton keys opening the locked filing cabinet. It only took a moment for Nick, an expert in lock picking, to have the filing cabinet open and very quickly he was expertly rifling through Hirst-Bergan's private and confidential paperwork. Most of it referred to his business empire, but there was one piece of information of great interest and that was a file labelled 'Bulgaria'.

In the folder they found that he was investing heavily into a fund out there and that he had built up quite a substantial network of contacts. One of the most interesting facts was that he had bought his yacht from the brother of an International Arms dealer. Also, according to the file, he had met up with members of the Bulgarian KGB and one person's name jumped off the page at him. He was the single most important leader in the Soviet Union, he was General Secretary of the Communist

Party's General Committee, and was none other than Yuri Andropov. In fact the whole file made interesting reading and Sir James Johnstone as well as Five could do with the information. *Perhaps I ought to borrow it* thought Nick, but instead he removed the documents, and very quickly and expertly photographed each one before returning them to the manila folder, which he then returned to the filing cabinet.

Alan, having placed a listening device under the desk, proceeded to install a similar device within the confines of a double wall socket and in a matter of seconds had done so and was now screwing back on the switch plate. They had now been in his office for close on ten minutes and they felt any longer would cause eyebrows to be raised and people to become curious as to what they may be up to. They unlocked the heavy oak door and without a sound made their way to the now deserted desk of Hirst-Bergan's secretary where they, as arranged, deposited the key in her top drawer. Having now completed their tasks they took the lift back to reception.

"All done?" the receptionist enquired upon seeing the two BT engineers emerge from the lift.

"Yes thanks. It was a noisy microphone." Alan said as he held up the small carbon filled disk he had removed from Hirst-Bergan's handset.

"Oh, I see. So everything's working now?"

"Yes that's right. He shouldn't have any more problems now."

"Thanks and bye." Alan and Nick raised their hands in acknowledgement as they made their way out through the main doors.

Chapter 6

The King David Hotel's restaurant had, as usual, produced a top quality culinary delight that had not been lost on Hirst-Bergan, a man who enjoyed champagne and some of the finest cuisine the world had to offer.

"Come gentlemen, it's a fine evening and a walk in the hotel's gardens may help the digestive system, wouldn't you agree Andrew?"

"Well why not Uzi and perhaps you could tell me a little more about your…umm…your project whilst we walk." Hirst-Bergan dabbed at his lips with his napkin and flicked off any crumbs that may have inadvertently dropped on to his trousers.

"Of course Andrew. Amir, are you coming?" Uzi asked his Mossad colleague as he pushed his chair back and got up from the dining table. The three men headed towards the open French doors and out onto the raised terrace that overlooked the carefully tended gardens. As they descended the steps onto the path that wound its way through the never ending pergolas with their overhanging tropical flowers, the media tycoon could not resist asking further about PROMIS.

"Tell me how the system worked once you had sold it to the Jordanian Intelligence Service, I mean how did you know it was successful?"

"Well, we just knew it was. Really there's not a lot more to add."

"But Amir how could you know, can you give me an example?" Amir fell silent. He wasn't keen too keen to tell Hirst-Bergan the 'ins' and 'outs' of PROMIS just in case the media boss 'let the cat out of the bag' at some stage. But Hirst-Bergan was not a man to be put off and tried another tack. "When you sold it to Jordan surely you were not able to track Arafat because I thought he was security conscious, in fact so security conscious that he was renowned for it."

"You're absolutely correct," replied Uzi, "that is why we specifically targeted him. For instance whenever he moved, the details were entered on a secure PLO computer. He constantly changed his plans, he never slept in the same bed two nights in succession and he even altered his mealtimes at the last moment. With PROMIS we managed to hack into the PLO computer and discovered what aliases and false passports he was using. We even obtained his phone bills and were able to check the numbers he called. We could then cross-check the calls, he made to those numbers with other calls made from those numbers, and in that way we soon had a 'picture' of Arafat's communications."

"For example," Amir took up the story, "we had a resounding success when an Intifada commander who had moved to Rome called a Beirut number that we had already listed as the home of a known bomb maker. Evidently the Rome caller wanted to meet our Beirut bomb maker in Athens. Once we had this piece of information it was a simple task for our computers to check all the travel offices to find out the travel arrangements of both men." Amir went on to describe how Mossad, with the aid of PROMIS, carried out further checks on the Beirut connection, which revealed that the bomber had got the local utilities to suspend supplies to his address. "Once we knew all services to his home had been suspended, we knew he was on the move and a further search by PROMIS of the PLO computers showed us that he had, at the last minute, switched flights. But my friend, that did not save him. We had one of our *kidon* pay Beirut a visit and he died on the way to the airport. He was killed by a car bomb." Andrew Hirst-Bergan gave a low whistle as the enormity of what Amir had told him began to sink in. He was absolutely amazed at the capabilities of the project and its potential.

If there's one thing I can do it is marketing, and this baby is dynamite!

"So what about the commander in Rome?"

"Oh, didn't I say! That was a little remiss of me; he was killed in a hit-and-run accident." Amir gave a smile. "They never did trace the driver."

In the post-war years, whilst building up his scientific publishing business, Hirst-Bergan had built a network of contacts in and around Berlin and Eastern Germany. This he had continued to build upon and it was not long before his network extended deep into Eastern Europe and the Eastern Bloc satellite states of Moscow.

Once back in his hotel suite, Hirst-Bergan began to formulate some sort of marketing strategy, and it was whilst thinking about how to market the software his thoughts turned to the network he had already created with his publishing business, and the germ of an idea started.

Maybe I ought to contact Kristoff, after all both Amir and Uzi suggested that he could be very useful. Now if that's the case then he could introduce me to his people in Bulgaria. Also there's my own network of people through the publishing business. Hmm this could definitely work. I think I can get the information that Mossad needs.

It was these avenues he would initially use, and because he could speak their language and understand their customs he knew that he would not fail to get what he wanted. It was this determination which had, after all, enabled him to build his media empire. Failure was not a word in his vocabulary.

Hirst-Bergan was a very astute businessman and at the meeting with Amir and Uzi he listened carefully to what they had to say and asked questions with a shrewdness that was part of him. He learned a lot about his Jewish friends, little snippets of information gathered here and there during their conversation were stored away in his memory to be recalled at some later date. He had the uncanny ability to store endless facts in his memory which meant that at meetings he never took notes or taped comments for reference. It was this ability that stood him in good stead as a 'spy' for Mossad.

Svetlana Zaslavsky was now a fully fledged KGB operator. As a young graduate in Moscow, she had met Mikhail Trepashkin who had convinced her to follow in her father's footsteps and join the KGB. Mikhail had appealed to her sense of loyalty towards her country, her father and most of all to her conscience. He not only felt she had promise, but he also had an eye for her beauty and thought that this would be her ultimate weapon, and as such he had convinced his superiors to send her to the KGB nine-month school. During her time at the school she had blossomed. She was no longer that 'young girl' he had met in a Moscow café, she was now self-assured and very confident; a beautiful, blonde, green eyed woman, who would be welcomed at any level of society. Mikhail was impressed by the changes he saw and convinced the officers above him to send her on a further two year course on deception, defence and assassination techniques.

Whilst on the two year course she was taught how to draw a gun whilst seated in a chair, how to cut a concealed opening into her skirt or dress in order for her to gain easy access to her weapon. She was taught how to shoot with deadly accuracy by emptying a full clip of ammunition into a target. She was shown how to pack her handgun inside her knickers, on her hip and into the rear of her waistband. She became proficient in a number of languages but predominantly English to a point where she had no trace of an accent. She learned how to create a dead-letter box, how to perfect the art of concealing a strip of microfilm to the inside of an envelope. How to disguise herself and how to alter her appearance by using cotton wadding inside her mouth to fatten out her cheeks so subtly changing the shape of her face. She was taught how to steal cars, act and pose as a drunk, use her charms to flirt and chat up the male sex. She was taught the importance of sex – how to use it to coerce, seduce and dominate. This she was particularly good at.

Once she had completed her training, Svetlana was given the name Cheryl Brooks as her code-name and was then assigned to the overseas section within the Lubyanka where she could liaise with various embassies. Her specific task was to provide cover – as a girlfriend or a wife for KGB, or Intelligence officers who were on active service throughout Western Europe, and with her impeccable English, she could easily pass as American, Canadian or English. Her task was to target senior officials and western diplomats, using her training and knowledge to obtain useful information for her bosses back in the Kremlin. Svetlana entered into her work with enthusiasm, she travelled around Europe and even went to America where she was attached to the Russian Embassy as a fully fledged Intelligence Officer. Mikhail Trepashkin had not been wrong when he said he saw her as a rising star through the ranks of the KGB. In less than four years she had gone from a raw recruit to the level of Colonel – a meteoric rise indeed.

Being a past master at marketing it wasn't long before Hirst-Bergan had proved himself to his Mossad masters and using the sales pitch 'PROMIS is better and cheaper than any other product currently available', he was soon turning in orders from all points of the globe. With success following success Hirst-Bergan's next target was to be none other than the mainstay of the Swiss banking system. Armed with a copy of PROMIS he set up a meeting with Credit Suisse with a view to having them install it on their computers. By the end of the meeting he had them hooked and the very bastion of the Swiss banking system was unwittingly providing Amir and Mossad with its sensitive information. In a very short time Mossad held data on many Israeli millionaires who had opened bank accounts overseas, a move that was highly illegal under Israel's financial rules. Armed with this information Mossad paid those concerned a visit and made them an offer that they would not refuse. Each and every one was to make a donation to help Israel. Should they refuse to make a sizeable donation then they were threatened with exposure which automatically guaranteed a very heavy fine and imprisonment. Not one of them refused.

Another detail that came to the attention of Amir and Mossad was that the respected Credit Suisse was being used by both the CIA and organised crime – the Mafia – in their various financial transactions, passing many millions of pounds a day through their respective special accounts; money that came from drugs and prostitution. Within days Amir and Mossad had tracked down the numbers of every single CIA and Mafia account. They soon had in their grasp the name of the CIA operative in overall charge of the agency's secret money laundering methods, how he moved covert funds in and out of Credit Suisse and sent them around the worldwide banking system by means of complex transfers that made it impossible to track his electronic signature. However Mossad now had it and by watching how he operated, how he used a special coded system that he had devised to give instructions to certain bank officials in various banks around the globe on how money was to be transferred – either by cheque or by courier - made certain that no transaction stayed in any one account longer than three days. In Tel Aviv Amir noted how foolproof this method was and as soon as the first profits from the sales of PROMIS arrived he began to use the same route and system as that used by the CIA operation. This method was so successful Amir even told Hirst-Bergan to use it for hiding his own profits made from PROMIS as well as any other venture. Now was the time for Hirst-Bergan to aim his main thrust at the Soviet Union and its satellite states.

I think it's time that Kim Kristoff and I met up again. After all I did promise to get in touch and that was back in Tunis ...yes in fact I will do just that. I will contact him first thing on my return to London.

The Gulfstream executive jet set down on the tarmac and taxied to a halt at Hirst-Bergan's personal hangar, where his car was already waiting to meet him. The sky was leaden and as the stewardess opened the aircraft door, Hirst-Bergan gave an involuntary shiver as he stepped out on to the five steps that had been placed alongside the door of the aircraft. The fine persistent drizzle gave a cold damp feel to the day which chilled him to the bone. *Typical bloody English weather.*

"Who the hell are you, and where's John my usual chauffer?" he growled at the man standing at the bottom of the steps.

"Sorry sir, but John was unexpectedly taken ill, so I was sent as his replacement."

"Huh I see. Damned inconvenient if you ask me."

"Yes sir. Where do you wish to go sir?"

"Where do you think? My office of course," he barked at the chauffer as he got into the waiting car and shut the door. In a matter of minutes the car purred out of Biggin Hill\Airport and headed off towards the city.

"Good morning sir," the receptionist greeted Andrew Hirst-Bergan as he swept in through the main entrance. He nodded curtly and grunted as he headed towards the lift that would whisk him up to his office on the tenth floor.

"Tell Kevin to come to my office now," he called back as he entered the waiting lift.

"Certainly…" but the lift doors had already closed before she had finished. *Mr bloody Hirst-Bergan, certainly. Three bags full your highness…*

"Sophie need you in my office now…oh and get some coffee."

"Yes Mr Hirst-Bergan." She picked up her telephone and called down to the floor below to the general office: "Ah Penny would you arrange for a pot of coffee for two and biscuits to be sent up to Mr Hirst-Bergan thank you." She then picked up the morning's mail, her shorthand pad, and smoothed down her skirt and made her way to his office.

"Come," his voice boomed out in reply to the gentle tap on the door. "Sophie, bring me up to speed on what's been happening whilst I've been away."

"The circulation figures are up again against The Sun. The returns for the last quarter are in for the group, oh and a gentleman called, the man who was here last month…"

"What was his name?"

"He didn't say, he just said he will call you back and to tell you it was the Doctor. I hope there is nothing wrong Mr Hirst-Bergan." He allowed a brief smile to touch his lips.

"No not at all. I think I know who you mean…had he a trace of an accent…Germanic accent?"

"Hmm, I think so."

"In that case I know who you mean. Also I am expecting a very important call from a Mr Kristoff, as soon as he calls put him through regardless. If I'm already on the phone interrupt, take the call back, and put Kristoff through. In addition keep my diary clear for the next few days as I may have to go out to the USSR at short notice, is that clear?"

"Yes Mr Hirst-Bergan. If Mr Kristoff telephones you want me to put him through and should you be engaged on the phone you wish me to interrupt, take your call back, and put Mr

Kristoff through. You also wish me to keep your diary clear for the next few days."

"Thank you Sophie that will be all." At just after 11.00 Sophie put a call through to Andrew Hirst-Bergan's office.

"Hirst-Bergan speaking. Ah Kim, sorry I haven't been back to you since we met in Tunis, but I've been terribly busy. How is life treating you? Oh I'm fine just busy, busy, busy. Now about that meeting you suggested when I was in Tunisia, I think the time is now right for both of us…Umm…umm…I see. Yes I have a proposition to put to you that may well be of interest to you…Of course Kim. You do know that I have been talking to Vladimir on and off for some time now…Oh, you do surprise me! Vladimir is your boss?" *As if I didn't already know that Mr Kristoff.* "Yes that will be fine. So Thursday we will meet…OK…till Thursday…Goodbye Kim." *OK Andrew you've got it in the bag…well almost. Now I'm going to enjoy this.*

Hirst-Bergan's interest in Bulgaria had started before he met Kim Kristoff and well before his recruitment into Mossad; in fact it was at one of those earlier meetings with Vladimir in Moscow that Hirst-Bergan first raised the possibility of investing a substantial amount of money in Bulgaria, well away from inquisitive persons in the City and Wall Street. Vladimir, as head of the KGB, had been surprised as he had assumed that 'someone of Hirst-Bergan's standing had already taken care of such things.'

But Hirst-Bergan was adamant that he would like to use Bulgaria as the country in which to store large sums of money in hard currency. But it would have to be readily available to him for withdrawal on demand at anytime. Then that would mean a Bulgarian bank would be a personal vault, and his accounts would be even more inaccessible than those in Switzerland.

Vladimir, a very cautious man by nature, looked over the thick lenses of his heavy-rimmed spectacles; his small piggy eyes searched Hirst-Bergan's face suspiciously. "Hmm I see," was all he said initially, his face bland and expressionless as he stared at Hirst-Bergan. "Of course I would need some time to see if we could accommodate such a thing, but on the face of it I don't see any problems," was Vladimir's reply.

Of course this would be good for us provided I can convince the Kremlin. After all no other entrepreneur from outside has ever asked such a thing, and I assume Andrew Hirst-Bergan that as you are asking for this then the money you wish to bury here would cause a lot of difficult questions for you.

Vladimir could also see major advantages for Russia with such an arrangement as it was Moscow that effectively controlled Bulgaria's banking system. The more he thought about it the more advantageous it seemed.

If Hirst-Bergan is allowed to keep his money in Bulgaria then the KGB would have an inside view of how he operates. Also there would be a financial aspect to this because we could charge him a 'handling fee' for offering the service, which would be paid into the KGB's bank in Moscow. Yes Vladimir, there are many possibilities and advantages for all.

With this in mind Vladimir consulted the most important leader in the Soviet Union, his own boss and predecessor as the head of the KGB, none other than Yuri Andropov, General Secretary of the Communist Party's Central Committee.

The party chief, Andropov, peered over the rims of his spectacles at Vladimir as he sat across the desk from him in his Kremlin office and recounted what Hirst-Bergan had asked. Andropov knew Hirst-Bergan better than anyone in the Soviet Union as they both shared the same background of poverty. Each had risen to prominence through a combination of hard work, ruthlessness and deception. There was also one other common denominator. They were both Jews. But unlike Hirst-Bergan, Andropov had carefully concealed his cultural roots. To be of Jewish origin in the Soviet Union's pecking order was almost as dangerous as being one in Hitler's Germany.

Hirst-Bergan had learned about the Russian's background from his Mossad friend Amir. Just like Amir, he had also filed that information away in his memory bank. Without telling Vladimir, he had contacted Andropov on the Jewish Day of Atonement and intimated that he would like to help develop Bulgaria because as a Jew he always wished to see an underprivileged country begin to prosper. After all he had himself grown up in similar circumstances, and now he had the money he would like to help others where he could.

However Hirst-Bergan knew that Andropov was already in the advanced stage of kidney disease and that once he died Vladimir would certainly be a most influential figure. To that end he began sending gifts by courier to his office in Lubyanka, and it was these gifts that eventually came to the notice of MI6 causing some of the officers to wonder about his motives.

Chapter 7

Located in the central business and diplomatic district, the Sheraton Tunis Hotel & Towers overlooks the entire city of Tunis, and is about a ten minute drive from Tunis Carthage Airport. Andrew always stayed at the Sheraton when visiting Tunis. It was the Sheraton hotel where he first met Mike Weatherall all those years ago and where Mike had originally introduced him to Kristoff, a business acquaintance, a man of many faces and an arms dealer to boot. A man whom Amir said was not who he purported to be, a man who was from the Bulgarian KGB. With this information firmly in mind Hirst-Bergan had pressed ahead with the meeting as he was convinced that Kristoff and his contacts could assist his own cause in some small way.

The phone on the desk rang incessantly. *Oh for goodness sake, do wait a minute,* a disgruntled head of DP4 thought to himself as he reached out his right hand to pick it up.

"Hello, DP4 section…Yes Sir James…straight away." He pushed back on his chair, picked up a pad and hastily scrabbled through the top drawer in his desk for something to write with. "Damn," he muttered to himself as he searched. "What is it about this place that pens and pencils are never to be found?"

"What's up Harry?" Steve, a fairly new member to the team, enquired.

"Bloody pens in this place. They just keep disappearing, or when you do find one it doesn't work. Ahh, there you are." He hastily retrieved a biro he had found under a pile of paperwork and tried it on a scrap of paper – it didn't work. "Bloody typical, you find one and it's run out…"

"Here Harry take this." Steve handed him a pen.

"Thanks Steve. Keep an eye on things I've been summoned…" He jabbed a finger towards the ceiling, and rolled his eyes upwards. "Still he who pays the piper...etc...etc." He really wasn't having a good day, his computer had crashed and he had only just started to retrieve the information he needed when Sir James had summoned him. *I could really do without this*, he thought to himself as he entered the lift that would whisk him up to the next floor and to 'C's' office. Although the boss was Sir James, by tradition the head of MI6 was always known as 'C'. Harry was of average build and height, a man in his mid forties with a regulation hair cut - short back and sides. His hair had at one time been light brown, but that was some years ago, now it was turning grey. The lift eased to a stop and the doors slid silently open to reveal a corridor that ran the full length of the building, the walls of which were thick triple-glazed plate glass panels which gave the office workers at either side the impression of space and light. The reason for the triple glazing was as an aid to soundproofing as well as a security measure against eavesdropping. After all this was the nerve centre of the UK's Secret Intelligence Service.

Sir James looked up as Harry entered his office. "Good, pull up a chair Harry." Sir James pressed a button on his phone. "Elaine, can you bring me the information we received from our man in Tunis. Thank you."

"The reason I've got you to come up Harry is that we have been receiving a lot of traffic with reference to our wealthy media mogul Mr Hirst-Bergan." Just then the interconnecting door opened and a middle-aged lady entered carrying a bulky file labelled 'Hirst-Bergan'.

"The latest traffic from Tunisia is on top Sir James."

"Thank you Elaine. Have we heard anything further from the chauffeur?"

"Only that he took him to his aircraft early this morning, apart from that nothing."

"Thank you Elaine." Sir James picked up his phone and punched in a number on the keyboard. "Hello Jimmy, can you join Harry and me up in my office, thanks." He looked at Harry with half-closed eyes and started to tap the desk with his fingers. "Harry," he said suddenly, "Hirst-Bergan seems to be causing quite a stir one way or another. I think we need to be getting up close and personal with him." At that point Jimmy, a young man in his late twenties, entered the office. "Ah Jimmy, grab a pew. I was just saying to Harry that our friend Hirst-Bergan seems to be causing a bit of a stir and I think it is about time we got a little closer to him. What's the latest from your perspective?"

"Well I can confirm that the techies have been tracking every conversation he has had on the telephone – his direct line - or any meetings he has had in his office. The system is working fine. For instance we know that he is working closely with Mossad. We know that he has interests in Tel Aviv, in fact his computer company AHB Computers is based there and we have had our man keep tabs on movements there. We know he left for Tunisia this morning, based on a conversation he had earlier in the week with a Kim Kristoff."

"Who is Kristoff, do we know?"

"Not yet Sir James we are having that angle checked out."

"Hmm…We need to know who this contact is, what he does, where he fits in. In fact make that a priority. Get someone on to it straight away. Also find out who we have in the field out in Tunisia and get them to arrange a covert surveillance on Hirst-Bergan and this Kristoff…whatever his name is. What about our American cousins, have we heard anything of interest from them yet?"

"Nothing specific. Our man in Washington confirms that the CIA have a field operative – Mike Weatherall – who has been known to associate with our target from time to time, otherwise nothing more specific."

"OK, then let's see what Tunisia brings. Thanks Jimmy." *Hmm, I wonder what your game is Mr Hirst-Bergan.* "Right Harry, I think it may well be worth us making contact with our media boss, what do you think?"

"I'm not sure Sir James. I agree he has spent quite a lot of time travelling backwards and forwards behind the Iron Curtain...."

"Harry, I've decided. When he gets back to this country we'll meet with him. In fact we will get our chauffeur to take us to meet him at Biggin Hill and we could have a very brief chat with him on the way back here. I think it is about time we made him an offer. Dig out all you can on his interests in the Soviet Union countries, I believe I'm right in saying that he owns a Scientific Research and Reference Publication. Maybe there is some mileage in that. See what you can come up with. Thanks Harry."

Sir James gave a slight wave of the hand to indicate that the head of DP4 was dismissed.

Outside the Tunis Carthage Airport a queue of taxis waited patiently for the next aircraft to disgorge its passengers. On the opposite side of the road from the terminal a beige coloured car parked in the shade of the overhanging roof. Inside the car sat a dark skinned Tunisian who seemed to be watching for someone, a passenger maybe or a relative. A Police car drew alongside. The occupant signalled to the driver to move. The driver smiled and waved in acknowledgement, then pointed to something at the front of his car. The policeman immediately edged forward so he could view whatever it was that the Tunisian had pointed at, took a note of the registration number and promptly called his superior on the radio. In a matter of minutes the reply came back. He raised his hand and drove off. The Tunisian in the beige car once more settled down to wait. His patience was soon rewarded as the portly frame of

Hirst-Bergan made his way to one of the taxis, opened the door, tossed his bags in the cab and got in. With a judder from the clutch the taxi – an old Mercedes that had definitely seen better days – chugged and wheezed its way along the terminal road heading for the centre of Tunis and the 'old town'. At a discreet distance behind, the beige coloured Mercedes from the airport followed. The covert operation was under way.

Having checked in, Hirst-Bergan's first port of call was his bathroom to take a shower to freshen up and get into something a little more lightweight and cooler. Within half an hour of arriving he had freshened up and without giving the Tunisian, who was standing near the lifts, a second glance he boarded the lift for the ground floor. As the lift door closed, the Tunisian turned on his heels and headed for the stairs, and taking them two at a time he made it to the entrance lobby well before the lift did. He moved a short distance away, just far enough not to be too obtrusive and yet close enough to be able to pick up his quarry quickly should he head out towards the town. He waited patiently for his target to emerge from the lift. Meanwhile a man of Eastern European extraction checked in at reception. The man's name was Kristoff.

In Lubyanka Vladimir had now come to a decision about Hirst-Bergan's request, *after all he seems to know Andropov personally,* he thought to himself *and Yuri was all for it.* He had decided to provide him with his secret bank account in the Bulgarian capital, Sofia. There was a certain poetic justice; a twist that made Vladimir smile. The bank account was to be with the Bank of Bulgaria, which was also the bank that the KGB used to finance its global traffic in drugs and terrorism. There was one condition that Vladimir had imposed upon himself and that was he needed someone he could trust to *watch over* Hirst-Bergan, so he sent for Andrei Lukanov, his most trusted operator in Bulgaria. Before he was prepared to give Hirst-Bergan his special coded account Vladimir sent for Andrei, who like Hirst-Bergan, had long since lost his peasant background. He now dressed, walked and talked in the most eloquent way. His manner was nothing less than aristocratic and as such, those he favoured he greeted accordingly, a hug for the men and a kiss on the hand for the women. As for the others that he did not favour, well they often disappeared from day to day, never to be seen again. Nobody would ever know how many people had disappeared after just a few whispered words or a slight nod of the head. He was cast in the style of a Mafia godfather.

Upon receipt of Vladimir's invitation to attend Lubyanka he wondered with some trepidation if he was about to suffer the same fate of many others – a KGB execution. In fact his fear could well have increased when he arrived at Moscow's airport because the limousine that had been sent to transport him from the plane to Lubyanka drove in through the side entrance known as 'Traitors Gate'. It was through this very same gateway that many a dissident or Russian traitor, who had been caught spying for the West, had entered.

"Andrei, good to see you." Vladimir gave him a customary hug.

"And you too Vladimir, you too," he answered with some relief.

"Come, follow me." With that Vladimir wasted no more time on jovialities and with a perfunctory wave of his hand he turned on his heels and set off along the passageway towards the stairs. The staircase led to the basement with its labyrinth of cells and chambers. He led Andrei along dimly lit corridors, past closed doors without names or numbers. Eventually he stopped at one such door and opened it to reveal a small cell furnished with only an old pine table and one chair. On the table was a bulky file. Vladimir waved Andrei into the room and pointed to the file. "You have one hour only. Sit here and read it from cover to cover and digest its contents." With that he left Andrei sitting at the table in the small cell-like office, and closing the door behind him, he retraced his footsteps back along the corridors from whence he came.

As soon as Vladimir closed the door Andrei opened the file named 'Hirst-Bergan' and started his task of reading the contents. The file was bulky and stuffed full of details about Hirst-Bergan, hundreds of pages of transcripts of telephone calls from his penthouse in London, and from hotels across the globe. Interspersed with the papers were vivid descriptions of Hirst-Bergan's sexual indiscretions. It was a dossier about someone that the KGB had more than just a passing interest in.

Within the hour Vladimir returned and found Andrei staring at the now closed file, completely immobilised by what he had read. Vladimir looked at the Bulgarian and with a thin half smile frozen to his face, he picked up the bulky file and led Andrei to his own comfortable, well-equipped office suite situated on an upper floor, where one of his aides served them both with coffee. As soon as the aide had left the room and had closed the heavy door behind him Vladimir said "Hirst-Bergan has enough money to buy most countries. The more he invests here, the better it is for our image, both here and in the West. He has contact with people in the highest places, those in high places of power in Moscow, and he has their approval. So Andrei help him all you can. If you need to involve anyone else in this then you must keep me informed. I want a record kept of all his financial dealings and of his lifestyle. In fact you must treat him like one who is very important; you must look after his every little need." He gave that thin half smile once more before continuing: "You know what I mean. You know how to handle him."

Andrei flew back to Sofia and the next morning he met with the President and told him exactly what had gone on in

Moscow. How he had been met at the airport and was whisked away by limousine to meet with the head of the KGB. How Vladimir, the head of the KGB, had shown him Hirst-Bergan's file and told him that the Media mogul was ready to place a large sum of money in Bulgaria. The prospect of Hirst-Bergan investing huge sums of money in Bulgaria was not lost on the President. "But Todor, you must be careful. Treat this man with respect as he will be the biggest investor Bulgaria has ever seen and he is no fool."

Todor was excited at the prospect. For quite some time, years in fact, Todor had been robbing his own country; he had been depositing large sums of money in Swiss bank accounts, all the time using the same route out of the Bank of Bulgaria that was used to finance terrorist activities. Whilst Hirst-Bergan would invest major capital in the economy to finance different projects – a deal already brokered by Vladimir – he would also conceal many millions of his own money. "Be rest assured Todor, he will watch over his hard currency like one of those predatory birds found high in the mountains beyond Sofia, so be warned. We cannot touch that money, however there will always be plenty of money left to 'skim off the top' from the projects in which he will be investing."

Upon arriving at Sofia the first time, Hirst-Bergan was treated with a deference usually reserved for the Chairman of the Soviet Socialist Republic, or at the very least high ranking officials from the Politburo. A ceremonial guard waited on the tarmac and a red carpet was prepared ready for when he descended the aircraft steps. His limousine was escorted by motorcycle outriders as it swept from the airport and on to the palace that was set on the slope of Mount Vitoshi overlooking Sofia. That night he was treated like a king, and as he stood on the balcony and looked down on the twinkling lights of Sofia, he thought *I now have two spiritual homes, my suite in the*

King David Hotel in Jerusalem and here, but this is the biggest and grandest one.

When Andrei realised the magnitude of what Hirst-Bergan was planning to do, he felt he needed to bring in an additional person to help in the management of it. He was known by his code name Oleg. At one time he may well have passed as good looking but over the years excess gave him a debauched look, but he still had a needle sharp brain and a shrewd mind. Like Andrei and Todor he always recognised a deal when he saw one, especially a deal that he would personally profit from. In Hirst-Bergan he saw the proverbial cow to be milked and on one occasion during a telephone conversation to Andrei he commented as such. The telephone conversation had been recorded by the Bulgarian Secret Service and from then on it would eavesdrop on Hirst-Bergan every time he visited. However the Bulgarians were not the only people interested in the media tycoon. In London, MI5 and MI6 had more than just a passing interest in what Hirst-Bergan was up to and in Tel Aviv Mossad was doing likewise. Each agency had their own reasons for doing so and Hirst-Bergan who craved for both secrecy and publicity was now one of the most watched individuals in the world.

Harry's Pub at the Sheraton Tunis Hotel offered a large bar set in convivial surroundings and it was here that Mike Weatherall had first introduced Kim Kristoff to Andrew Hirst-Bergan. On this particular night a soft-spoken gentleman with a broad Slav face, dark hair, and of average height and build made his way to the bar and ordered a cold lager. He spoke in English with a slight American accent. Kristoff picked up his drink and selected a table not too far away from the entrance where he could keep a watchful eye out for Hirst-Bergan, who he had arranged to meet at 7:30. He glanced at his watch, it was 7:25 *better to be five minutes early rather than two minutes late* he thought to himself. *At least I won't miss him sat here.* Dead on the dot of 7:30 the lift doors slid open and Hirst-Bergan stepped out into the lobby. A quick look around to confirm that Kristoff was not waiting for him there and it was off to Harry's Pub. Had he cared to have taken more than just a cursory look he may well have noticed the Tunisian gentleman sitting not too far from the lift, promptly get up and casually saunter along behind him towards Harry's Pub.

"Ah, Andrew there you are." Kristoff immediately rose to his feet as Hirst-Bergan entered the bar. "What may I get you, a beer or maybe something a little stronger perhaps?"

"Hello, Kim. Pleased to meet you again. A cool beer will be fine. Shall we sit outside?"

"Why not? Would you like a large or a small beer one?"

"A large one. I'll go and find a table."

Hmm, I wonder who your friend is Mr Hirst-Bergan? the Tunisian thought to himself as he watched the two men discreetly from a chair near to the entrance. He fumbled inside his voluminous shirt that hung loosely over his loose fitting trousers and surreptitiously produced a miniature camera. Without drawing attention to himself he manoeuvred into a position that gave him an uninterrupted line of sight to the Slavic-looking Kristoff. Another quick glance assured him that neither Hirst-Bergan nor Kristoff had noticed his action and within a split second he had taken a series of shots of both men. Having managed to obtain a number of photographs he placed the camera back inside his concealed pocket and resumed his seat, safe in the knowledge that they could not leave without being seen.

Hirst-Bergan headed towards the open patio doors that gave hotel guests access to the grounds and the outdoor swimming pool. The Tunisian watcher looked about him as if he was searching for something, then his eyes alighted on a large silver tray. *Just the thing.* He picked up the tray and placed it under his arm then boldly walked into the bar and looked for Kristoff. *Ah there you are.* He was over at the bar just paying for Hirst-Bergan's drink. The Tunisian quickly picked up Kristoff's drink, which he had left on the table where he had been sitting, placed it on the tray and walked purposefully over to where he was standing at the bar. "Thank you sir, pleeze allow me," he said in his best Tunisian accent as he addressed Kristoff. "Pleeze, I take your drinks."

"No it's OK," Kristoff drawled in his slight American accent.

"No pleeze sir, allow me." He gave a little bob of his head. "Pleeze sir, I insist or I get into big trouble with the management for no doing my job."

"Well, if you insist."

"Much, no, I mean many thanks. Pleeze sir follow me." With that he bobbed his head again and walked towards the open patio doors through which he had seen Hirst-Bergan go a few minutes earlier. Outside on the terrace he paused and casually looked around as he waited for Kristoff to join him. As a professional operator he had already noted where Hirst-Bergan was sitting over to his right near the pool, well away from everyone. He had also made a mental note that there was a table close by, partially hidden by the large ornate earthenware tub containing a large plant of some description. *If I deposit their drinks on their table I could casually walk around the corner to that other table and I may just manage to catch a little of their conversation.*

"Ah, there's my colleague." Kristoff pointed over to where Hirst-Bergan was sitting smoking a half corona cigar.

"Pleeze after you sir. I bring your drinks now." Kristoff led the way with the Tunisian following close behind. The man placed the drinks on the table bobbed his head once again and was about to withdraw when Kristoff tossed a handful of change onto the silver tray. "Many thanks sir, many thanks." He bobbed his head up and down a number of times as he backed away. *Blimey mate that was an unexpected bonus. Now it's time to make yourself scarce.* He picked up the money, put the tray under his arm and headed off towards the patio doors. At the doors he checked on the two men who were by now in deep conversation and completely oblivious to him or his whereabouts.

Later that night a Tunisian in a voluminous shirt and loose fitted trousers left the Sheraton Hotel, as he did so he nodded to an impeccably dressed businessman entering the lobby and said "target at table near the pool." Nobody noticed as a Tunisian in baggy shirt and loosely fitted trousers drove off in a beige coloured car and headed down the road towards Les Berges du Lac and the British Embassy.

Chapter 8

The secure high speed telex terminal chattered into life, spewing out the latest report from the 'firm's' field section based in the district of Les Berges du Lac, Tunis. The report was headed URGENT - UK EYES ALPHA thus alerting the admin section that it was to be treated as 'specific to British Intelligence' and not to be shared with 'the company' otherwise known as the CIA and read:

MTKZXMNDFXWBTUHLLFXMPBMALXHGWMTKZXM
GTFXDLBLMHHFXGMBHGXWTELGAXTKWGTFXPXT
MAXKTEEBLVHFLTGRTZXGMLHLLBUERATGWEXKH
KYKBXGWNDMTKZXMLXXFL2DGHPUHMALAHMHHY
MTKZXM2LXGWURLXVNKXYTQ

The message, a Caesar cipher with a shift of seven, was immediately copied and sent to the 'Codes and Ciphers' section for translation before continuing on its ultimate destination – Sir James Johnstone.

The internal phone buzzed. "Hello Johnstone speaking…"

"Sir James I/Ops desk. We have received information from our man in Tunis which I think you would be interested in, shall I bring it up?"

"Certainly Simon, say ten minutes."

"Thank you Sir James." The phone clicked as the duty officer of I/Ops replaced the handset.

Perhaps this might clear up a few questions, Sir James thought to himself as he cleared the line and then punched in his secretary's number. He heard the ring tone twice before it was picked up. "Elaine, get hold of Harry Frank and tell him meeting, conference room, say ten minutes. Also alert Jimmy and tell him that we need up to date info on the Hirst-Bergan operation. Incidentally, which of our team have we got on standby?" There was a pause as Sir James waited for his secretary to check down her standby list.

"We have three on leave Sir James, but two of them should be back in the next few days. We also have four others who are due back from overseas duties by the end of the week…apart from those, there's nobody else unless you wish me to recall Richard James?" Sir James thought about it for a moment or two before he replied.

"No. We'll leave Richard out of this for the moment, but I'll bear him and his team in mind for later…"

"Or, I could cancel all leave if it's really urgent." Elaine waited for Sir James to reply.

I suppose a few more days won't hurt!

"No don't recall anyone or cancel any leave, it'll keep but make a note in the diary to get I/Ops to release two of their people from overseas duties and to put them on standby in case we need them."

"Would that be all Sir James?"

"Err…let me think," he paused as he mentally ticked off the various items in his mind's eye, *refreshments!* "Ah yes, one other thing Elaine, refreshments for the conference room."

"Certainly Sir James, in ten minutes?"

"Yes that will be fine. Thank you Elaine."

Sir James poured himself a cup of coffee whilst he waited for the arrival of Harry Palmer Head of DP4, Jimmy from Technical and someone from I/Ops. Jimmy was the first to arrive.

"Ah Jimmy, thanks for coming up. Help yourself to a drink whilst we wait for Harry and the duty officer from I/Ops."

"Thank you Sir James."

No sooner had they both sat down when the door to the conference room opened and Harry closely followed by Simon from I/Ops entered.

"Grab a drink you two and we'll get started." Sir James waited until both his colleagues had helped themselves to coffee and sat down before he spoke. "OK. Simon," he glanced across to the young man sitting opposite him, a man in his early twenties, slim build and athletic looking with a physique of someone who regularly worked out in a gym. "You said you had received something from our man in Tunis that I ought to know about..."

"Yes Sir James, this." He passed a neatly folded sheet of A5 paper across the table to 'C'. "As you will see Sir James, the top half is the original message headed urgent and UK Eyes Alpha, so on seeing that I thought it might be important.

"Huh-huh," muttered Sir James as his eyes scanned the document held in his hand.

"You will see that I've already had it deciphered Sir James..." Sir James cast his eyes to the bottom half of the page and read the contents:

TARGET UK MEDIA BOSS MET WITH SECOND TARGET NAME KRISTOFF MENTIONED ALSO HEARD NAME WEATHERALL THINK WEATHERALL IS COMPANY AGENT POSSIBLY HANDLER OR FRIEND UK TARGET SEEMS TO KNOW BOTH PHOTO OF TARGET 2 SENT BY SECURE FAX.

"So do you have a photograph?" Sir James looked questioningly across the table at Simon.

"Yes," he answered and slid a black and white copy of a photograph of a man with Slavic features.

So this is the mysterious Mr Kristoff.

"Has anyone managed to dig anything up on him?" he asked as he slid the photograph and the message across to Harry Frank. Simon shook his head. "Not yet Sir James but we are still checking it out."

"Well let me know as soon as you've completed your checks. Does he mean anything to you Harry?"

"I can't say I readily recognise him, but that's not to say we haven't come across Mr Kristoff before. What about 'Five' have they anything on him or the *'company'*, our friends from across the big pond, and who is Weatherall?"

"Now, I can answer that one, Weatherall is definitely CIA and what's more, I wouldn't mind betting he's known to our Mossad friends. He was even around when I was overseas staff and that's going back a few years."

"So if he's one of the *'company'* boys do you think Kristoff knows, or do you think that he is just targeting Kristoff?"

"What makes you think he may be targeting Kristoff?"

"Ah, come on James, it's obvious from the photograph the man's Eastern European, bah I've seen enough nationals from the Soviet Bloc to recognise one when I see one…yeah, I'd say Weatherall is targeting him."

"Hmm, I'm not so sure. Something…I don't know what it is…a gut feeling maybe, but something tells me that we could well be barking up the wrong tree here. Mind you if we're not then why would Hirst-Bergan be interested in him and why would Weatherall."

"Could he be working for Weatherall?" Both Harry and Sir James turned to look at Simon. "Well…maybe not…"

"No wait a minute Simon…"

"Come on James…I don't think so…" Harry started to smile then stopped himself when he realised that Sir James was serious. "You really think that it's possible don't you James?"

"Well, why not? After all some of our top people have defected so why not the other way round? You know, as well as I do, that we have turned KGB agents before, so why couldn't our friend Weatherall have done the same? Eh...well come on Harry, why not? Never say never until we know for definite."

"Are you suggesting that Kristoff is working for the West?"

"I'm not suggesting anything for the moment. I think that we could be jumping to unnecessary conclusions and we need to check him out thoroughly. After all the main concern is not him, but Hirst-Bergan and whether or not he is doing a Burgess or a Philby. In other words is he defecting? Now that's the burning question, and it is this that we are trying to find the answer to. So Harry, you check with any of your sources about Mr Kristoff, and Simon you do likewise. Jimmy have you any input that you would like to add?"

"Well as you know we have already got eavesdropping devices installed in Hirst-Bergan's office and we have a phone-tap in place. We have heard the name Kristoff mentioned a number of times by Hirst-Bergan both on his phone and to his secretary, but as of yet there has been nothing concrete to suggest he is defecting. In fact from the phone calls we've eavesdropped on I would suggest that far from defecting, he is building an empire, the main thrust of which is behind the Iron Curtain. As for Kristoff, well, he just seems to be another contact. I think I'm right in saying that the link between Kristoff and Hirst-Bergan does not go back too far, but far enough for them to be reasonable business contacts." A silence descended on the meeting as the four of them pondered on what had been discussed and what, if anything, they had so far. Sir James looked up at the ceiling for a minute or two, deep in thought, then he spoke. "OK. My gut feel is we do not have a potential defector. However I do think we still need to talk to our target so, Simon, I want to know as soon as Hirst-Bergan leaves Tunis. Ideally we need to have sight of his flight plan, can that be arranged?"

"I think that's possible. However we may need to use a little persuasion of the monetary kind."

"Good then I'll leave you to organise that. Oh yes, one other thing, get a copy of Kristoff's picture out to everyone in the *'firm'*, especially those in the Soviet Bloc countries. Ask them to obtain any information they can about our Slavic friend and mark it urgent. Harry, we still need to have a chat with our Mr Hirst-Bergan because, if I am right about this, then Hirst-Bergan with his business contacts could well prove a useful person to us." There was a slight pause before he continued: "Has anyone got anything else to say?" Sir James looked around those present. "Well, in that case gentlemen, thank you very much for your information and keep me posted as and when things develop."

The sun, already low in the Moscow sky, gave way to a cool breeze as Mikhail Trepashkin escorted his protégé Svetlana from Lubyanka. They headed out into the hustle and bustle of the city commuters as they made their way home.

"Come Svetlana let us take a walk."

"OK, but where do you propose Mikhail?"

"I thought perhaps as it was your last night in Lubyanka for a while you would enjoy a nice walk in the park, you know, I like to just walk and think. They say that Chistye Ponds is nice this time of the year and a favourite place for lovers," Mikhail gave a little chuckle. *Yes my Svetlana I would dearly like to be your lover.*

"And if we go for a walk in the park then what Mikhail?" she asked coyly.

Mikhail blushed and felt embarrassed as he stammered "Oh…umm…I really only meant a walk as a friend."

"Oh Mikhail and I had hoped…" she left the sentence unfinished. Once again Mikhail looked uncomfortable and embarrassed. "Oh poor Mikhail, I've embarrassed you."

"No, I mean yes…" Then he saw her laughing and realised she was teasing him. "Svetlana Zaslavsky you are nothing but a tease." *How I wish you had meant it. Ah but I am married and you are a young beautiful woman, the daughter of a retired KGB Officer and I should show more respect for my comrade.* "Come Svetlana we go for that walk in the park and then I insist that I take you for a meal before you leave on your assignment to America." Then, without a second thought, he caught hold of her hand and started to walk briskly along the busy Myasnitskaya street, leaving Lubyanka Square behind. She didn't resist. She had grown fond of this man, although deep down she knew that it was wrong, and for one night she let her feelings rule her head.

"Then I must say 'yes' Mikhail Trepashkin, I will go with you to the park and I will let you take me for a meal," and in a low voice almost to herself she said, "and I will miss you my very own *gentle bear.*" Mikhail squeezed her hand gently as they walked on in silence; she squeezed his hand back in reply. He gently released her hand and slid his arm around her waist and pulled her toward him. She knew it was wrong, but she could not help herself as she also slid her arm around his waist and they walked like this past the Chistye Prudy metro and into the park.

As Svetlana walked through the Danish airport her thoughts returned to her last night in Moscow, how she and Mikhail had walked through the park, and from Chistye Ponds towards Taganka into the residential area of Moscow and the embankment of the Yauza river. It was here they lingered and Mikhail had kissed her. At first he was unsure and hesitant but she had responded and returned his embrace. She imagined she could still taste him on her lips as she remembered every last detail of their lovemaking in the hotel room he booked for her last night in Moscow.

She had a few hours to wait before her onward flight so decided to spend some time in the Danish capital. Everywhere she turned virtually exploded before her very eyes with colour, it was a far cry from the drab grey and monochrome of Moscow and the Soviet Union. There were beautiful shops everywhere and she was overwhelmed by the cleanliness of the city and the sights and sounds that greeted her. She had of course witnessed such culture but it had only been on film and not in the flesh so to speak. So in a way she was quite unprepared for this culture shock.

It was late in the afternoon when she eventually passed through the boarding gate to start the last leg of her journey, a fourteen hour flight to New York. For much of the trip her eyes were glued to the window and she wondered if the twinkling lights below were those of Ireland or Iceland.

Eventually her eyes closed and she fell into a fitful sleep, her mind drifting back to the previous night in the hotel room with Mikhail. How he had made her laugh. They had eaten well, gone to the ballet then on the spur of the moment booked a hotel room. In the bedroom they drank vodka and champagne, eaten caviar and laughed. She had teased him. They had embraced. He kissed her neck and nibbled her ear. Slowly he undid her blouse and exposed the delicate whiteness of her breasts. His mouth moved down across her left breast. She felt the fire within her body start to consume her very soul. Suddenly she woke with a start, her eyes quickly focused.

"Would you like some dinner madam?" *Dinner, what…oh of course dinner.* She realised where she was. *Of course Svetlana you're on the way to America.*

"I'm sorry, I was just dozing. Yes dinner of course thank you." The SAS stewardess passed her a dinner menu.

"And would you like some wine with your meal?" she asked.

"Yes please, may I have some red wine?"

"Of course madam." The stewardess turned to her trolley and retrieved a small bottle of red wine from one of the drawers and passed it with a plastic glass to Svetlana.

With the continual whoosh of the air-conditioning feeding the passenger cabin and the swish of the air slipping past the fuselage outside once again Svetlana could feel her eyes closing once again, but for all her body screamed out for sleep she was far too excited to succumb completely. All she could do was to doze, and as dawn approached and the sun started to burn off a light fog, she could see a land mass beneath her and suddenly realised she was over America. She at last saw the landscape of Russia's old rival – there below her were thousands of tiny suburban houses, endless freeways and brightly coloured cars and trucks. The plane banked and levelled out. The 'Fasten Seatbelts' sign lit up, and over the speakers came the disembodied voice of the stewardess: "Ladies and gentlemen, the seat belt sign is on and we request that you return to your seats immediately as we will soon be arriving at Kennedy Airport New York. We hope you have enjoyed travelling with us and we look forward to being at your service in the future. On behalf of Scandinavian Airlines, Captain Larsen and his crew we wish you a safe onward journey and please remember to take all your personal belongings from the aircraft when you leave. Once again thank you for travelling with us."

Svetlana watched out of the window with pounding heart and pent-up excitement, as the runway rushed up to greet the quickly descending aircraft. There was an almost imperceptible bump as the wheels touched down, a roar from the engines as the thrust was reversed and the aircraft quickly lost momentum. The roar was cut to a low whistle as the plane turned off the main runway and trundled slowly towards the terminal where it eventually came to rest. Within a short space of time Svetlana was soon being greeted by a smiling immigration officer.

"Welcome to the United States," he said as she produced her passport. "Enjoy your stay." As she made her way to the baggage hall she suddenly realised how far from home she really was. She had a momentary pang of regret but then it was gone.

Chapter 9

Before leaving Russia and the Lubyanka it had been decided that Svetlana, as a cover, would initially work for Radio Moscow as a journalist. There was no doubt in her mind that both the FBI and the CIA, or 'company' as they were known, almost certainly knew that most of the Soviet journalists in America were there for only one reason and that was to gather information for Russia and that they were spooks. Svetlana was under no misapprehension on that score and was sure that the US officials had little doubt as to what she was doing there.

One of the covers the KGB used in New York was to house their 'employees' in a high-rise block situated on Third Avenue, which they call "UN Mission". The mission was in fact the headquarters for a number of Soviet personnel, diplomats and support staff attached to the United Nations and of course KGB spies and intelligence officers. Svetlana and her colleagues, including technical staff and specialists, occupied an entire floor within this large, high-rise brownstone building where security was tight. It was within this high security area that the KGB's New York station was situated and this, along with several other rooms, was dutifully protected against electronic eavesdropping and it was here that all top-secret talks were held. The security was so tight with so many jamming devices installed, that even if one of the officers had been 'turned' and entered the building wired for sound, then there was no way he or she could have transmitted to the outside world.

Svetlana was given a very apt code name 'Felix'; matching her figure which was lithesome like a cat's. She was initially tasked to obtain Political Intelligence which meant that she was to target promising Americans who could supply the KGB with information about foreign and domestic policy. The main targets to penetrate were the White House, Congress, State

Departments, the CIA, the Pentagon, the FBI, leading scientific and research centres, major corporations and think tanks. Svetlana was assigned to concentrate on major corporations as well as scientific and research establishments.

During her time in New York she heard about the impending court case against Hirst-Bergan the British media tycoon. In fact the 'UN Mission' fairly buzzed with excitement about him and the fast gathering storm clouds surrounding his attempted business fraud. According to one of her colleagues, he had entered into negotiation with a very wealthy American to sell his scientific and reference book publishing company but in doing so it appeared as if he had artificially inflated the value of the company by using his private family business interests, which it seemed was illegal. The following morning the head of the New York station sent for her.

"Svetlana, I have received fresh orders from the Kremlin. They need you to find out about this businessman Hirst-Bergan. Find out what other interests he has and where his money comes from. They want to know everything, his strengths, and more importantly sexual preferences or deviations, in fact anything that may be regarded as a weakness. This order has been signed by Yuri Andropov himself and takes priority over anything else you are doing. From now on you are Cheryl Brooks, a British citizen and marketing manager for Andromeda Research – a European based company trying to break into the American market place with an office here in New York."

"Fine, but what if someone gets curious and decides to check out Andromeda Research?"

"It won't be a problem. We already have our legal department dealing with it. You have an office here in this building, in fact three rooms, they are a little small I grant you, but nonetheless you have an office suite. The company, on paper, employs fifty or so sales and marketing people. Of course they are all paid on 'commission only' which is normal out here, but the main thing is you do have a sales force!"

"What if someone visits Andromeda Research?"

"Even that's catered for. You already have a receptionist and secretarial staff in your offices downstairs. We have installed and connected the necessary telephones. New office furniture and filing cabinets have already been moved in and even as we speak a brass external name plate is being fixed to the outside wall near the entrance."

"And if someone takes it into their head to try and contact one of our sales guys, then what?"

"No problem, any phone calls come through the main switchboard – your office – and are passed on. Someone here will always follow up any such calls. Don't worry Svetlana all angles are covered."

The first thing Svetlana had to do, as Cheryl Brooks Marketing Manager, had to do was to find herself a new apartment, a new car and a new wardrobe, all of which had to portray the lifestyle of a successful high-flying executive. Svetlana Zaslavsky, for now at least, no longer existed and that chapter of her life was closed. Long live Cheryl Brooks!

Whilst masquerading as the Marketing Manager of Andromeda Research, Cheryl spent many hours poring over magazines and books at the Science Industry and Business Library (SIBL) in Madison Avenue. The SIBL is found just off 34th Street south of the Mid-Manhattan Library and is a useful resource on anything to do with science or business contacts. It also offers more specialised areas such as a comprehensive collection of United States and foreign documents, patents and local laws. Also foreign and US directories and buyers guides as well as extensive international trade and business resources, all of which proved to be very useful indeed. One area in particular that caught her eye was the 'Corporate annual reports' section for both the domestic and foreign industry, along with financial information services and reference works. Her aim was to find out as much as she could about the sector that Hirst-Bergan's science publishing company fitted into. It wasn't long before she had built up quite a profile about Hirst-Bergan's business interest in the science and research sector. It was certainly apparent to anyone with a modicum of business sense that Hirst-Bergan was not only a ruthless and devious person in his business dealings but he was also incorrigibly suspicious of other people.

According to her research, the scientific journal and reference book publishing business had its profits inflated by as much as a third and was sold initially for a sum of $446 million. The more she investigated this the more contradictory it became. It was like a spider's web. On many occasions, according to the financial reports, the share price was continuing to rise even though nobody seemed to be buying the stock. The share price had been rigged. This factor alone intrigued Cheryl and prompted her to trace the history of Hirst-Bergan's empire. It wasn't long before she unearthed the DTI saga and the threatened court case by the prospective purchaser of the business. According to one of the articles, the London corporate watchdog committee found Hirst-Bergan's "apparent fixation on his own abilities causes him to ignore the views of others if these are not compatible." Hirst-Bergan's reports to shareholders betrayed "a reckless and unjustified optimism," it said, that sometimes led him "to state what he must have known to be untrue."

Well, well, well I do believe you've been a naughty boy.

She continued to read further damning evidence about his dealings. According to the report "he invented deals between his private and public companies. He was incapable of distinguishing between other people's money and his own." In particular, the report criticized his inflation of the so-called sales of the encyclopaedia business and the sales of ILS

Corporation and went on to say "he sold a lot of scientific journals to related private companies and inserted them as profit." Cheryl wasn't quite sure what all this meant in real terms but she was sure it would be of interest to her bosses in the Kremlin. She carefully noted the salient points, and having returned the documents to their rightful place, she left the library and headed back to her apartment in West Village Manhattan where she put together a full report on her findings. In the morning, once she had given her report to the New York station chief for transmission to Lubyanka, she would return to the library to continue her research.

The secure phone on Sir James Johnstone's desk rang noisily. "Johnstone…I see, put him through Elaine." The phone went dead for a moment or two before a voice at the other end spoke. "Hello this is Tunis office; we have ascertained that Mr Hirst-Bergan plans to return to the UK later this evening. His flight plan has been lodged with Air Traffic this end; it states Biggin Hill as entry with an ETA of 19:30 hours. I hope this is of some assistance."

"Thank you Tunis. Any news on Kristoff, his contact?"

"Not as yet. We have our man at the airport checking flights out of Tunis but as yet nothing."

"Has he left the hotel?"

"Negative, unless he has managed to give us the slip."

"Thank you Tunis. We will be in touch."

"Anytime London, glad we could be of assistance." The phone clicked and went dead. Sir James glanced at his watch, it was nearly 4:00 pm. That gave him at least one and a half hours before they needed to leave. He picked up his phone and punched in Harry's number and waited for him to answer.

"DP4 Palmer speaking."

"Hello Harry, James here. We have an estimated time of 19:30 at Biggin Hill. Suggest we leave at…say five to five-thirty. That would give us a couple of hours to get through the rush hour and on to Biggin. Can you make the necessary arrangements with transport? Thanks Harry."

The thrust from the engines on the Gulfstream slowly moved the aircraft along the taxiway and out on to the main runway and its holding point.

"Hello flight hotel bravo one eleven, you are cleared for take-off." The metallic voice of Tunis tower came through over the headphones.

"Roger Tunis over." The pilot eased the throttle forward. The engine note changed as the power built up. He released the brakes and the Gulfstream started on its path down the runway, its speed increasing by the second. The engines hit a screaming crescendo as the nose lifted up and the wheels left the tarmac behind.

Hirst-Bergan released his seat belt, slipped off his shoes and settled back into the soft leather of his seat. "Susan," he summoned the stewardess.

"Yes Mr Hirst-Bergan, what can I do for you?"

"Fetch me some champagne from the cool shelf there's a good girl."

"Certainly Mr Hirst-Bergan."

"And ask the pilot what he estimates our time of arrival in Sofia to be?" There was a distinct pop from the galley and a few minutes later an attractive dark haired, brown-eyed stewardess appeared, carrying a silver tray upon which stood a single glass filled with champagne. Andrew had always had an eye for the ladies and Susan was yet another example of his taste in women; tall, slim, unmarried and attractive, with an hour-glass figure. Having handed him the glass of champagne she went back to the galley only to return a few minutes later with the opened bottle in a silver ice bucket packed out with ice.

"When would you like to eat Mr Hirst-Bergan?"

"Oh, leave it for now."

"Thank you Mr Hirst-Bergan, will that be all?"

"Yes Susan. I'll give you a call should I want anything else."

"Very good sir." Susan then headed in the direction of the cockpit to ask the pilot for his estimated time of arrival.

The evening had turned decidedly chilly now the sun had gone down. Sir James looked at his watch. It was nearly 7:30 pm and still no sign of Hirst-Bergan's aircraft.

Where the hell had he got to?

"You did say 7:30 didn't you James?"

"That's what our man in Tunis told me. He said the flight plan had been filed for Biggin Hill and estimated time of arrival here was 19:30." Both men peered skywards scanning all around for the merest speck that might possibly be an approaching aircraft.

Ah there it is. Or is it?

Sir James strained his eyes to focus on a tiny dot. He opened the car door and retrieved a high-powered pair of binoculars.

"Have you got something James?"

"Might have, over there at two o'clock," he said as he lifted the binoculars to his eyes and proceeded to sweep the sky above the horizon where he thought he had seen the dot. He was on it. He adjusted the focus and the fuzzy dot came into sharp relief. "Yep, it's an aircraft all right. Might be him…hmm can't be sure as it's too high to tell." He passed the binoculars to Harry, "here you take a look and see what you think." Harry swung the binoculars on to the distant dot in the sky and immediately an aircraft sprung into view. He readjusted the focus for his eyes.

It was a Gulfstream all right and heading this way, but surely it was far too high.

"It could be him but if it is then he has a lot of altitude to lose, unless he's landing elsewhere."

"Ah yes you can just see it with the naked eye."

Harry passed the binoculars back to his boss, who once again focused them on the Gulfstream high up in the evening sky. "Harry, nip over to the tower and find out what's going on, there's a good chap." Harry, with coat collar turned up to give an element of protection against the keen wind that had sprung up, headed across a large expanse of tarmac that served not only as a vehicular approach to the hangar but also as a taxi path to the main runway's dispersal area.

"Hello there, is it all right for me to come up?" he called as he climbed the short flight of stairs that led up to the main consoled area of the control tower.

"Who the bloody hell are you?" the senior controller demanded as Harry appeared on the platform. "Go on hop it, this is a restricted area," he said as he reached for the telephone. "I won't tell you again, this is off limits to the public and if you don't bugger off I'll send for security. Did you hear, I said bugger off or I'll call security."

"Hang on, hang on. Don't get excited. My name's Palmer and I work for the Government."

"I don't care if you're the Queen, you're still not allowed in here. Now for the last time bugger off!"

"Listen to me, I work for Government Security." Harry pulled out his wallet and flashed *the firm's* card at the man. "Look this is my identification," he said pointing at his MI6 establishment card. The irate air traffic controller examined the card that Harry had thrust under his nose.

"Hmm, looks genuine enough but how do I know that's not a forgery?" he asked sullenly.

Harry removed it from the plastic pocket in his wallet and turned it over revealing an address – to return the card to should it be found – and a general telephone number for members of the public to use. "Look if it makes you feel any better then get your mate over there to phone this number and ask them." He paused, then in a brusque tone that meant business. "Now sir, I need some answers if you don't mind and pretty damn quick."

The controller was about to protest but then had second thoughts. "So what is it you want to know?" he asked rather sheepishly.

"That's better!" Harry barked. "Hirst-Bergan, do you know the man?"

"Well...yes but what about him?"

"We were given to believe that he was due to land here at 19:30," Harry glanced up at the clock on the wall above the man's head, "and according to your clock it is now 19:38 and there is still no sign of his aircraft, so have I been misinformed?"

"Yes, I mean no..."

"What my mate is trying to say sir," the second controller intervened, "is that he was due to land at 19:30 but..."

"He has been stacked," the senior controller cut in.

"Stacked you say, stacked! What do you mean by stacked? This isn't Heathrow this is Biggin bloody Hill." Harry was rapidly losing his patience.

"Well sir there was a major problem earlier this afternoon."

"Where?" Harry interjected.

"In France sir."

"In France, so how does that impact on the arrival of Hirst-Bergan's plane?"

"Well sir because of that and its associated problems...there has been a knock-on effect and..."

"Look, don't try explaining it all to me. Is he or is he not landing here?"

"Well yes of course sir."

"So what is his estimated time of arrival? Is it five minutes, ten minutes or an hour?"

"When would you expect Colin?" the senior controller asked his colleague.

"He should be cleared to start his descent in the next fifteen minutes or so."

"So when would you think he will land?"

"Oh once he is on his descent path we'll bring him straight in. So what's your interest in him?"

"I'm sorry sir that's something I can't discuss, and whilst we are on the subject, this conversation is subject to the Official Secrets Act, and as far as both of you are concerned it never took place do you understand, this meeting and our conversation never happened?" Harry said emphatically.

"Oh yes we understand all right don't we Colin?"

"Yes of course," he answered nodding his head at the same time.

"Because should any of this get out, or I get as much as a whiff that you even thought about it, then you'll both be in serious trouble and end up in prison. So my advice to you both is to forget everything about tonight. OK?" Harry gave them both a stony stare. "Thank you gentlemen and on that note I'll leave you to your work."

Mike, the senior of the two men, waited until he heard the outer door close behind the uninvited guest before he spoke. "What do you reckon Colin, do you think Hirst-Bergan has been up to something or what?"

"I don't know. Maybe he's one of them."

"How do you mean one of them?"

"You know…a spook…a spy."

"Hey…you could be right."

Harry, with his coat collar turned, up walked quickly back across the open expanse of tarmac to where the boss was watching the aircraft high above them, as it slowly turned and headed back the way it had come and once again it became no more than a speck in the distance.

"Fifteen minutes."

Sir James lowered the binoculars from his eyes. "Fifteen minutes you say?"

"Yep, that's what the tower said. They said something about a major problem this afternoon, something to do with France, so his aircraft is stacked or something. Anyway that is him and I think they are just waiting for his flight to be handed over to them. From what they said they are suggesting it could be another fifteen minutes or so before he lands."

"In that case we might as well get back in the car and wait."

True to the air traffic controller's word, fifteen minutes later Hirst-Bergan's executive jet touched down on the main runway and ten minutes later it had come to a halt outside the hangar where the black limousine was parked. As the pilot killed the twin jet engines Harry and *the firm's* driver, who passed as a chauffeur, walked over to the Gulfstream and waited patiently for the fuselage door to open and the built-in steps to be lowered. They didn't have to wait long before the large frame of Hirst-Bergan appeared in the exit. As he came through the door into the cool evening air, unaware that anyone was there, he slid his arm around the stewardess and stroked her thigh as he gave her a peck on the cheek.

"Good evening Mr Hirst-Bergan."

He turned to see who was addressing him. "Who the hell are you?" he asked Harry brusquely.

"I will explain everything when you come down," Harry answered quite unperturbed by Hirst-Bergan's gruff manner.

"The hell you will!" Hirst-Bergan replied belligerently as he descended the steps. Once he was on the ground he pushed Harry to one side and headed straight for the waiting car. As he reached the car he turned and glared at Harry, who was now standing close behind him. "If you don't bugger off and get lost I'll …" His threat was curtailed as out of the corner of his eye he noticed the car's rear blacked-out window half open, through which a man's voice spoke to him.

"Mr Hirst-Bergan do get in the car. We would really appreciate your company and a chat."

"Who the hell…" he growled. By now the chauffeur and Harry Palmer were standing either side of him. The chauffeur opened the back door wide to allow Hirst-Bergan to enter.

"Now Andrew, it is Andrew isn't it? Do get in there's a good chap," a well spoken voice from inside the car addressed him. Hirst-Bergan leaned down in order to see who the owner of the voice was. Too late he realised that both the chauffeur and Harry Palmer were behind him so he had no option but to obey the mysterious person in the back of the car. Although Hirst-Bergan vehemently protested at this treatment, his protestations fell on deaf ears as the party set off for a quiet drive in the country. This was DP4's chance to make the media tycoon an offer he felt would appeal to the man's 'larger than life' ego.

As the limousine cruised effortlessly down the A25 towards Hosey Hill, Harry Palmer told their reluctant passenger what *the circus* already knew about him and his movements, the meeting he had with Kristoff in Tunis and his recent flights to and from the Soviet Bloc.

"Now Mr Hirst-Bergan in my job it is very necessary to know all about what goes on in the countries behind the Iron Curtain and also to 'advise' and 'help' businessmen who travel throughout the Soviet Republic on what to look out for. You see Andrew, I hope you don't mind my calling you Andrew?"

"I suppose not," Hirst-Bergan answered, now resigned to the fact that it was pointless arguing.

"Good. Now as I was saying, it is part of my job to advise people travelling to the Soviet Bloc on what to be wary of – for instance you maybe approached by very attractive young ladies whose job it is to entice businessmen into compromising situations."

"I guess you mean that they get you laid!"

"Well…yes. I couldn't have put it better myself. So they try and get you into bed, usually in their place where you are filmed having sex and the first you know of this is when they threaten to expose you etcetera, etcetera, but I am sure you are only too well aware of such matters. By the way, does your wife know about your little indiscretions?"

"What indiscretions, I don't know what you mean!" Hirst-Bergan snapped angrily.

"Come, come Andrew. We know all about these things. We know how lonely life can be when you are away. We are all adults and realise that sometimes a man has a few drinks in the company of a young attractive woman and sometimes one thing leads to another. I mean to say, that young stewardess on your plane, well I think any red-blooded male would enjoy her company as I'm sure you have on many occasions. Now all I am interested in is that when you visit your friends behind the Iron Curtain you keep your eyes and ears open. Now should you hear anything, or find out anything…"

"Such as?"

"Anything, let us be the judge of its usefulness, but mainly we are interested in their technology. How far advanced they are; the computer systems they use; any technical innovations that you may come across, and of course should you happen to fall over any military information on your travels then that could be very useful indeed."

"This is Leigh isn't it Mark?" Sir James addressed the driver.

"Yes Sir."

"Good, then there is a nice little country pub I know. I think it's called the 'Plough', do you know the one I mean?"

"Is that the one on Powder Mill Lane?"

"Yes that's right. I believe that they do quite a nice meal and I could certainly do with something to eat, how about you Andrew?" Without waiting for Hirst-Bergan to reply, Sir James told the driver to stop at the inn in question and to enquire about a table for the four of them.

Andrew Hirst-Bergan, for once in his life, had lost his natural exuberance and was very subdued as he stepped from the lift into his London penthouse apartment. His mind was in turmoil as he went over and over what Harry Palmer and Sir James Johnstone had said. The seed had been planted and he knew that his future was now in their hands.

Chapter 10

The sun glinted on the golden dome of the Alexander Nevsky church that stood not far from Sofia airport, located southeast of the city, on the border of the Druzhba district. The first international scheduled flights from the area took place as early as 1949 connecting Sofia with other European capital cities. Between 1951 and 1965 a massive improvement programme took place, extending the single runway and modernising the terminal building to enable the airport to cater for the rapid growth in air travel. During this period many different features were added for the comfort of its customers not least of all the addition of a business class lounge. The business class lounge, which is situated on the second floor of the passenger terminal, offers a level of comfort and exclusivity reserved only for those who were fortunate enough to be granted a special invitation card issued at the check-in desk of the airlines concerned. Unless of course your name is Andrew Hirst-Bergan, a personal friend of the most senior and influential members of State, in which case you, and your guests, are welcomed at any exclusive venue in Sofia.

It was in the business class lounge that a lone passenger, a short stocky man of Slavic features, was sitting reading a copy of the Financial Times. An article headed 'AHB Computers Expands Its Customer Base and Overseas Operation' jumped off the page at him. According to the article Andrew Hirst-Bergan, the media tycoon, was holding talks with the Bulgarian government with a view to expanding his computer and software manufacturing facility. A spokesman for AHB Computers, when asked for a comment, stated: "It is anticipated that a multi-million dollar deal with the Bulgarian Government will be forthcoming in the very near future and this will necessitate a new production and servicing facility being set up either in Sofia or close to the capital. The opening of such a facility will provide a number of jobs for the local population." A spokesperson for the British government's Department of Trade and Industry, declined to comment on what could be viewed as a potential 'risk' for the West by offering its technological expertise to a country within the Soviet Bloc.

Now that is interesting, I wonder who your contact or contacts are Mr Hirst-Bergan?

"Ah there you are Kim." Hirst-Bergan ambled over to where the lone person was sitting. "Did you have any problems getting in here?"

"None at all. I'm impressed. Now how on earth did you swing that?"

"Ah, I have friends in high places…" Hirst-Bergan smiled. *Little do you know how high my friends go Mr Kristoff. But more to the point how high are your contacts?* "Here let me give you a hand, my car's just out front," he said grabbing hold of Kristoff's bag as they made their way from the peace and quiet of the lounge out into the hustle and bustle of the main body of the terminal. "Tell me, have you eaten yet?"

"No not yet."

"Good. I've booked a table at Chevermeto; if you've never eaten there before then you'll enjoy it. It serves good food and has an excellent wine list, in fact even the Russian President has eaten there, that says something for it. There's the car, over there." Hirst-Bergan pointed to a large powerful Russian car parked in a restricted area reserved for VIPs and visiting dignitaries. As the two men approached the highly polished black vehicle a Bulgarian government chauffeur stood smartly to attention, took the bag Andrew was carrying and opened the rear door for him and his guest.

"Restaurant Chevermeto." The chauffeur gave a quick nod of his head, stowed the bag in the boot and immediately set off for the main highway into the city.

"So Kim, who have you arranged for me to meet whilst you are out here?"

"I thought I would introduce you to someone very special…a very senior member of the …umm…the government," was all he said, then he fell silent. No matter how hard Hirst-Bergan tried to inveigle further information from Kristoff about his contacts, Kim would not play ball other than to say, "all will be revealed in due course when we meet tomorrow."

"Good morning Andromeda Research how may I help?"

"Good morning," a female voice answered, "I have been asked to return a call to Ms Cheryl Brooks – you do have a Cheryl Brooks working there don't you?"

"Yes certainly ma'am. May I have your name please and the company?"

"Sure you can honey. My name is Jodie and the company is NIR, that is the National Information and Research Corporation in Washington, and my boss Jim Sullivan asked me to phone Ms Brooks."

"Just one moment I'll transfer your call."

"Well I thank you honey." The phone clicked as the switchboard operator transferred the call to Svetlana, otherwise known as Cheryl Brooks.

"This is Cheryl Brooks speaking."

"Hi there Cheryl," a man's voice came through the handset, "this is Jim Sullivan from NIR Corporation in Washington. I received your message with reference to the possibility of meeting with you next week. Tuesday would be good, shall we say 11:20, I always book appointments off the quarter and half-hour, that way people remember me as the awkward one." Svetlana smiled to herself as she wrote the time in her diary.

"Of course Jim. 11:20 it is and I look forward to meeting with you."

"OK Cheryl, see you next week, bye."

"Sure thing. Bye."

Good, perhaps this will give me a starting point. The word from Mikhail is that there are two people who could help find Oleg. One is somebody called Weatherall; the other as yet is unknown.

"Natasha," she called through the open door of her office to the Russian girl on the reception desk, "will you please book me on the flight to Washington D.C. and arrange a hotel. I need to be there Friday night onwards."

"OK it will be done."

The flight from New York to Baltimore Washington had proved uneventful. The first thing Svetlana needed to do was to pick up a hire car. It was necessary to portray herself as a very successful, high profile executive of an international scientific and media company, and the Mercedes 500 sports coupe would fulfil the role admirably. With the paperwork completed she made her way to the shining white Mercedes parked in the hire car parking lot, and within minutes she was on the 1 – 95 heading south towards the Baltimore to Washington Parkway and the Grand Hyatt hotel in downtown Washington. She needed to get checked in as soon as possible so that she could spend some time getting to know the local area, where and where not to go, where and where not to be seen. She needed to know about places of interest which could be useful topics of conversation and have a good general knowledge of her surroundings. She needed to fully prepare herself for what could turn out to be a long and arduous task, one that would require the many skills she had perfected whilst at the KGB school, even down to her feminine intuition, charms and sexuality if she was to find her man. Svetlana's first test would be on Tuesday when she would meet Jim Sullivan, the Marketing Manager for the NIR Corporation, whom she hoped would be able to shed further light on Mr Weatherall, his friends and their whereabouts.

Andrew was awakened by the sun streaming in through the partly open curtains. It was yet another nice sunny morning in Sofia and today he was due to meet Kristoff's mystery contact. Slowly but surely he was building up a databank of important key figures, not only within the local KGB but also within the Bulgarian government; any of whom could prove to be useful. His aim was to sell the software package known as PROMIS and make money. The best way to achieve his aims was to produce a complete system out here in Bulgaria and that was as good as done. All he had to do was to put his signature on the dotted line. Once his factory was up and running he knew that not only would he be able to sell into Bulgaria, he would also be able to target Russia and the rest of the Soviet Bloc. In addition to the potential sales, he also knew that having an operation here in Bulgaria gave him, his Mossad partners and their operators under the guise of being employees of AHB Computer Systems, a door through which they could pass unhindered. This would be the perfect vehicle that would enable Mossad to learn many things about the technology used behind the Iron Curtain. It went without saying such information would be priceless to Israel's Intelligence Service.

Hirst-Bergan gave an exasperated sigh. It was nearing eleven o'clock and still no sign of Kristoff. He had not heard or seen anything of the man since the previous night.
Damn it man where the hell are you?
Again he looked at his watch. He was rapidly losing his temper. If there was one thing that annoyed him more than anything else it was lack of punctuality; people who make an arrangement but never stipulate a time came a close second. In anger he grabbed the keys to his room and rapidly walked to

the door, then just as he reached out for the handle the telephone rang.

"Yes," he answered sharply, "who is there?"

"Andrew, it's Kim."

About bloody time.

"Oh, I thought you had died," he said sarcastically, but the sarcasm was wasted as Kristoff treated the remark with the contempt it deserved.

"Sorry I've been so long, but I had a slight problem."

"Oh, and what was that?" Hirst-Bergan asked, his voice showing some concern.

"Nothing for you to worry about as it's all sorted out now. Anyway I've arranged a meeting with a highly placed individual tomorrow."

"Good, at what time and where?"

"Midday in Moscow."

"What...did you say Moscow? But we are here in Bulgaria...and...and..."

"What about your plane, can't that be used?"

"Well yes...but..."

"Sorry old chap, I thought you would be pleased...I suppose it is rather short notice...tell you what I'll cancel..."

"No don't do that," he said quickly, "I'll get hold of my pilot and get him to sort out the plane. I'll call you when I know a time." He slammed the phone down.

Who the hell does he think he is? Bloody idiot...imbecile...absolute arse!

Two hours later Hirst-Bergan telephoned Kristoff's room to announce that the jet would be ready for take-off at 09:30 the following morning.

"Good afternoon Kim, is this the man you spoke of?" The man, dressed in a grey shirt, blue suit and matching tie addressed Kim Kristoff in Russian.

"Yes, this is Andrew Hirst-Bergan," he answered in Russian. The stranger looked Hirst-Bergan up and down through his half-closed eyes trying to weigh him up. Suddenly his look of suspicion fell away and he smiled.

"Andrew, it is good to meet you," he said in English. "I am known as Semion, Simeon, Semon, Shimon or plain and simply Seva and I can get many Jews out of the Soviet Union. I have many interests right here in Moscow."

"Pleased to meet you Seva. Kim told me your interests stretched as far as Israel, is that true?"

"Well of course. I have over fifty companies, legitimate of course, but there are some other interests...umm...shall we say...sidelines of mine."

"Oh yes and what are they?"

"A little prostitution, drugs, money laundering, contract hits and of course arms dealing," he announced in a matter of fact way as if to see Hirst-Bergan's reaction. But if he had expected to get one he would have been disappointed because Hirst-Bergan's face remained impassive. "Of course my other companies, the legitimate ones, are throughout Europe, Britain and Israel. So you see my friend I am also a truly international entrepreneur just like you." At this he gave a raucous laugh. "Also, like you, I have a number of family business interests, but my family is called the Rising Sun!" Again he laughed only this time it was because of Hirst-Bergan's naivety and ignorance. After all the Rising Sun was one of the biggest criminal families in Moscow.

There were two things that immediately interested the English media tycoon about the short, overweight criminal sitting opposite him, and that was the access to arms and his claim that he would be able to get Jews out and smuggle them to Israel. Both of these factors, he felt, would be of great interest to both Amir and Uzi. His mind was working way ahead now.

Once I have set up the computer company in Bulgaria and sold the system into Russia then Mossad would track down the Jews and Seva would get them out.

"So Seva, you say you would be able to get Jews out of the Soviet Union?"

"Of course, but I will need a little help…"

"What do you call a little help?"

"I need to set up more companies and in order to do that I need another passport." At this point his voice softened, "you see mister, just like you I was born a Jew, a Ukrainian Jew, but I do not have a Jewish passport and that is something that would help enormously."

Hirst-Bergan thought for a moment or two about the implications of what he had just been told about smuggling Jews out of the Soviet Union and the illegal arms, the financial gain to him and the risks involved; he thought about the possibility of getting this man a Jewish passport. His mind was made up. "Right," he said, "leave it with me. You shall have your Jewish passport but I need to be a part of your organisation and get a cut from the proceeds. Is that agreed?"

Seva thought about the possibilities. He poked and prodded it; in the end he agreed.

"OK Andrew, it's a deal. So when can you arrange my new passport?"

"Is there a phone I may use?"

"Of course my friend, in my office, please come and I will show you," he said in broken English. "Excuse us Kim. You are my guest so order some drinks, a woman maybe or perhaps something to relax the mind… a little coke to snort…or just some whisky." He slapped Kristoff on the back and laughed out loud as he led Hirst-Bergan to his office. A quick telephone call to Tel Aviv was all it took and Seva had his passport. Now he could travel anywhere he wanted - to Gibraltar, Cyprus, the Channel Islands and even the Cayman Islands where money and a 'no-questions asked' policy went hand in glove. Seva would soon be able to avail himself of these new opportunities.

Cheryl Brooks once more checked her appearance in the mirror before making her way back to the reception area.

Perhaps I should undo one more button.

She leaned forward to check the final result.

That's better, just enough cleavage showing to keep his eyes occupied.

A quick check of her make-up, the merest trace of lip gloss to give her that wet lip look and she was ready to meet Jim Sullivan.

"Good morning, my name's Cheryl Brooks and I have an appointment with Mr Sullivan."

"Thank you ma'am, what time is your appointment?"

"11:20."

The receptionist glanced up at the clock and noted that his visitor was dead on time. "Thank you ma'am. Hello Mr Sullivan, your 11:20 appointment, Ms Cheryl Brooks, is here. Shall I send her along to your office, or will you come down to reception? Thank you." She looked over to where the blonde visitor was sitting. "Excuse me ma'am," Cheryl looked up, "Mr Sullivan says he will be down for you in a couple of minutes. Can I get you a coffee?"

"Yes please."

"How do you take it, straight or with cream?"

"With cream please and no sugar."

"OK, give me a couple of minutes." With that she went over to a small room just off the reception area only to reappear a moment or two later with a cup of filtered coffee topped with cream. "There you are ma'am compliments of the house."

"Why thank you." Just as Svetlana took a sip of the hot coffee a tall dark haired good looking guy approached her.

"Hi, you must be Cheryl," he said as he extended his hand as he introduced himself. "I'm Jim, Jim Sullivan." Cheryl got to her feet, shook the man's hand and smiled. "Pleased to meet you Jim." His handshake was firm and strong. *Hmm, not bad at all,* she thought to herself as she secretly admired his rugged outdoor physique.

"Would you like to follow me through to my office?"

"Sure," she said as she followed him out of reception.

Jim Sullivan's office was at the back of the main NIR office block and looked out on to an area of neatly tended grass, that gradually sloped towards a line of trees which served as a natural boundary between NIR Corporation and the interstate highway. Cheryl cast an expert eye around her surroundings noting the layout of his office and committing it to memory. She noted the fact that there was no visible intruder alarm fitted, but that didn't mean a thing. She had already made a mental note of how far it was from reception and approximately how long it had taken to get here. On the way they had passed two elevators and a set of double doors that appeared to give access to a stairwell. On his desk was a computer screen and presumably there was a filing drawer housed in the desk plinth.

No filing cabinets though, so I wonder if he has a secretary? Her mental note-taking was rudely interrupted by Jim inviting her to sit down.

"Please Cheryl, take a seat." Jim indicated the leather chair adjacent to a small coffee table. She carefully manoeuvred herself into such a position that when she placed her half-drunk coffee on the low table, and her blouse fell open, he could not possibly fail to see the natural curve of her well formed breasts. She looked up just in time to see him ogling her natural feminine charms and smiled at his embarrassment at being caught out. From that small reaction he had signalled his vulnerability and she immediately knew from her days of training, that by skilful manipulation and her sexuality she was certain to get what she wanted. Her next move was to sit in the seat nearest to his desk so that she could check out the rest of the office for what it was worth. As she sat down she allowed her skirt to ride up as if by accident. Once again she smiled sweetly as if she was completely unaware of what had happened. Jim swallowed hard and sat in the chair opposite her.

"Now Cheryl, what was it you wanted to see me about?"

"As I told you on the phone," she leaned forward to pick up her coffee cup, "Andromeda Research is an international company interested in the scientific and technology field, and as such I was interested to meet with you to discuss your company's involvement in the recent innovative design of the new software package everyone is talking about."

"Ah, you mean the one that was trialled by the United States Department of Justice office?"

"Yes that's the one, it seems to be just the sort of innovative idea that our readership would like to know more about and I wondered if your company would be interested in us doing an article about the project...umm...what's it called again?"

"PROMIS it's an acronym for Prosecutors Management Information System."

"Thank you, PROMIS ah yes that's the one, I remember it now," she said glibly, "so do you think such an article would be possible?" She once again smiled sweetly.

Jim pulled a wry face. "Err...I'm not too sure. I'll need to think about the implications of such an article, especially as it is still being tested and hasn't been released as such. Tell you what, leave it with me and I'll give you a call," he said. Cheryl gave him another smile and nodded her head as if to agree with him, but her mind was working overtime.

No Mr Sullivan that is not an option. I need to get a line on Weatherall and I think you or your company can help.

"I understand your reticence, but rest assured I think you are losing a great opportunity. Just think what a boost an article like this would do for your company."

"I agree, but until the trials are finished we are in no position to do anything." A long silence ensued whilst she considered her next move, but it looked as if she had completely misread the signals and had now hit a brick wall.

There's only one thing for it, plan B. I will have to find another way to get my information even if it means a night time visit.

"Supposing I agreed to do something with you after the trials are finished?" Jim asked. Suddenly there was a light at the end of the tunnel.

Perhaps if I get him away from here… all right Cheryl play it cool.

"Well…that may not be a problem. Tell you what, I'm staying at the Grand Hyatt in downtown Washington perhaps you could join me for a drink after work and we could discuss it further?" Again she smiled as she leaned forward and picked up her coffee cup watching him as he snatched another look down her blouse. "What do you think Jim?"

"OK, you win. What time shall we meet?"

At last, now reel him in real slow.

"Around 6:00 or is that a bit early?"

He seemed a little unsure.

"On second thoughts could we make it 7:30?"

"Yeah, that would be OK."

"Good that's settled then." *Slowly, slowly catch the monkey.* "I have just had an idea - I've got to eat, so why not join me for dinner…"

"Umm…"

"Come on…I'll put some proposals together after I leave here and run them past you over dinner, what do you think?"

Damn it man what's stopping you…she's a gorgeous looking woman and…

"Come on Jim, as I said, I'll put some ideas together and we could discuss them over dinner, then maybe afterwards you would show me around the area, what do you think?"

At last he weakened and with a broad grin on his face he agreed to her proposition.

Time to go Cheryl Brooks you have sowed the seed.

She stood up and smoothed down her skirt and smiled seductively at him. "I'll see you at 7:30 then."

"Sure thing, I'll take you back to reception."

"No that's all right; I'll find my way back."

You stay there; I need to have a nose about.

"Well if you are sure. It's left from here through the double doors then right you can't go wrong." He opened the door and watched her as she headed toward the double doors. Having made sure that she knew her way Jim closed his door and continued with his day's work.

As Cheryl reached the double doors, she paused long enough to glance back but Jim had already gone. Making sure that there was nobody else in sight she immediately headed back the way she had come. At the lifts she paused, once again she checked up and down the corridor making sure that her way was clear before taking one of the two lifts to the top floor, where she felt some answers may be found, in her search for Mr Weatherall and his contact the mysterious Mr X.

The lift stopped with an almost imperceptible jolt and a metallic voice announced to Cheryl that she had arrived at the top floor. There was a slight sigh from the doors as they slid back to reveal a light and airy corridor not unlike the one on the ground floor. Cheryl stepped from the lift and checked both directions to see if there was anyone around, but thankfully everywhere seemed deserted.

Which way shall I go?

Suddenly there was the sound of approaching voices to her left. The decision was made. She had no time to waste if she was to remain undetected so she set off down the corridor to her right. When she felt that she had put enough distance between herself and the lifts, and she couldn't hear the voices anymore, she assumed that they had either got in the waiting lift or had entered an office somewhere, but just to be on the safe side she made sure by looking back along the corridor – there was no-one in sight. Cheryl gave an inward sigh of relief. *Thank goodness I can now get on with the job in hand.*

Having walked the full length of the corridor she still had not found what she was looking for. She had passed a stationery store, a cleaner's room, a large research and development area with a computer suite, but no secretarial or director's office. She had passed through a set of double swing doors and started to walk along the next corridor when suddenly an office door opened and she was confronted by a young woman.

"Hi, you look lost, can I help?" she asked.

Come on Cheryl think…

"Err, actually you probably could. I'm new here and I was sent up to get some information from Mr…oh what's his name, the President …Mr…"

"Oh you mean Mr Weatherall."

"Yeah, that's it Mr Weatherall."

"Well, whoever told you it was along here was wrong. You need to be right around the other side, you know past the lifts and along that corridor, it's about the third or fourth office. You can't miss it; it has 'NIR Corporate President Mike Weatherall' on the door."

"Thank you." Cheryl turned and headed back the way she had just come as quickly as possible to avoid any unwanted questions.

"Oh that's…" the young woman started to say.

Huh, I wonder what her rush is. It must be important, she thought to herself as she set off about her business in the opposite direction.

Cheryl smiled to the receptionist as she passed through the reception area.

"Goodbye honey and have a nice day."

"Thank you and you too," Cheryl replied as she stepped out through the front door of NIR Corporation and into the midday sun.

Not a bad day's work. I have landed Mr Sullivan and I've found the main director's office, all I need to do is to return here after dark and take a closer look around, I only hope that the window I have doctored is not discovered.

Chapter 11

At 7:30 dead on the dot the telephone in Cheryl's hotel room rang. "Hello, yes. OK please tell him I'll be down in five minutes. Thank you." *Right Jim Sullivan let the party begin* she thought as she replaced the handset. She checked around the room to make sure
she hadn't forgotten anything, one last check in the mirror and she was ready.

The dinner proved to be uneventful but went according to plan. Jim Sullivan, now away from his office, appeared to be far more relaxed, in fact the proposed article that Cheryl had used as bait to get him to meet her was never mentioned once, apart from when she spoke about it.

"Ah that was a lovely meal, thank you Cheryl."

"I'm pleased you enjoyed it, now the ideas I had about the article…"

"Aw forget the article, it's not that important."

"But you agreed…"

"Yeah and why not, you can do an article if you wish, and I'm sure you'll do a good job but the truth of the matter is I was more interested in seeing you again."

"Ahh, I see, in that case Mr Jim Sullivan you can just escort me to one of your best clubs around here and show me the nightlife," she said and smiled impishly at him.

It was two in the morning when Jim and Cheryl Brooks entered the foyer of the Grand Hyatt hotel.

"Let me get you a drink Cheryl."

"No thanks Jim, honestly I really need my bed."

"Aw come on. Just one then I'll leave you in peace."
Cheryl appeared to think about it, but only for a moment. "Mr Sullivan, you're incorrigible. OK but just the one!"

"I promise." *Hmm, perhaps you'll let me take you to your room!*

"On second thoughts, why don't we take the lift to my room and have a drink there?" she said and laughed.

Great minds think alike.

"Are you sure?" he asked her innocently.

"Of course I'm sure. Come on race you to the lift."

Cheryl slowly and carefully lifted Jim's hand from off her naked breast and slid out from underneath the duvet. She gently lowered his arm and re-covered it. Then on tiptoe she moved across the luxurious bedroom carpet, all the time keeping her fingers crossed that he would not suddenly awaken. As she moved across the bedroom floor a floorboard creaked underfoot. *Damn!* She paused with bated breath waiting to see if he stirred. She strained her ears for the slightest tell-tale sign of him waking, but nothing. His breathing was still regular and he didn't move a muscle. She felt a slight twinge of guilt. After all, in training they had always said you used sex for the job, there was no mention of enjoyment but she had enjoyed it. She allowed herself a few moments to savour her memories before pressing on with her plan.

First things first she thought as she felt inside the rear pocket of his trousers for his wallet. *Ah there it is.* Next with bated breath she crept forward towards the bathroom where she had earlier stowed a change of clothes – a pair of black jogging pants, trainers and top.

Just a few more steps to the bathroom and relative safety.

Suddenly she froze, he was starting to stir – *please don't wake up!*

"Cheryl, are you all right?" he called to her in a sleepy voice.

"Yes I'm fine, just going to the bathroom, go back to sleep," she called back to him softly.

"OK, but don't be too long."

"I'll try not to be." She waited until she heard him breathing regularly once again, then waited a few more seconds just to reassure herself that he had gone back to sleep. She then slipped into the bathroom, closing and locking the door noiselessly behind her. Once inside the bathroom she expertly rifled through his wallet and found exactly what she had hoped she would find – a swipe card that would allow her access into the offices at NIR Corporation. Now with lady luck shining on her, she could perhaps find out what she needed to know.

On her return from NIR yesterday she placed her suitcase in the Mercedes and paid her hotel bill, using the excuse that she had an exceptionally early morning start. The only thing she had to do now was to bundle her clothes into her bag pull the room door closed and head off back to the NIR office block for her night time visit before returning to New York.

Within half an hour she was back inside NIR Corporation, the swipe card that she had found in Jim's wallet had proved invaluable. Not only had it got her into the main building, but it had also been useful for access to the corridor where Mike Weatherall's office was situated. In a matter of minutes she had his office door open and she was going through his desk with an expert touch. She knew exactly what she was looking for, anything to connect Mr X to NIR. There was nothing. She had drawn a blank. There was one last chance and that was the filing cabinets in his secretary's office. As an expert in these things it only took her a couple of minutes to open up the locked filing cabinets. Her nimble fingers rifled through the buff-coloured folders stopping at one labelled 'personnel & contacts'. A quick glance at the clock on the wall told her that time was getting on and that she would need to hurry. She pulled out the folder and flicked through the alphabetical list inside, running her finger down the list of names. Suddenly she paused at a name listed under 'H' that seemed somehow familiar but she didn't know why. The name was Hirst-Bergan but there was no other information except a number.

Was it a telephone number?

She hastily wrote the name and the number into a little jotter that she had in her pocket. Unfortunately there was no mention of anyone other than Hirst-Bergan.

Maybe I'm wrong, maybe he has nothing to do with this company at all.

She had worked right the way through to 'W' where she located Mike Weatherall, the name of the boss. Against his name were two interesting pieces of information, one was his home address, the other was that there was a second factory in California.

Hmm, interesting. Now why didn't Jim mention this and more to the point why wasn't it listed in the library back in New York?

She was now convinced more than anything that her hunch was right. Apart from these two pieces of information nothing spectacular had been revealed, so Cheryl replaced the files, re-locked the cabinets and checked that she had left everything as it should be. Then she made a quick check on the time and realising it would soon be daybreak decided it was time to leave. She closed the door behind her and quickly made her way back down to the ground floor.

As the early morning sun penetrated through the bedroom curtains at the Grand Hyatt hotel, Jim Sullivan began to stir. He stretched out his arm to feel the warmth of Cheryl whose bed he had shared for the night. His hand fell on a cold sheet. Suddenly he was wide awake.

Where are you Cheryl?

He rubbed the sleep from his eyes and looked around the room. There was no sign of her. *Perhaps she's still in the bathroom, perhaps she's not well.*

That last thought galvanised him into action. He threw back the duvet and swung his legs out of bed. "Cheryl, come on where are you?" he called but there was no reply. "Cheryl, are you all right?" he called, but without waiting for a reply he was across the bedroom to the bathroom door in no time at all.

Goddamn it speak to me!

He pulled open the door nervous at what he might find.

Well we did have a fair bit to drink.

He stopped dead in his tracks and let out a sigh of relief. Cheryl wasn't there, the bathroom was deserted. His relief suddenly evaporated and gave way to anger. He hit the wall with the side of his fist giving vent to his hurt pride and his feelings. "Fuck, fuck, fuck."

Why have you done this Cheryl?

Slowly his anger subsided and as he became more rational he looked around the room for clues as to where she could be. The first thing he did was to open the closet. It was empty, not even her suitcase remained. He pulled open the drawers in the dressing table; there wasn't a piece of clothing anywhere to be found.

No shoes, no clothes and no suitcase.

He looked all round the room for clues then he saw it, an envelope resting on the pillow where earlier she had slept. He immediately picked it up and tore it open, inside was a single sheet of paper on which was a hastily scribbled note: -

Dear Jim,
Sorry for not saying goodbye, but I have an early morning flight to catch and you looked so peaceful sleeping there. Thanks for a great night, and the sex was amazing. I hope

that our paths cross again sometime - till then goodbye and sweet dreams.

Cheryl xx

He read and re-read the note as it slowly sunk in that she had gone out of his life.

Well Jim there is only one thing for it and that's to have a shower and grab a cab home. Pick up your car and get off to work. Just put it down to experience and a great night out.

It was now over a week since Svetlana, masquerading as Cheryl Brooks, had returned to New York with what little information she had managed to glean from her illegal entry into the office of Mike Weatherall at the NIR Corporation. There was one piece of information that she still found puzzling, that was the name Hirst-Bergan which she had found in the file of contacts. She still did not know why this name was so familiar, then like a bolt from the blue *of course he owned one of the newspapers out here in New York, he was that media tycoon from Britain who had a court battle for pumping up the share price of his scientific publishing company. Also he is one of the main people I need to get close to. Now what is his connection with NIR?*

"Natasha," she called to her colleague, "can you book me a seat on the first available flight to Los Angeles and book a hotel in the name of Cheryl Brooks again. Also I need a full kit to take with me, and can you ask the New York desk if there are any reliable contacts that I could use in L.A?"

"OK Svetlana."

I think it is about time I paid you a visit Mike Weatherall.

"In fact let's change that Natasha, can you book me on a flight to Boston, then down to Fairfax from Boston. Don't book it via Boston but as two separate flights."

"So you want a single from here to Boston then a single from Boston to Fairfax IAD?"

"Yes, that's right."

"What about California, do you still want that?"

"No I'll book onward from Washington DC if I go, but book me on the Fairfax flight in a different name."

"How about Sheri White?"

"That's fine."

Two days later Svetlana, now known as Sheri White, arrived in Fairfax Virginia, her target this time was Mike Weatherall the president of NIR Corporation. She needed to know more about his movements and more to the point his connection with Hirst-Bergan. Her first job was to find his address, a place called Gainsborough Court, Jermantown Road in Fairfax. This time she hired a fairly nondescript vehicle as it was her intention, that once she found his home, she would keep a watch on his movements and see where that would lead her.

She hadn't been waiting too long before, out of the corner of her eye in her rear-view mirror she caught sight of a red Chrysler as it turned into Jermantown Road, heading towards her and Gainsborough Court. As the Chrysler approached her parked car, Svetlana, thinking that she may well be seen, sank as far down in her seat as she possibly could and held her breath. Then as it drew level with her, it suddenly slowed right down. For a moment she thought the driver had seen her and that the game was up, but then he drove on and turned into one of the driveways further along the road that led to Gainsborough Court. He then disappeared from view. Immediately the danger was past Svetlana, adrenalin pumping, was out of the car and running quickly to the vehicular entrance into which the red Chrysler had turned. She got there just in time to see a slightly built, fair haired man about 5' 10", get out of the car and head for the big detached house 'Gainsborough Court' that gave the development its name.

So you are Mike Weatherall!

She paused to get her breath and thought carefully about her next move.

Do I wait for him to leave and follow him, or do I check out his house?

Whilst she was considering her options her hand was forced as the front door reopened and the fair haired man reappeared. He was carrying an overnight bag which he tossed onto the back seat of his car, then he got in the drivers side. She could have kicked herself for being caught off guard *damn, too late to do anything now* she thought to herself ducking back into the shadows as the red Chrysler swept past her. The one saving grace was that from her vantage point she managed to get his number, this she hastily jotted down in a little notebook that she always kept just for such an eventuality. With Weatherall out of the way for the night Svetlana knew what she had to do - she would return later.

It was a little after midnight when a black Ford saloon car turned into Jermantown Road and headed towards Gainsborough Court. As Svetlana neared the access drive into Gainsborough Court she doused her lights and pulled up onto the private entrance. Fortunately for her it was a clear night and the moon gave sufficient illumination for her to negotiate the vehicular access into the grounds of Weatherall's home. As she approached the house she killed the engine and let her momentum carry her forward into the shadows cast by the trees and the surrounding buildings and here she parked. Then she took a number of items out of her bag; a set of skeleton keys, a miniature camera, a small pencil light and a small electronic gizmo used to override alarms. Now she was ready.

I wonder if there is a Mrs Weatherall or for that matter anyone else at home? she thought to herself as she placed the tools of her trade in the pocket of her black jogging pants, pulled on a jet black sweater, black ski mask and black leather gloves. Slowly she opened the car door and living up to her code name *'Felix'* she slid catlike from the car, closing the door silently behind her. Standing in the shadows, the darkness enveloped her and in her black attire she melted into the night and became invisible. She took two or three deep breaths to calm the butterflies in the pit of her stomach and waited for her eyes to become accustomed to her surroundings before slinking quietly off in the direction of the house.

Slowly and quietly she made her way through the garden, past the front door and around the side of the house. *So far so good!* She checked along the side of the house using her torch sparingly to ascertain whether or not there appeared to be any form of intruder alarm fitted, she also gently tried each of the windows on the off chance that he may have left one undone, but to no avail. As she rounded the corner to the back of the house she again momentarily switched on her torch.

What's that?

She shone the light on a heavily armoured cable that appeared to run from a junction box under the eaves and down the wall to about a couple of feet above her head. She shone the pencil light on the junction box and noticed what looked to be telephone cables coming away from it.

Shit it must be alarmed, but why isn't there an external alarm? Hmm a silent alarm, so where does that go?

Svetlana made a mental note of the fact that not only was the property alarmed, but it was unusual in as much as it was a silent alarm.

Gradually she made her way around the perimeter of the property, testing each ground floor window as she did in the vague hope she would find one undone. The house seemed to be as tight as a drum which only left her with one option and that was to break in at the rear of the house, risk the alarm, give it a maximum of ten minutes to find whatever she could and be out. With her mind made up she returned to the rear of the house where for some unknown reason, call it sixth sense or woman's intuition, she just happened to glance up towards the roof line and low and behold there was a bedroom window open. This discovery could mean one of two things, either he had been in such a hurry that he had forgotten to close it, or there was somebody on the premises. If that was the case then it could prove to be quite useful. With this latest revelation Svetlana changed her plans and turned her attention to the garage where she felt sure she would find some ladders.

The plan was now to enter the house via the upper story window, which if someone was in there would mean that the alarm downstairs would be on a walkthrough delay. If, on the other hand, there was nobody there then this would indicate that the alarm was either not set, or it was only partially set. Her reasoning was that if it was a silent alarm, and there was no reason to believe it was otherwise, then it would be quite a sophisticated system. This would either warn the operator that a window was still open and could not be set, or else it would downgrade to a partial '*system set*' which would only detect a forced entry. Either way was good for Svetlana's purpose.

With her lock picking skills carefully honed at the KGB school, it took Svetlana little or no time at all to gain entry into the garage where she found the set of ladders that she had hoped would be there. Within a couple of minutes she had them placed up against the wall just high enough for her to ease the window off its catch and open it fully. She paused and listened to see if she could hear anyone breathing, but all seemed quiet. Slowly she pulled herself up and slithered across the windowsill, her lithesome body entered the room head first. With arms outstretched she slowly lowered herself down onto the floor and as silent as a cat she rolled forward and sprung up onto her feet. Again she paused and listened for the slightest sound. *Is that breathing I can hear?* She switched on her pencil torch and shielding the light behind her hand crept forward across the floor. Now she was sure she could hear breathing. She extinguished the light, paused and listened carefully.

Yes it was off to her left, so there is a Mrs Weatherall or someone else after all.

Stealthily she moved away from the breathing until she found the wall and followed it around until she came to the door. She felt for the door handle, but her luck was in, the door was already open. Silently and on tiptoe she crept from the bedroom and out onto a large landing. Once outside the bedroom she again risked switching on her torch. In the narrow beam of light she could see the stairs and a hallway below. She swung the light around the landing and noted that there were seven other doors apart from the one she had just come through. She extinguished the torch and turned back to the bedroom door and very carefully and silently closed it behind her. Now she could get on with the job in hand. Her first task was to silence the alarm. She knew that the panel would be somewhere close to the front door but she would have to work fast as there would only be a short time delay to allow the inhabitants time to enter the alarm zone from upstairs and disarm the downstairs with the correct code.

Holding the flashlight between her teeth, Svetlana placed the little gizmo, which had been designed in Moscow specifically for the KGB's use at Yasenovo, against the alarm control panel and pressed its trip button. In milliseconds it had scanned the electronics housed inside the panel and came up with a six digit code. Svetlana immediately punched the code into the keypad of the control box and the low level buzzing, which had been emanating from the box as an audible warning, now ceased. Svetlana exhaled a big sigh of relief now safe in the knowledge that the alarm system was disarmed. She now moved around almost carelessly to a degree, but still silently. She checked out the room off to the left, but that held nothing of interest it was a games room with a full sized snooker table. The next room she checked was adjacent to the games room and turned out to be a library. Her third selection proved to be the right one for it was here in the beam of her torch she discovered a large roll top desk. She cast the light quickly and skilfully around the room picking up on a number of large oil paintings, heavy drapes at the windows, a number of leather bound books on shelves and various antiques. This room had promise. She quietly closed the door behind her, checked that all the heavy drapes were closed then switched on the standard lamp close to the desk for additional light. She then turned her attention to the desk and with skilful manipulation of the skeleton key set she had it open in no time at all.

Although there were some interesting facts about the company NIR Corporation there was nothing that she felt was of use, except maybe the address of the Californian plant which could be her next port of call. Having now satisfied herself that there was nothing further of interest Svetlana turned her attention to the drawers. The top drawer only housed accounting books for NIR; still there was nothing of interest. It was similar for all the drawers she went through, nothing at all except papers concerning the company. She was about to give up when a small cash box caught her eye. Upon opening it she found a key and a few business cards but nothing untoward. *Now where do you belong?* She carefully studied the key that she had discovered and wondered what it unlocked. She tried it in each of the drawer locks but to no benefit. She tried the lock on the desk with the same result. She searched inside the desk for a hidden drawer but drew a blank. Then she ran her hand under the top of the desk but still nothing.

She sat down at the desk and tried to imagine herself as Weatherall and where he might hide things. The obvious answer was a safe, but this key wasn't a safe key. It had to be in or on the desk somewhere. With her fingers she carefully tapped the underside, listening to the noise it made. As she moved along there was an imperceptible change but nonetheless a change. She tried again. Yes she could definitely hear it. In the centre it sounded hollow. She got down onto the floor and shone her torch under the desk and there it was, a keyhole, carefully concealed behind the inlaid edging of the front of the desk. *Very clever indeed.*

The key fitted and a section of the underside slid noiselessly back to reveal a small box held in place by two arms on pivots. Svetlana had a feeling about this and she was not wrong. Inside the box were a number of things of interest. One was a little black address book listing a number of telephone numbers throughout the United States as well as overseas. One number of specific interest was the one against Mr Andrew Hirst-Bergan. Svetlana wasted no time at all in photographing the information. Another telephone number was a company called AHB Computers in Tel Aviv and it also had Sofia written against it, but no address or telephone number. There was a name Kim Kristoff with a note saying "*introduce to Hirst-Bergan when in Tunis could be useful.*" This last name was interesting but she didn't know why, could he be Mr X?

There was another black book which didn't at first make any sense whatsoever. All it contained was a series of numbers, some codes and nothing more except at the back it listed various amounts of money. Little did Svetlana realise at the time that she had unwittingly discovered the CIA's controller of money laundering. Nor did she realise how important the series of numbers was. She replaced the book without giving it a second glance. A third book again proved of little immediate interest but this gave coded information about his contacts in both the CIA and Mossad. Again Svetlana failed to realise its importance, but this time just as a precaution she photographed its pages. The final thing in the box was a small handgun, a Berretta, the gun favoured by Mossad, especially the *kidon* which was the equivalent of the KGB Department V or *'wet department'*, the unit for dispatching traitors, dissidents or others unspecified. Suddenly it dawned on Svetlana that Mr Weatherall must be CIA, FBI or Mossad, this had to be a bonus. Elated by her discovery, she carefully replaced her finds back in the box, making sure everything was as she found it; replaced the box back in its secret compartment, slid the drawer back into place and re-locked it. She put the key back where she had found it and with the skeleton keys carefully relocked the drawers and the desk. Next she switched off the standard lamp and with torch in hand she retraced her footsteps to the hall. The only difference now was she could go out through the front door once she had re-armed the alarm.

With the bedroom window placed back on its catch, the ladders restored to their correct place and the garage relocked Svetlana's job here was complete, but she still had to find Mr X, perhaps the British media tycoon held the secret.

Chapter 12

Time had moved rapidly since the day that Kim Kristoff had introduced Andrew Hirst-Bergan to Seva, the overlord of the *'Rising Sun'* family in Moscow, and a lot had happened since then. AHB Computers was now a firmly established international company and under Andrew's guidance it was rapidly expanding its customer base. There was one thing that Hirst-Bergan could do well and that was selling. So far, in conjunction with his Mossad partners, he had legitimately managed to sell his system with the 'doctored' PROMIS software into a number of the Soviet Bloc countries and by using AHB Computers as a vehicle, Mossad operators and katsas (case officers) had now managed to successfully infiltrate behind the Iron Curtain, something that they had never done before. And by posing as computer specialists, technicians and engineers of AHB Computers, Israelis were able to move freely between Tel Aviv and Sofia, making it possible to set up a fully functioning covert operation right under the noses of the KGB. This enabled them to gain not only useful information about the Soviets' technical abilities as they moved freely around the satellite countries of the Iron Curtain, but also any other information that they may or may not require at any one time. By successfully carrying off such an audacious operation Amir and Hirst-Bergan between them had managed to make Mossad one of the most powerful Secret Intelligence Services in the world, and Amir's credibility with his masters was at an all time high.

William H Weinberg had for many years followed an uneventful legal career and it came as a great surprise to many people when he was appointed as the director of the Federal Bureau of Investigation – commonly known as *'the Bureau'*. The local media watched and waited with bated breath when he took up his post, half hoping that there would be more of the headline-grabbing stories just as there had been about his predecessors, but the worst that any reporters could write about him was that 'Weinberg was a safe pair of hands'. He had now been the Bureau's Director for quite some time and had long since developed the skill of walking an invisible tightrope which was constantly being tugged one way or another by either the Director of Central Intelligence at Langley or the President's National Security Advisor in the White house. If it wasn't them on the phone calling him, then it was their assistants.

On this particular morning, sitting in the back seat of his chauffeur driven Lincoln, he mused about the current ongoing secret FBI investigation and he knew that many of the men that he frequently spoke to on a day to day basis had been touched by it. The investigation, which had already been running for a year, was so secret that he had all field reports sent directly to him on his own secure fax number. Based on the content of such reports and in the privacy of his own office he, and only he, would decide who should see the latest summarised evaluation.

Because of the sensitive nature of the enquiry both national security and international operations were involved; this had implications for both diplomacy and security, resulting in some knowing a great deal whereas others were only told as little or as much as they needed to know. Even the chair of the Senate Select Committee on Intelligence and the President's Foreign Intelligence Advisory Board were kept in the dark on this one.

Weinberg had a good reason for doing this as one of those being investigated was a powerful figure on the Washington political front, his name was Frank, John H Frank, a Texan Republican senator and very close ally of the equally powerful media tycoon Andrew Hirst-Bergan.

It was John Frank who opened the most important doors for Hirst-Bergan, including that of the President's Oval Office. Hirst-Bergan with Frank at his elbow, was often allowed to run over his allocated time slot, unlike Britain's ambassador to the United States and various government ministers from the United Kingdom who were strictly allocated time accordingly with no leeway. Even the Presidential staff were astonished by how Hirst-Bergan even with Frank's help, had managed to inveigle his way into the White House.

One of the many things that the ongoing investigation had thrown up was that Hirst-Bergan's relationship with John Frank went back quite some time. In fact Hirst-Bergan had realised some years previously that the only way to succeed in the United States was to use a lobbyist and he very quickly learnt that their wealth came not only from the generous salaries that they commanded, but also from the bribes that they collected. For instance when major corporations wanted something passed through Congress their lobbyist would use politicians who, in return for their votes, would receive exotic holidays for their families, or generous stock options. Often senators and congressmen were offered directorships and consultancy positions and suitably rewarded accordingly with both cash and gifts. Everyone had a price and Hirst-Bergan knew it. He also knew that if he were to succeed in the USA then he would have to follow a similar path of corruption.

One night, whilst in New York at the Four Seasons, Hirst-Bergan noticed one of the previous President's old advisors. Even though he was no longer at the centre of power he was nonetheless still useful and Hirst-Bergan engaged him in conversation.

"If you are to make your mark Andrew," the man said, "then I suggest you meet up with John H Frank. After all, he is one of the mainstays of the Republican Party and a past chairman of the Senate Armed Services Committee. You know

Andrew, after twenty five years on Capitol Hill John Frank has decided to call it a day. Now I wouldn't mind betting that he will resign within the year, and if that is so, then he could well be looking for an opening to maintain his current lifestyle."

Andrew, this sounds too good an opportunity to miss.

That night, from his suite at his hotel in New York, Hirst-Bergan called the private number of Amir in Tel Aviv.

"Hello Amir. I have heard on the grapevine that there is a possibility that Senator John Frank is possibly going to retire in the next twelve months and he could be worth approaching. What do you think?"

"Frank you say, he's a big fish you know. Wait until I've checked him out."

Mossad held files on all senior US politicians, constantly updating them with reports from its case officers or *katsas*. Frank's file held detailed information about his political opportunities, his numerous extramarital activities with different high-class hookers and his business dealings over twenty years. It also linked him to the assassination of President John F Kennedy.

After reviewing the file on Frank, Amir informed Uzi of Hirst-Bergan's hope to employ the senator. Uzi was enthusiastic in so far as he felt that even in retirement Frank would still be one of the major players on the Washington political scene. A man who would still have the President's ear and be a fount of information about US policymaking in the Middle East. He would know many things, even perhaps how far Washington was prepared to go in their support of Iran in their fight with Iraq and with this uppermost in his mind Amir called Hirst-Bergan at his hotel.

"Andrew, I've spoken with Uzi and we are in agreement. This man Frank will, I'm sure, prove to be a very valuable asset so you have our blessing. Employ him."

It began as simply as that.

Andrew Hirst-Bergan, ever mindful of the necessary protocol in such matters, did not go back to the contact he met in the Four Seasons, but instead decided to ask one of the American board of directors of his publishing company to arrange an introduction to Frank. He was an intellectual who was highly thought of in Washington and he contacted Frank and explained what was on offer.

"Tell Hirst-Bergan that I don't come cheap and already I've had a number of companies approach me so I'll only meet him as long as we're not talking small change," was his reply to the offer.

This blunt, straight talking no holds barred response brought a smile to Hirst-Bergan's lips, as it was nothing less than he'd expected from him and that night he phoned Amir.

"What is the rate for a retired senator such as Frank?"

"I would say whatever it takes, Andrew. Just get him."

John H Frank's background was impressive, as Amir knew from Mossad's files. He was born in Houston Texas the son of a preacher. After graduation he joined the US Navy. During the war he served in the western Pacific on an amphibious gunboat and in Hirst-Bergan, a man who owned a yacht larger than the vessel he had served on, John H Frank would soon find a common interest. Like Hirst-Bergan, he had fought his way to the top and in doing so, like Hirst-Bergan, he had created many enemies but in Frank's case they were among old-money Republicans who felt that someone with more of a social standing should have been in his Senate seat.

Even his political friends were disturbed by John H Frank's arrogance and blunt manners. However no one could deny that it was his dynamism as he rose through the Republican ranks, that gained him seats on many important Senate committees to such an extent that he was regarded by his Democratic opponents as 'ruthless, rude and unscrupulous.' There was no doubt about it; he was a truly self-motivated person with the same energy that drove Hirst-Bergan. This was not the only similarity, they even had the same taste in crude jokes. So much so that when one of the Republicans' elder statesmen in the Senate as a seventy year old, married a twenty-two year old beauty queen, he said, "When they bury him, they'll have to beat his pecker with a baseball bat to keep the coffin lid down."

Upon first meeting Hirst-Bergan, John Frank cut straight to the chase. "My fee for acting as your personal consultant will be $200,000. No more no less, take it or leave it."

"Hmm, so what do I get for my fee?" asked Andrew.

"For two hundred grand I will guarantee to open doors to Capitol Hill, to defence contractors and even the Oval Office should you so wish. In fact if you want to visit the White House I can arrange it. If you have a product you wish to sell to the US armed forces I can open doors to people who control the purse strings. This is what you get for your $200,000."

Hirst-Bergan took a moment or two to consider what Frank was offering before he agreed. Of course he already knew it was a good investment and he would willingly pay this amount into whatever account Frank chose, but he didn't want Frank to think that he was too eager. That night he called Tel Aviv.

"I tell you Amir, this is a shrewd deal because he can open many doors and he is now on the payroll."

"OK, I hear what you say Andrew so tell him to open the door to Los Alamos and Sandia Laboratories because it is there that we want to install PROMIS."

"OK Amir he will do it," Hirst-Bergan replied confidently. "In fact he had better do it otherwise there will be trouble. I'll tell you what Amir, there is no way that I'm paying out these vast sums of money just for him to sit on his arse in Capitol Hill and that's a fact," retorted Hirst-Bergan.

Yes my friend, if he doesn't perform then I'll be talking to a few people so don't you worry on that score.

That evening Hirst-Bergan, not letting the grass grow under his feet, contacted John H Frank.

"John, I need you to get me in at the Sandia facility Albuquerque. I need a good audience. I need to have the main decision makers, the ones who will commit to the purchase of complex software, and the people who hold the purse strings as well as the project managers. I need anyone and everyone who has a say in the purchase of such things. Anyone who can influence such a decision needs to be there for me. Understand this John; there can be no half measures. This must be right first time make no mistake about that."

Within a few days of his conversation with John H Frank, Andrew Hirst-Bergan was on his way to the Kirkland Air Force base which was not far from Los Alamos and was the Sandia facility's airport.

The Sandia facility is situated in New Mexico south-east of Albuquerque and not far from Walker Air Force base. The Walker Air Force base, or Roswell Army Airfield as it was also known, was at the centre of a UFO report in 1947 when it was believed an alien craft crash-landed on a ranch in the Roswell district. It is the Sandia facility that is central to the defence of the USA and it is in their laboratories where research and design work of the most sensitive nature, concerning America's nuclear programme, is undertaken. It is this facility that is at the forefront of technological innovation and which helps America stay ahead in the arms race. As such it is protected by the best security systems ever devised. Sandia is at the core of America's nuclear defence and it is here that new weaponry systems are developed, with a power so unthinkable that few would wish to contemplate the outcome.

The Gulfstream began its descent towards Albuquerque and had Hirst-Bergan cared to look south-westwards he may just have just been able to make out a small dot in the distance that was the township called Truth or Consequences, a name that may well have brought a wry smile to his lips had he known of its existence, but Hirst-Bergan had more important things on his mind. After all he had good reason to be preoccupied. Even though he had sold PROMIS into a number of intelligence services and other agencies around the world, today's presentation would be different. As Amir had said the people in Sandia were highly skilled and trained to look for any signs of deception. They were trained to look for the problematic, the wrong move or the wrong word, the appearance of being too keen or being evasive, even for the most innocent of reasons. Anything could trigger alarm bells, so Hirst-Bergan was justified in being so pre-occupied because in a short space of time he would be inside Sandia making his case as to why they should purchase his software package.

As the private jet taxied to its resting place at Kirkland Air Force base Hirst-Bergan picked up his bulky briefcase which held the two copies of PROMIS doctored by Amir's programmers. He made his way to the exit, knowing full well that in a matter of minutes he would be on his way to what could well be the most difficult sales pitch of his entire life. Outside on the apron a stretch limousine and its driver waited patiently for the multi-millionaire media tycoon from England, as did the FBI agent whose job it was to log the movement of all visitors to Kirkland Air Force base including Hirst-Bergan and his entourage.

Hirst-Bergan had over time developed a well rehearsed presentation as his sales pitch. He told the engineers, executives and scientists gathered together in the boardroom of Sandia, that whilst they may know of him through his connection with John H Frank he was also well connected elsewhere. He proceeded to illustrate this by giving his audience a whirlwind tour from Russia to England, from the British Prime Minister at No. 10 Downing Street to the palace of the French President. He dropped names of European leaders and told them of his frequent visits to the White House and the time spent with the President.

"I have on many occasions visited your own nuclear air arm at Strategic Air Command Harwell, which I am sure you all know is Britain's own nuclear facility and of course NATO's headquarters in Brussels. Of course I do have a close relationship with Israel, America's ally, and Israel's leaders and I continue to support their economy." Now it was time for him to introduce PROMIS. "Gentlemen, I will not ask about what you do here, but suffice it to say that Senator Frank has told me enough for me to know that it is very important work. In fact, important enough for me to have travelled all this way in order to introduce you to this piece of software." Hirst-Bergan immediately opened his bulky briefcase and removed one of the two disks which he then held aloft.

"Gentlemen, on this disk you will find software developed in Israel to handle all aspects of project management. To date it is the most powerful software ever developed in this field of project management. It will, amongst other things, provide the user with all critical path networks; it will provide important and critical information, fully track information and offer a complete solution to project management problems. Gentlemen this is PROMIS - Project Management Information System. This total solution software package is only available through MIS, Management Information Systems of San Francisco right here in the USA, and they will handle all the negotiations from here on." Judging by the general discussions that ensued, Hirst-Bergan was almost certain that he had clinched a deal and was convinced that by the time he left Sandia his company, MIS, would have netted a cool $39 million of which his personal cut would be $3.9 million. Already his $200,000 investment in John H Frank had paid off.

Svetlana closely studied the photographs she had taken of the numeric codes and the data that she had discovered on the night of her visit to Mike Weatherall's house. But try as she might, she was unable to find anything that gave her a clue about Mr X or his identity. The only information she had was a reference to Kim Kristoff, Hirst-Bergan and ABH Computers all of which she had discovered in Weatherall's possession. The more she studied the photographs the less the information made sense, and this left her in a quandary as to what her next move should be. Should she make a return visit to Gainsborough Court in Fairfax in a further attempt to find more documents, or should she return to the NIR Corporation in Washington? Another possibility to consider was the NIR facility in California, should that be where she should concentrate her effort? Perhaps Hirst-Bergan, the multi-millionaire from England, should be the centre of her attention? All these options had possibilities but after careful consideration she decided that Hirst-Bergan should be her next port of call.

But that, Svetlana, may well prove to be easier said than done!

"Ah, Svetlana there you are." The voice of Alexei, head of the KGB New York station, interrupted her thoughts. "I just thought you might like to know that our man in Washington has heard a whisper that Senator John H Frank is about to join forces with Hirst-Bergan. In fact, he may already have done so."

"Did I hear you correctly? You did say Hirst-Bergan didn't you?"

"Yes Hirst-Bergan the media mogul from Britain."

With the mention of Hirst-Bergan and the possibility of him being linked to a senator on Capitol Hill Svetlana's interest was immediately aroused.

Now this could prove interesting!

"What did you say this…err…senator's name was?" she asked eagerly.

"Frank or Franks, something like that," Alexei answered in a matter of fact sort of way, but then he saw the fervour in her eyes. "I am curious Svetlana, why is he of great interest, I thought Hirst-Bergan was the important one?"

"Hmm, maybe," she answered quietly.

That's it. If I can get up close to the senator then that could help me with Hirst-Bergan!

"Look Alexei this is only an idea," she said having regained some of her composure, "I need to get to Hirst-Bergan so what better way than through someone he trusts!"
Alexei nodded his head as he began to see what she was driving at.

"This man, this senator, tell me again Alexei about what you have heard."
Svetlana, without thinking, tapped lightly on the desk with her carefully manicured finger nails as she listened to Alexei as he once more repeated what he had heard from the Washington station.

"Do me a favour Alexei," she asked once he had finished talking, "find out all you can about Senator Frank. His likes, dislikes, friends and associates, any weakness or deviation, everything, and I mean everything, you can."

"But Svetlana we already have a file on him."

"We have?"

"Of course."

"Is it up to date?"

"Well…as far as I know it is."

"Brilliant. So give me the file as I may just pay Senator John H Frank a visit. By the way, who is our main contact in Washington?"

"The head of section there is Ivan, Ivan Pedrosky. I know him well, in fact we trained together in Moscow. After our training he came here to New York whilst I spent a year in foreign counter-intelligence in Lubyanka before joining him. Since those early days he has been back home, and then to Europe – East Germany in fact. Eventually, after a short stint in Finland, he came back here as head of station for six months before moving to take over Washington station. After his move I was promoted and took over here. Yes Svetlana, Ivan and I go back a long way."

"So would you arrange a meeting with Ivan?"

"Of course, anything for my *Felix*, my Russian doll!" Alexei gave Svetlana a wave of his hand and smiled as he turned to leave her office. "I'll send Mr Frank's file down with my secretary," he called back as he left the office.

Huh, my Felix, my Russian doll indeed. Bah!

Ivan Pedrosky was lean and athletic-looking, with piercing blue eyes that seemed to see into the very soul of a person. His energetic manner belied his forty nine years and his boundless enthusiasm inspired those around him. His shrewd assessment of any situation came naturally to him and enabled him to side-step many issues, making him the envy of his colleagues. There was no doubt about it Ivan should have made general, but because he never kowtowed to Moscow, coloured his reports accordingly, or said what his superiors in Lubyanka wished to hear, he had never made that rank.

It was Friday afternoon when Alexei introduced Ivan Pedrosky to Svetlana.

"So you are *Felix*," he addressed Svetlana and smiled briefly. "Your beauty and reputation travels before you, and I have heard much." Svetlana looked at him curiously. "And what do you mean by that Mr Pedrosky?" she asked. He smiled and his eyes twinkled mischievously as he answered her. "Only good of course."

"In that case I am pleased to meet you Ivan; Alexei has also told me many good things about you…" With a wave of his hand he quickly dismissed Svetlana's comments. "Bah Alexei talks too much, I am nothing." She gave him a knowing look. "It is true. I just do a job for our masters back in the Lubyanka and that is all," he stated, playing down his role within the KGB as if it was a mere office job and quickly changed the subject. "I gather from Alexei that you wish to know more about what is happening in Capitol Hill?" Svetlana nodded her head. "Well let me see, where shall I start?"

"If I said to you that I needed to find some way of getting close to a man called Andrew Hirst-Bergan would that help?" asked Svetlana.

"Ahh, the man they call the 'media king', the man who has a large computer interest in Israel." He nodded his head knowingly. "I have also heard he has a company right here in America." There was the trace of a smile then it was gone. "So my Russian *Felix* why do you need to get close to him?" Svetlana opened her mouth to answer but he stopped her. "No, don't tell me let me guess." He thought for a moment then with eyes half closed he continued. "Our lords and masters have an interest in this man. Yes, that's it. Our lords and masters know that he comes in contact with the right people and, what is more, he has invested in our economy so they need to know more about him. Am I right?" he asked with a trace of a smile.

"Very good Ivan and of course you are right," she glibly said as that was *not* her real task. Her task was to track down the man known only as *Oleg* for he was the one that had betrayed her country. *He is the traitor in our midst*! That was what she had been told by her good friend Mikhail Trepashkin on that fateful day in Lubyanka and she remembered it as if it were yesterday.

It was Oleg who beat your father and raped your mother all those years ago. He is the man you need to find. For a moment she was that young girl again, witnessing what had happened all those years ago. She gave an involuntary shudder. She had to get close to Hirst-Bergan to find Mr X who she was sure would ultimately lead her to *Oleg.*

"So has Alexei spoken to you about the Republican – John H Frank?"

Ivan's voice brought her back to the present.

"Yes, he said that there was a rumour that a Senator Frank was now on the payroll of Hirst-Bergan, is it true?" she asked, pushing unpleasant memories to the back of her mind.

"As far as I know it is true. John Frank is retiring from the Senate and like many of his colleagues he needs an income to fund his life-style, and I have heard that Hirst-Bergan has taken him on as a consultant to his company in San Francisco."

"Do you know the name of the company?"

"I believe it's called Marketing Information Systems or something similar."

"What do they do?"

"It's a marketing company selling computer software."

Svetlana fell silent and thought. *I wonder if I could introduce Andromeda Research to them and get through to Hirst-Bergan that way.*

Ivan momentarily held her in his stare, his piercing blue eyes searched her face and then, as if he could read her mind, he said "I wouldn't consider getting to Hirst-Bergan through San Francisco."

"Why not?" she asked.

"Well to begin with it is run by his eldest daughter and her Bulgarian husband. In fact Hirst-Bergan has very little to do with it so if it is him you want to get to then the best way is probably through the senator."

"OK, but how?"

"That's easy. He has a habitual weakness for women," then as an afterthought he added, "especially beautiful green eyed blondes like you." Once again Ivan flashed his infectious smile and Svetlana lowered her eyes in embarrassment. *Ivan Pedrosky, you are incorrigible* she thought and felt herself blush. "He is what the British would call a womanizer. He has had many affairs, so Svetlana why not target that weakness of his, a girl of your talent and beauty could easily…." he left the rest of the sentence unfinished. "Get him into a compromising situation," she immediately answered. Ivan nodded his head in agreement. "Any suggestions as to how?" she asked.

He thought about it for a moment or two before answering. "How about a party, an exclusive 'do' at the embassy right here in New York, or at one of the hotels? I'm sure we could arrange such a thing and of course we could always bring along a number of …shall we say businessmen with their wives. We could then invite Mr Frank as the contact from Hirst-Bergan's company, or maybe even Hirst-Bergan himself who knows." Again she saw that fleeting smile and then it was gone.

"Now if you did manage to get Hirst-Bergan then that would be brilliant."

"Well stranger things have happened Svetlana so don't discount it. If we do get him then you know what to do, and if we don't… then you work on Senator Frank; either way I am sure that such a *krasavitsa,* or how the Americans say, such a beautiful woman, will get what they want in the end." Ivan gave Svetlana a broad grin and a knowing wink. "Do you not agree?"

Svetlana nodded her head and a faint smile touched her lips as she thought about the possibilities. "Yes, you are right Ivan. I will do my part provided you can set it up," she said confidently.

"Consider it already done my dear!"

Chapter 13

In order for Svetlana and her colleagues to be successful, it was necessary for Ivan to return to Washington to talk to his contacts. He desperately needed information about the different events that Senator Frank had attended. *Perhaps a fete or garden party* he thought, but both of these he quickly discounted as probably being too unlikely.

A party maybe, this would be more likely. Yes a party held at another senator's house, a dinner party perhaps, but...
Although it seemed a good idea and highly likely, it was far too intimate. What he needed was some sort of event where Svetlana and the senator could quite conceivably have met. An event that was formal yet informal, not too large and yet large enough to enable Svetlana to convince him that they had met using something along the lines of *' perhaps it has slipped your memory', or 'don't you worry it's probably a minor lapse as I'm sure a busy man like you meets many people during your working day!'*

He picked up the phone and dialled a number. He didn't have too long to wait before a male voice answered in Russian. "Boris that woman, whose name escapes me, the one on Capitol Hill that you cultivated for us...Ah yes that was her name Donna, well can you contact her and get her to supply us with a list of any official engagements that Senator John Frank's name appears on...no I need garden parties, fetes, fund raising events anything along those lines, in fact anything involving members of the public say... over the last couple of years, and I need it fairly quickly. Thank you Boris." With that Pedrosky replaced his phone. *Once Boris has the information,* he thought to himself, *we can move forward and Svetlana will have her basic cover story. Then all we have to do is to get him to our party in New York.* So that was Ivan's plan.

Donna was a single woman and a senior administrative assistant working in Senator Frank's office. She had previously worked in the American Embassy in Moscow. The KGB's internal counter-intelligence directorate, which amongst other things was charged with watching and recruiting foreigners living within the USSR, had decided to try and recruit her. To this end a young, good looking KGB officer was assigned to the operation and using his charms he had a torrid affair with her during her two year tour and subsequently had been able to ensnare her. Upon her return to America and her new post in Washington, Ivan Pedrosky's station was directed by Lubyanka to continue to cultivate the woman and so Boris, another young operator, was introduced to her at a diplomatic reception. Using the guise that he worked for a Foreign Ministry and was a great friend of her lover it seemed only natural that they should become friends, and it was not long before Boris, again using sex and romance, had the woman passing what she thought was harmless information.

Donna had, for the last few years, dealt with the senator's diary, arranging appointments and requests for his attendance at various venues and public events. When she was asked by her good friend Boris about past events she did not see any harm in telling him what she knew, in fact most of it had been covered in the media so was already in the public domain. Within a few days she happily supplied Boris with a list of some eighty to a hundred events and venues that John H Frank had attended over the previous two years, and safe in the knowledge that most of them were already in the public domain, she was sure she had not compromised security.

There was a tap on Ivan Pedrosky's office door. "Come," he called, and a tall good looking Russian sporting a neatly trimmed moustache entered. "Ah Boris, you have the information?" enquired Pedrosky.

"Yes sir. I have the list from Donna as requested," he answered handing over a brown envelope.

"Sit down Boris," Ivan said as he withdrew a single sheet of paper, embossed with the name Senator John H Frank, from the envelope. He quickly scanned down the typewritten list of venues, dates and events occasionally pausing to read some additional typed notes about certain venues or events. "Thank you Boris. Well done comrade I am sure this will prove very useful indeed." He smiled with appreciation, "and the woman, Donna, she was happy to give you this?"

"Yes sir. She said it was no problem."

"Good. Perhaps you should buy her some small token for her trouble, maybe a small pendant say up to $30, she is a good contact and we need to keep her happy."

"Yes sir." Once more Ivan smiled. "Good, then that is all Boris." With that the young KGB officer stood smartly to attention, gave a quick nod of his head in acknowledgement and left the room. As Boris pulled the door closed Ivan returned to reading the typewritten sheet that lay on the desk in front of him. Taking out his fountain pen he proceeded to edit the list by striking out some of the more formal engagements where guests would have appeared on a guest list. Next he turned his attention to small dinner parties with fellow senators or friends, these he drew a line through. *Too small and intimate.* Eventually he had reduced the list by about fifty percent, but it still left a good thirty to forty possibilities.

Ivan read and re-read the remaining list of engagements making his own additional notes against each event. At last he had the event, an annual Awards Dinner Dance held at the New York Marriott Marquis. The event in question was the platform used to present awards to individuals and organisations for their extraordinary efforts and notable achievements in improving the quality of life for all people who were blind or visually impaired. It was large enough for Svetlana to have possibly attended. Although it was a ticket only event, it was quite conceivable that Cheryl Brooks, Marketing Manager of Andromeda Research, could well have been present. There was also a distinct possibility that she could have met John H Frank at such an event and highly likely that he would accept it as fact.

So my Felix, we have your cover story of where and when you met him, all we need to do now is to find a suitable venue and create a function

The theme for such a function would need to capture the imagination of the senator and also to appeal to his ego. *So there needs to be a reason for such a party,* Ivan thought to himself. *It also has to make the man feel important, therefore the invite must be from a VIP.* Then it occurred to him, they could use Svetlana's cover, Andromeda Research - the fictitious company that had purposely been created by Alexei the head of New York stations KGB section. Slowly an idea started to form.

Andromeda Research in the USA has just secured a multi-million dollar contract with an overseas pharmaceuticals company and as a celebration the President of Andromeda Research and his Marketing Manager Cheryl Brooks request the presence of Senator John H Frank to attend an exclusive champagne reception and cocktail party.

Although it still needed working on he felt the basis was there and it was this idea that he proposed to his old friend Alexei. Now all they had to do was to decide on a suitable venue.

After much discussion with Ivan, Alexi decided that a small intimate party held in either the Manhattan Club or a local hotel, would achieve far more than a formalised function at the embassy. After careful consideration and being mindful of Frank's reputation for having affairs, it was felt that provided the owners were prepared to hire out the club exclusively for twenty four hours then the Manhattan Club, with its central location, easy access and intimate atmosphere would be the ideal venue.

For America to stay ahead in the arms race, the facility at Los Alamos known as the Sandia facility needed to stay abreast of leading edge technology in all aspects. Sandia, as a high security government facility and because their modus operandi dictated it, had a dedicated department used specifically to establish rightful ownership and copyright of any new software program prior to its use. The department, upon checking their extensive database would soon ascertain whether or not Hirst-Bergan's offer to supply them with the new software package - Project Management Information System – was in fact his exclusively to offer. It didn't take Sandia long to ascertain that the database of Hirst-Bergan's company, Marketing Information Systems of San Francisco, was actually linked to over two hundred computer databases. This enabled them to compile technical and business information via US government agencies. Further checks also revealed that MIS customers had to pay a subscription to have access to information held on its database and advice on how to obtain information from the American government databases. However it was apparent from Sandia's searches that none of the information obtained from these agencies or similar institutions constituted a risk, nor was any of the information obtained classified. Nevertheless security at the Sandia facility dictated that a certain protocol must be followed and as such it meant that the National Security Agency also had to run a security check on MIS.

A security trace was subsequently carried out by NSA who advised Sandia that MIS was owned by 'Hirst-Bergan, the British media tycoon and owner of the scientific publishing company that supplied various scientific establishments throughout the world with reference books, scientific papers and information.' It also stated to Sandia that a number of customers of MIS were from companies in countries behind the Iron Curtain. Based on this information, and as an added precaution, one of the technicians carrying out the searches within Sandia telephoned the FBI in San Francisco. This immediately triggered alarm bells and agents from the San Francisco office were despatched, without delay, to the offices of MIS where they questioned at length the president of the company. Whatever the outcome of their questioning, it was decided that the matter did not warrant any further action by them, but it was felt that it was important enough to refer the matter upwards. However, instead of going to Albuquerque, the agent in charge felt it to be so serious that he contacted Weinberg, the FBI Director, and outlined his worries in a memorandum classified SECRET.

In his communiqué to Weinberg he outlined his concerns stating that 'San Francisco indicates negative regarding Hirst-Bergan and his scientific publishing arm. President of MIS interviewed and business described as "a marketing and information research system company", which supplied information to its subscribers'. The final paragraph of the document confirmed that 'AHB Computers in Tel Aviv had been a client of MIS for many years and as such it would be impossible to recollect all the information that had been requested by them'. His report then concluded by stating that the president of MIS had *'fully cooperated with the FBI and that San Francisco was taking no further action'*.

Exactly twelve months to the day after the communiqué from San Francisco was sent to Weinberg, Albuquerque FBI regional office submitted a similar memorandum classified SECRET. In their memorandum they stated that they had been conducting certain investigations into the activities of Andrew Hirst-Bergan and *'that in light of information brought to the attention of FBI Albuquerque regional office, the NSA had stated a wish to establish liaison with the Bureau, but to date we have had no further word from NSA. In view of this lapse we feel that perhaps it should be brought to the attention of Director Weinberg for his personal attention.'*

From Director Weinberg's point of view suddenly there was another agenda, something he couldn't rightly put his finger on, but someone somewhere was blocking his investigation. There were some very powerful people involved at the highest level and it was made very clear by the powers that be that the investigation into Hirst-Bergan and his dealings had to be dropped. With Hirst-Bergan having John H Frank on board to open various doors right up to the President's Office it was obvious that it was possible to exert pressure in all kinds of places, from the White House to the top of the CIA and NSA. This resulted in the NSA deciding not to pursue further investigations, leaving Director Weinberg with no option other than to direct Albuquerque to advise Sandia that 'they were taking no further action and this matter was now closed'.

The Manhattan Club lobby with its distinctive marble floor and leather settees immediately gave the feeling of opulence and exclusivity, *just the right sort of venue to hold this evening's reception and party,* thought Alexei as he checked on how the team was progressing with its preparations. Already the caterers were on site preparing the caviar. Champagne had been put on ice in the members, bar and the toastmaster had been briefed. The embassy had taken over all thirteen floors and every suite on each floor in order to maintain privacy and security. Each floor had been swept by the Russian security service during the morning and Alexei knew that there were now no problems with regard t security. All they needed now was confirmation from Senator John H Frank's office that he would be attending, but as of lunchtime Andromeda Research had still not heard a word. *This is not good* thought Alexei as he took the elevator up to the penthouse where Svetlana was going through her preparation as Cheryl Brooks ready for the evening.

I hope this is not a complete waste of time Alexei; otherwise you could have a lot of explaining to do!

As the elevator approached the thirteenth floor a soft female voice announced "floor thirteen and Penthouse suite." The elevator came to a halt and the doors slid back noiselessly giving access onto a luxurious hallway that even Trump Tower would be hard pushed to equal. Alexei stepped from the lift out into the hall and headed through the open oak door into an expensively furnished lounge.

"Svetlana," he called.

"Through here Alexei. I'm on the phone."

Alexei followed the sound of Svetlana's voice as it drifted through the double doors that opened into the lounge from the large well appointed bedroom.

"Are there you are, any news from Washington?" he asked as he entered the bedroom just as Svetlana was putting the phone down.

"That was Natasha; she has just received a fax from the senator's office confirming his acceptance of our invitation and states that he hoping to be with us a little after 20:30. She said that he apologised that he couldn't get here before '*but unfortunately he has a late afternoon meeting which requires his attendance so he will be delayed and offers his apologies.*' Well that was the gist of it."

"Phew, thank goodness for that." Alexei's relief was apparent. "I was beginning to think that maybe I was going to have to answer some very difficult questions and explain why I had authorised such expenditure to our masters in Moscow."

"What do you think to this?" Svetlana waved her hand around the room, "do you think it will do?" she asked.

"Hmm, very nice," he answered appreciatively. "Very nice indeed." He slowly walked back into the lounge and looked around at the high class reproduction antique furniture and the expensive décor. "Just the right setting for that intimate drink at the end of a busy schedule, yes very good indeed."

"Oh, and did you notice in the bedroom, we have very discreet microphones and cameras installed just so that we can exert a little pressure on the senator should the need arise. Also Ivan Pedrosky is close to hand with a couple of his men should I require help at anytime."

Alexei nodded his head approvingly. "I think you and Ivan between you have thought of everything." He glanced at his watch, it was already showing just after 17:00. "Ah my *Felix* time marches on, and with just over three and a half hours to go before our guest of honour arrives I have much to do and I am sure you have also. So we will aim to have everyone in position by 19:30 so the good senator senses that the party is well under way. And don't forget - use whatever it takes to get at Hirst-Bergan and his empire." With that Alexei started to walk towards the hall. "Oh, I almost forgot," he called back over his shoulder as he reached the door, "I had a telephone call from a Mikhail Trepashkin in Lubyanka today..."

"Really!" Svetlana answered enthusiastically, "and what did Mikhail have to say?"

Alexei turned to face her. "Oh, not a lot. He wanted to know how you were, how things were going. Just this and that really."

"Oh, is that all?" The disappointment in her voice was obvious.

Alexei smiled. "There was one other thing he did say..."

"Yes and..." she asked expectantly, "what was that?"

"He said your father and mother are very proud of their daughter and he said his thoughts are with you every day."

Alexei smiled broadly. "You know I think Major Trepashkin is a little bit in love with our *Felix*, don't you?"

Svetlana, under Alexei's gaze felt embarrassed and looked away. "Oh, don't talk rubbish. I think you read too much into what he said." *But I hope you are right* she thought to herself.

Having now received confirmation from Senator John H Frank's office that he was going to attend the party at the Manhattan Club, Alexei, head of New York KGB station and his good friend and colleague, Ivan Pedrosky head of Washington KGB station, devised a plan by which they could alert Svetlana to Frank's movements. This was a simple plan involving low level surveillance and the embassy security staff, a job that was well within their capabilities. The main body of the security personnel, who would be discreetly wired with concealed microphones and earpieces, was to circulate amongst the invited guests in the bar and function room, where they could easily keep track of both Svetlana and the target. In addition to the main team, two other members, also discreetly wired like their colleagues, would be on duty at the entrance. Their job, to all intents and purposes, was to make sure that those attending were bona fide guests and had in their possession a personalised invitation, and that their name appeared on the guest list. However this was only a cover as their primary role was to notify the co-ordinator, Ivan Pedrosky, as soon as the senator came into view. Alexei's role for the evening was to act as the boss of Cheryl Brooks and President of *Andromeda Research* and he, like the security personnel, was also discreetly wired. Svetlana had the most difficult job of them all. It was her job to use whatever means she had at her disposal, including sex if necessary to cajole, extract or entice information about Hirst-Bergan and his empire from the senator. In addition to this she had the agenda set by

Lubyanka as well as her own personal agenda to find *Oleg* and *Mr X*.

At six thirty the team gathered at the Manhattan Club for their final briefing by Ivan. "This is the target, this is Senator John H Frank," Ivan said as he flashed a picture of the American senator up on the screen. "You will look at his photograph and commit it to memory," he picked up a small pile of photographs and passed them to one of the security team, "here pass these around. Now for the two on the entrance, I need to know as soon as he arrives so that I can pick him up. Keep him chatting until you get the clearance from me OK?" A man and a woman nodded their heads. "As far as the rest of you are concerned, remember this is discreet surveillance nothing more and nothing less. Also as co-ordinator I will always take priority over anything else on the communications and that is a definite, unless of course there is an emergency. Should an emergency arise then the code is *security, security, security* spoken three times in quick succession and that, my comrades, takes precedence over everything including me. On hearing the code all other communication will cease immediately and the person issuing the emergency code assumes control, advising us as to the nature of the problem and how we can help, how many required and his or her position. At all other times keep talking to a minimum. Understood?" There was a murmur of assent. "Then that's all until 19:30."

Svetlana was dressed in a low cut azure blue evening dress with sapphire earrings and a sapphire drop pendant to match. She looked stunning as she circulated amongst the guests, pausing now and then to talk to different people, supposed guests of Andromeda Research, about this and that in the pretence of being the hostess. It was whilst she was engaged deep in conversation with Natasha that another guest's arrival was announced by the toastmaster.

"Ladies and Gentlemen, Senator John H Frank."

On hearing the announcement Natasha gave Svetlana the briefest of smiles and an almost imperceptible nod of the head and glanced over towards the door. "It looks as if our man has arrived," she whispered to Svetlana, "and he is alone."

Svetlana smiled. "And what does he look like?"

"Pretty much as his photograph." As Svetlana went to steal a glance at the new guest, Natasha gently took hold of her arm and steered her away across the room.

"What's wrong?" Svetlana asked Natasha in a hushed voice.

"Nothing it was just that he was right behind you and I thought it a bit obvious that's all."

"OK *Felix* to your right is the senator," the soft voice of Ivan Pedrosky came through the earpiece that was carefully sculptured into the body of her blue sapphire earrings.

"Please excuse me," Svetlana said loud enough for those close by to hear, "I've just seen someone over there I must say hello to." Hoping that her staged excusal was not too obvious Svetlana, with half a glass of champagne in her hand, headed towards the tall dark haired well built stranger whose back was toward her. As she drew close to the target she heard someone call her.

"Cheryl, Cheryl Brooks."

She turned to see who was calling to her and as she did so, so did the unsuspecting senator. His arm came into contact with her hand and the glass of champagne she was holding went everywhere but mostly over the senator. The ruse could not have worked better.

"I'm so sorry," said the senator, "how clumsy of me."

"No not at all, I should have been looking where I was going." Then, as if she had just recognised him. "Why it's you, I mean Senator Frank. It is Senator Frank isn't it?"

"Yes I am John H Frank, should I know you?" he asked looking puzzled.

"Yes John, don't you remember? We met a while back, surely you remember?"

His brow furrowed as he tried to remember her face but he drew a blank and slowly shook his head. "Nope I can't say I do…"

"Sure you do, it was at that awards dinner," she paused but the senator still looked blankly, "you know the one, the one at the New York Marriott Marquis. I was introduced to you."

"Ah yes I remember it now but your name escapes me."

"Sorry, how remiss of me, I'm Cheryl Brooks the Marketing Manager for Andromeda Research. Now do you remember me?"

"Of course," he lied, hating to be caught out like this, "you were the lady I spoke to during a break in the proceedings."

Nice lie mister, but a good line anyway thought Svetlana. "Good I'm pleased we've cleared that up," she touched his arm, "oh dear, you're jacket is soaked, come with me and I'll sort it out," she said grabbing hold of his hand.

"No it's fine honestly."

"But I insist, and you wouldn't want it said that I threw champagne over one of my guests now would you?"

John Frank looked at her beautiful face and grinned. "OK, you win."

"Now that's better," she said as she led him from the room to the elevator that would whisk them to the penthouse suite where hopefully she would get the information she needed.

Chapter 14

Svetlana and John H Frank stepped from the elevator into the luxury of the penthouse suite.

"Is this where you're staying?" the senator asked incredulously.

"Of course why?"

"Well all I can say is your company must pay you handsomely because I could never afford such luxury."

"Nonsense, you are worth a fortune," she retorted. "Anyway, this isn't getting your jacket sorted out, come on through here." She led him into the lounge. "Take your jacket off and make yourself comfortable whilst I try to get the worst of the champagne out." The senator removed his jacket and without saying a word handed it to Svetlana.

Good man, now I wonder what if anything your jacket will reveal.

"Thank you John, I hope you don't mind me calling you John?"

"No that's fine, really."

Svetlana took the senator's jacket and went to the bathroom where she proceeded to dab a wet cloth along the sleeve in an attempt to remove the champagne before it stained. "I won't be long," she called to him through the open door. "While I'm doing this help yourself to a drink and put some music on if you wish." She carefully adjusted the shaving mirror above the wash basin so that she could view a large section of the sitting room through the open door. Once she had ascertained that John H Frank was safely out of her view and she was out of his, she left the tap running and tiptoed over to the bathroom door and gently closed and locked it.

Now let's see what revelations your pockets hold

Quickly and skilfully she went through his pockets to see what, if anything, she could glean from their contents.

However, John H Frank did not get to be in his position in life by being careless, so just as she expected there was nothing of any consequence to be found, except a small complimentary box of matches. On the front of the box was the silhouette of a naked lady under which was emblazoned the name *The Silhouette Night Club*. On the back of the box was the telephone number and the downtown address. As she turned the box over and over in her hand she wondered where she had seen that logo before, then like a bolt from the blue it struck her. The club had recently been the lead story in the media after an undercover operation by the FBI had raided the premises of the supposed owner and his son, linking them to extortion, prostitution and the sex trade of women and children. The indictment of the supposed owner had shown that the club was linked with one of the biggest criminal families in Moscow, the one known as the Rising Sun.

Ah yes it is all coming back to me now. I remember Mikhail telling...

But her train of thought was rudely interrupted by a knock on the bathroom door.

derr`mo, b`lyad'! She uttered the two Russian profanities under her breath at the interruption. "Just a second," she called as she quickly looked for somewhere to hide the matchbox. There was nowhere accessible, so as a last resort she pushed it behind the shaving mirror and the wall keeping her fingers crossed that it would stay where she had lodged it. "Just coming," she called as she tiptoed to the toilet and flushed it, then hurriedly turned off the tap that she had left running before opening the bathroom door. "Sorry about that John, I desperately needed...you know," she smiled at him sweetly.

Slowly the smile faded as she realised that the senator, who stood at the door, was purposely barring her exit. "John, come on now, stop messing around." She gave a slightly nervous laugh. He moved his hand down lower on the door jamb and stared deep into her green eyes, a stare that was, even for her, a little unnerving. "Come on John, why are you staring at me like that?" she asked a trifle nervously as he slowly shifted his gaze to her plunging neckline and her cleavage. Slowly he licked his lips in anticipation. She could feel the sexual tension in the air as he leered at her.

"I think you know why," he said his voice croaky with lust.

"I don't know what you mean John." She gave him a weak smile. "Please let me pass so I can dry your jacket," she said, her voice almost a whisper as she feigned fear, but she knew exactly what he meant and she knew exactly what she needed to do. He didn't move, he just continued to stare at her cleavage mesmerized by her breasts and her sexuality. Slowly she nodded her head and pushed her way past him. She felt his breath hot on her face as her breasts pushed hard up against his chest as she forced her way out into the lounge. He never flinched, just lowered his gaze and stared at the bathroom floor for a moment or two, before turning round. He then followed her as she made her way from the lounge into the luxurious bedroom, where she would hopefully get some answers.

"Is everything OK?" the soft low voice of Ivan Pedrosky, situated in the suite of rooms on the floor below, came through the miniature earpiece concealed in Svetlana's earring. She glanced up at one of the miniature cameras and nodded.

"Yes fine, but we need something on him," she answered in little more than a whisper.

"OK, leave that with me," Ivan replied as he watched the picture of Svetlana on his screen as she moved across the bedroom. "Boris, that reporter friend of yours, has he any dirt on our friend the senator?"

"I'm not sure, but if he hasn't I'm sure something could be found," he gave Ivan a knowing wink, "leave it to me." With that he disappeared into the next room where there was a telephone. He dialled the area code for Washington followed by an ex-directory number and waited.

"Hello," a young man with a Texan drawl answered, "who's there?"

"Jimmy, it's your friend Boris. Can you talk?"

"Sure, what's the problem?" he asked.

"Senator John H Frank, he's the problem. What have you got on him?"

"Such as?"

"Anything at all, photographs, scandal, girls…anything along those lines."

"OK, so where can I reach you?"

Boris looked at the number on the phone. "I'm at the Manhattan Club in New York so you can call me here on 888 201 6711. I'm in room 503, and it's urgent so please come back as soon as you can."

"OK man, I'll dig out what I can and I'll call you back within the hour."

"Good, thanks Jimmy." With that Boris replaced the handset and returned to the surveillance room to give Ivan the news.

As Svetlana kicked of her shoes John H Frank entered into the bedroom. His heart pounding in anticipation of what was about to happen. Again that lascivious look and he licked his lips as he pictured her naked and astride him.

Ah yes you are so young and desirable and those beautiful nubile breasts of yours just crying out to me…

She turned to face him. Momentarily he held her at arms length, and then suddenly pulled her to him, but she was too quick by far. She smiled at him, twisted away and in a flash was out of his arms.

"Now what do you think you are doing Mr Frank?" she playfully admonished him. Again he made a grab for her, and again, like lightning, she twisted and ducked out of his reach. "Now, now Mr Frank, this is not very becoming of a senator is it?" She laughed as she leapt barefoot onto the bed and stood provocatively before him. Again he lunged at her, again she sidestepped him and danced lightly out of reach as he overbalanced and landed on the bed with his face buried in the duvet. Slowly he raised his head up and grinned.

"Cheryl Brooks you are a bad, bad woman leading me on like this."

She laughed out loud as she playfully teased him.

"Keep him dangling Svetlana." The soft voice of Ivan percolated through her earpiece. "We should have something within the hour so play along with him. In fact we are recording on video right now."

Svetlana gave a quick glance up at the discreetly positioned camera and gave an imperceptible nod in its direction before turning her attention back to John H Frank. Suddenly he grabbed her ankle and with a quick yank he pulled her foot from beneath her and she collapsed, laughing and giggling, in a heap on the bed. In a trice he was on her, his mouth covering hers. Initially she tried to push away from him but slowly her fight subsided and she surrendered to his embrace. Her lips parted slightly as she returned the kiss and she could now feel his hardness as he pressed his body hard up against her. She felt his hand move across her stomach and up to the neck of her azure blue dress. Suddenly she felt his hand cup her breast and start to fondle her in such a way that, try as she might, she could not stop her body's physical reaction to the attention his fingers were giving to her sensitive erect nipple.

Please John, please stop this is not good...

He gently bit at her neck which only served to heighten her arousal.

God, how he wanted her now...

As he lay alongside her on the soft quilted duvet he slowly transferred his hand from her breast to her neck as he gently kissed her once again. She moved her hand down to where his hardness was pressing against her thigh, and slowly rubbed him there.

Please, oh pleas Cheryl...

Gradually his hand moved down from her neck, across the flatness of her stomach and slowly at first, very slowly he started to push her dress up exposing her firm thighs. Gradually he moved his hand around onto her inner thigh and gently, ever so gently he pushed her legs apart. Suddenly she broke away from his embrace and rolled out of his grasp. Once more she was in full control and, living up to her codename *Felix*, just like a cat she sprung up from the bed.

"No John this is not right," she said feigning guilt. "You, I mean we, must return to the party."

"Cheryl, Cheryl come on. Nobody will miss us," he more or less pleaded with her, his arousal now at fever pitch. All he wanted to do was to release the sexual tension within his body, but she wasn't going to play. She looked at him coyly and shook her head.

"I'm sorry John, but they will miss us. I'm sure they will," she said almost demurely.

"Nonsense," he said his voice soft and low, "they won't even realise we have gone."

How little you know senator.

"Are you sure?" she asked quietly.

"Of course." He got up from the bed and moved towards her. He cupped her face in his hands and lightly kissed her on the lips. Once more, he slowly moved from her lips to her neck, kissing her gently, nibbling at her, moving down her neck, around the front and down to the gentle swell of her breast. Gradually she relaxed and he could feel her body begin to respond to his touch. His mouth moved up her neck gently teasing and nibbling at her the whole time. Slowly his hands unzipped her dress and once again she felt his hardness rise against her. Now she responded. Now her hands grappled with the buttons on his shirt as she kissed him passionately. Suddenly she seemed on fire. Her dress fell around her waist and he skilfully unhooked her brassiere which she now allowed him to remove from her completely. His eyes drank in her beauty as his hands, once again, gently fondled her young full breasts. Her hands tore at his trousers and in no time at all she had them down around his ankles. In a frenzied moment he pushed her back onto the bed thinking she was so aroused, but he was mistaken. Suddenly her moans, as he fondled and caressed her, became questions.

"John, wait. I need a favour," She said and for the second time she broke away from him.

Come on Cheryl, don't stop me now.

John Frank was so aroused that in a moment of passion he agreed to help this blonde green eyed beauty that lay beneath him. "Of course Cheryl, I will help you. I will do whatever you want," he answered breathlessly his mind but on one thing.

The telephone in room 503 jangled incessantly.

"OK, OK I'm coming," shouted Boris as he made his way into the lounge. "Hello...Jimmy you have something for us?"

"Yeah man. Your friend Senator Frank was caught in a motel room with two naked fourteen year old schoolgirls two years back."

"Was he indicted for it?"

"No. The man knows people in high places and he has some powerful and influential friends."

"Have you any proof of this taking place?"

"You mean like photographs or something?"

"Yes something like that."

"Yeah, I spoke to a contact in the local feds department and he sneaked out a copy of their witness statements and sworn affidavits. They also managed to get me copies of photographs taken on the night by a private detective. Evidently one of the girl's parents suspected something and paid this private detective to keep tabs on their daughter, so he followed her to this motel and bingo her parents were right, there was something going on, big time."

"So how come he got away with it?"

"Like I said he is powerful and knows the right people. According to my contact he was charged with offences against minors but the DA's office dropped all charges. It was rumoured that he bought off the parents but it's only a rumour. At the time this was dynamite - it still is!"

"Can you wire the information across to my office and ask them to wire it to me up here in Manhattan?"

"Sure I can. I'll get that off to you now. By the way it cost me a couple hundred bucks."

"No problem I'll get you reimbursed when I get back. Cheers Jimmy."

"Cheers Boris."

"Any good?" Ivan called from the other room.

"Sure we have photographs, affidavits and statements on the way to us." Boris called back as he replaced the receiver. "Evidently two years ago our friend was caught with his trousers down in a motel room with two minors, two underage girls but it was squashed and hushed up. Jimmy says it's dynamite so perhaps we can get Senator Frank to play ball with Svetlana after all."

Ivan glanced up at the screen and smiled to himself as he watched a very frustrated senator try to coax their Russian doll *Felix* into letting him have sex with her.

"*Felix,* we now have our means to an end. We can definitely lean on your amorous Senator Frank, so you can get dressed again. Oh by the way they were right about you. You do have a beautiful sexy body!" He grinned when he saw Svetlana's look of annoyance as she glanced up at the camera.

"Cheryl, are you there?" the voice of Alexei percolated through to the bedroom.

"My God, who's that?" John H Frank asked in a hoarse whisper as he rolled off the bed on to his feet, grabbing his pants and trousers as he did so. In one swift movement he caught up Svetlana's clothes and tossed them to her and in that split second, his ardour subsided and any sexual thoughts he had were gone. Svetlana put on her underclothes and hissed at him to stay calm and be quiet.

"Give me a few minutes and I'll be down."

"OK Cheryl. I just wondered where you had got to that was all."

They both waited in silence until they heard the hum from the lift announce its departure back to the function room. What Senator Frank hadn't realised was, that at the same time as Alexei had entered the penthouse so had Boris and Ivan Pedrosky who, based on the evidence now in their possession, were about to make John H Frank an offer he couldn't refuse.

With the deal in Los Alamos safely concluded Andrew Hirst-Bergan, driven with desire to be one of the wealthiest and most powerful men in the world, looked towards Bulgaria and a possible further expansion of his empire there. It was whilst he was back in Sofia he arranged to meet up with his old friend Andrei who had told him about a young man who had come to his attention. The young man in question was a member of the Bulgarian secret service who, over a period of time, had voiced his ambition to become very wealthy. In order that their meeting did not raise any suspicions or look out of place, Andrei suggested that they should meet in a well known bar that was popular with both top ranking officials of the Bulgarian Government and the KGB, for it was quite normal for the media mogul to be seen in the company of such people. Just after eight thirty Andrei, accompanied by Ivo the young Bulgarian, paused inside the entrance to the busy bar and looked around for his friend Andrew Hirst-Bergan.

"Ah there he is Ivo, over there chatting to some comrades," he pointed to a small group of men deep in conversation with a tall, heavily built dark haired man who was his friend from England, Andrew Hirst-Bergan. "Come Ivo I'll introduce you." Andrei, with Ivo close behind, set off towards the small group over by the bar. They hadn't got very far before Andrew Hirst-Bergan noticed their approach.

"Gentleman and comrades please excuse me, there is Andrei and I need to speak to him." He gave a curt nod of his head to the small group of officials and moved away to greet Andrei. "Andrei, my friend, how are you?" He immediately embraced Andrei in greeting. "Come let me get you and your young friend a drink."

"Thank you, but first of all let me introduce you to Ivo, a colleague of mine." Andrei ushered the young man forward. "Ivo, this is Mr Hirst-Bergan a very good friend of mine from London in England."

"Pleased to make your acquaintance Ivo," Hirst-Bergan said as he warmly shook his hand.

"I thought it useful to bring Ivo along to meet with you Andrew."

"Oh in what way do you mean useful?" asked Hirst-Bergan his curiosity aroused.

"Well for a start Ivo is an officer in the secret service here in Bulgaria and like everyone he is ambitious and I wondered if…how should I say…if there was some way that you could use his expertise?"

At this revelation Andrew was suddenly very interested in the young Bulgarian and wanted to hear more about what Ivo did. However Andrew felt that the main bar area was not the right place for a frank and honest discussion as it was just a little too public. What they really needed was to find a quiet corner, and there it was, a table set back in a small alcove well away from the main body of the building. "Come my friends let's sit over there it's not so public and we can talk without interruption," he pointed to the table he had seen and without waiting for them to answer he headed off towards it. He waited patiently for Andrei and Ivo to sit down before speaking. "So tell me more Ivo, what do you feel you can bring to the table?" Hirst-Bergan listened carefully to Ivo as he expanded on his career and experience to date within the Bulgarian Secret Service. "And how do you feel your experience and expertise, as such, will help my quest?" Hirst-Bergan asked the young man.

"Well sir, to start with I have many contacts all over the place, which I can make great use of..."

"Hmm, I see," interrupted Hirst-Bergan, "and what exactly do you mean by all over the place?" Hirst-Bergan asked as he took out his cigar case from his inside pocket.

"Well sir Moscow and Budapest are two of the main areas," Ivo answered as Hirst-Bergan carefully removed one of his half coronas from his case and rolled it gently between thumb and forefinger alongside his ear before wetting the end and placing it in his mouth.

"Cigar Ivo?" Hirst-Bergan asked as he offered him his open cigar case.

"No thank you sir," Ivo answered politely as the media tycoon applied a lighted match to his unlit cigar. Andrew Hirst-Bergan drew in a lung full of cigar smoke relishing the taste of the half corona before he replied.

"You say you have contacts all over the place, give me an example of where exactly."

"In those two cities I know many people."

Already Hirst-Bergan had the beginnings of a plan, as he watched through half closed eyes, the pale blue cigar smoke curl above his head.

Hmm with contacts there you could act as my frontman, especially when I need to deal with Seva and his family.

The more he thought it through the more he felt it could work, he could see it being a very useful partnership indeed.

Another aspect to all this is that you could make contact with the Russians who I know, especially those who I know have businesses in the West. Yes my friend it could well be a worthwhile partnership.

"OK Ivo, I think with your contacts and mine we can go far. I'll tell you what I'll do. In the not too distant future I will introduce you to one of my business associates and, if I'm not wrong, between the three of us we could make a lot of money. How does that sound to you?" Ivo's grin said it all.

I can just see it now: Ivo the millionaire - big mansion, big powerful car - maybe I would have a chauffeur - and the women, oh yes, I could take my pick of the beautiful women in Moscow, perhaps a different one each night!

"It sounds good to me Mr Hirst-Bergan, in fact very good, so when do we start?"

"Not so fast my friend. I need to consider different things…"

"What sort of things…I come with good contacts and I know many things and many places so what is there to consider?"

Hirst-Bergan did not reply straight away because he was already considering 'things' such as how best to use him, who to introduce him to and when he, Hirst-Bergan, should 'expand' his interests!

Within a few months of meeting Seva and being introduced to Ivo, Hirst-Bergan - driven by his ambition to become one of the wealthiest and most powerful businessmen in the world - started to carve out another niche for himself as he entered the sordid world of international crime. This was a world that differed from that of his media world in one big way. In his media world he had a bevy of people looking after his every wish, from personal assistants who organised his diary to secretaries who were on hand for note taking and other 'personal services'. In this new business venture his new found business partners did not bother with such niceties as sending notes to offending persons, instead they had their armed bodyguards close at hand to make sure that no one spoke out of turn. As to having fun and relaxing, Hirst-Bergan would always enjoy having a good meal, good champagne and the company of a beautiful woman. Seva and Ivo's idea of fun would be to force their way into a night spot where they would terrorise the customers, and do whatever they wished, whenever they wished. Having no scruples or conscience they would manhandle their women in public for the simple reason that nobody dare say a word for fear of being shot or given a severe beating. They played rough all right with no holds barred!

The business that Hirst-Bergan, with his new found partners, found himself involved in was that of prostitution, drug running and trafficking in men and women. In fact the criminal aspect of their partnership was so bad that when Seva entered the UK and visited London, MI5 made it their business to find out about him and his business operations. They reported their findings to the Home Office, at which point the Home Office took immediate action and deported him from the UK stating that he was 'one of the most dangerous criminals in the world'.

Despite the intervention of MI5 and the Home Office, Hirst-Bergan continued with his 'sordid love affair' of the dark and evil empire in which Seva and Ivo operated, for this was a partnership made in Hell. Should someone even dare to cross Seva's or Ivo's path on the odd occasion, then a phone call was all it took and a short time later a person or persons corpse or corpses would be found in either a back street in Moscow or floating downstream in the river. Both men were as ruthless as each other and as such they had a team of killers who, at all times, were only a phone call away.

As to Hirst-Bergan and his involvement well, this was a paradox, an absurdity, call it what you will. Here was a wealthy media tycoon whose pleasure it was to be seen rubbing shoulders with Hollywood stars and kings and queens the world over. His photographs filled not only his papers but those of his rivals as well. When he met with his new business partners Ivo and Seva, he dared not even be photographed in a Sofia nightclub. He only ever dared meet them in the shadows or in one of their fortified palaces where even he had to undergo a full body scan before being allowed access. He knew their business was corruption and pornography of every kind. They made fortunes from their rackets; prostitution, trading men, women and children for the sex industry, mass marketing of pornographic and obscene films, contract killings, blackmail, drugs and extortion. Why was he involved, for here we have a man not averse to hiding behind all that was respectable suddenly fronting two of the most powerful godfathers in the world? The answer was money, his insatiable desire to be the richest man in the world and it was Ivo and Seva that offered him the means by which to come closer to his goal.

*   *   *

"Ah, good evening Senator Frank, allow me to introduce myself. My name is Ivan Pedrosky and this is my very good friend and colleague Boris Kournikova."

"What the hell is going on?" growled the senator.

"Oh I am sorry senator; let me explain, as I said my name is Ivan…"

"Yes I heard all that, now cut the crap and tell me what this is all about before I call the feds."

"Oh dear oh dear senator," Ivan said shaking his head, "I wouldn't do that if I were you."

"And why the hell not?" he asked, his annoyance showing.

"Well to start with what will you say, '*I was forced to come to this party*' or something along those lines. No I don't think so senator, as we see it you came to this party of your own volition, nobody forced you to, now did they?"

"Hell no," he retorted. "No one forces me to do anything."

"So, as I said, you came along of your own free will and I, Ivan Pedrosky and my colleague here, Boris Kournikova, have been watching you very closely. In fact you have been our star turn!"

"What do you mean by that?" he asked angrily.

"Haven't you guessed senator?" Ivan smiled. "Let me introduce you to this young lady."

"There's no need to do that I already know her." Slowly he started to realise something was wrong, "her name…her name is Cheryl," he stated falteringly.
Ivan shook his head.

"Aw shit…so what is her name?"

"My name is Svetlana," she smiled at him sweetly, "Svetlana Zaslavsky and I work with these gentlemen." Suddenly the smile was gone. "Now John, I need your help," she said in a business like voice, "and this is how you can help me…"

"Fuck you!" He fairly spat out the expletive as he cut her short. "There's no way I would help you now, you bitch! Bloody Russian bitch."

"Oh dear, oh dear senator now that's no way to talk to a pretty young lady like Svetlana," Ivan said shaking his head.

"By the way, have you seen these?" Boris tossed a couple of photographs of a naked man kissing a young schoolgirl stripped to her waist, whilst on the bed next to her lay another partially clad young girl. Frank paled as he realised that the naked man was him.

"W-w-where did you get this?" he stammered.

"Never mind where, but suffice it to say we have them."

"And there are plenty more where these came from," interjected Ivan.

"Now this is the deal," Boris continued in a soft voice, "you help our colleague Svetlana get close to Hirst-Bergan and no more will be said."

"And if I don't do as you say?"

"If you don't do as we ask then we will release these, and the others, to Reuters. The media will have a field day and your wife, your poor wife, well does she know about this sordid little escapade with minors?"

Frank, now a broken man, slowly shook his head.

"Also, just as an added incentive to help us, we have video taped your little escapade in the bedroom tonight and don't forget you have already promised to help this beautiful Russian girl. Now how do you think the American press will react to one of their trusted senators having a sexual fling with a Russian diplomat?"

For once in his life John H Frank was silent. He knew he had been very foolish and that the only way to play it was their way but he still tried to bluff his way out of the situation.

"Who's going to take your word over mine, an important senator, who has the ear of the President?" he asked half-heartedly.

"Well shall we see, are you prepared to risk such an exposé John?"

"Just one more thing," said Svetlana.

He turned to face her. "And what's that?" he asked in a whisper.

"The Silhouette Night Club," she said looking straight at him.

"What about the Silhouette Club?"

"Well wasn't that the club that the FBI raided and found it to be a front for the 'sex for sale' scandal linked to one of the biggest criminal families in my country. The Rising Sun family in Moscow? Now I suspect that if we dug around a little more, we may find that the good senator, John H Frank, may well have some connection there. What do you say John?" Svetlana eyes were no longer burning with desire but were now cold and calculating as she went on "I'll tell you what Senator Frank, Ivan, Boris and I will give you just a few minutes to think over what we have said and to consider our offer then perhaps you would be kind enough to give me your answer."

Realising that there was nowhere to run John H Frank reluctantly nodded his head.

"OK, you win. Yes I was at the club and yes, I do have a loose connection with it." He then proceeded to explain how he worked for Hirst-Bergan and that the *Silhouette Club* was part of the media tycoon's American business operations and how he did not realise until the FBI raided it that it had any links to Russia. But he had found out in the last week or two that this venture was part of a group owned by Hirst-Bergan and a Russian known as Seva.

"That is all I know. I will help you but only if you keep it from Hirst-Bergan."

"No problem senator, we do appreciate your situation in all of this but we all have a job to do not least of all you and Svetlana, so we will keep our side of the bargain as long as you keep yours," Ivan stated in a matter-of-fact way.

"And what about the film and the photographs?"

"Those we retain as our insurance, until the job is done of course."

"Then what?"

"Then you may have them."

For a few minutes the senator thought about his predicament and wondered exactly what their demands would be, he didn't have to wait long before his thoughts were answered.

"Here's the deal senator," Ivan Pedrosky was the first to speak. "Over the next few days you will put together a complete dossier on Andrew Hirst-Bergan, his likes, his dislike, his taste in women and the background to all his business ventures. In fact everything that you know about Hirst-Bergan and especially anything that you feel would be of use to Svetlana."

"And if I refuse?" he asked.

At this juncture Svetlana picked up the pictures and the rest of the damning evidence and stared at the senator through half closed eyes. "What a shame," she said in almost a whisper. "Now should these accidentally fall into the wrong hands…" the tone of her voice suddenly changed, "do we need to spell it out to you senator?" she added menacingly.

"Well senator, perhaps you need a few minutes to consider the consequences," added Ivan.

The senator looked at the three Russian diplomats and realised from the determined look on their faces that they meant every single word. There was no negotiation, no manoeuvring and no diplomacy to be used and in that split second he knew he had no option but to go along with their plan. Yes it was blackmail at the highest level, but there was nothing he could do.

"OK, how long have I got?" he asked in a subdued voice.

"Let's say a few days, maybe a week at the most. Boris will call you to arrange a drop zone."

"One other thing John," Svetlana spoke quietly. "The man Kim Kristoff, have you ever heard of him?"

His brow furrowed as he tried to recollect where he had heard that name before. *Kristoff, Kristoff I'm sure I know that name... I remember Hirst-Bergan speaking to me about someone in Tunisia, was that Kristoff?*

"I'm not sure, but I think I heard Hirst-Bergan mention the name."

"Well think harder!" snapped Svetlana her patience wearing a little thin.

The senator tried hard to recollect what Hirst-Bergan had told him.

I'm sure he said he was introduced to him in Tunisia.

Suddenly it all came flooding back to him.

Yes of course he was the man in Tunisia, and some months later they met up again only this time it was in Moscow where he introduced him to a man called Seva. "That's it!" John exclaimed jubilantly. "I remember it clearly now. Hirst-Bergan told he met Kristoff in Tunisia, he was in export or something, worked for an import/export company." John H Frank smiled triumphantly.

"And?"

"How do you mean and?"

"What specifically did he deal in of course?"

"Oh I see. Well according to Hirst-Bergan almost anything from arms to leading edge technology. I suppose he was some sort of broker."

Svetlana shot a sideways glance at Ivan.

"You said, 'leading edge technology', what exactly did you mean by that?" asked Ivan.

"He never really said. I assumed computers or something along those lines. Why?"

Svetlana looked thoughtful. "Could it be software?" she asked.

"I suppose it could. Why?"

"Have you ever heard of National Information and Research Corporation in Washington?"

"Well yes of course..."

"And what about a product called PROMIS?"

At the mention of PROMIS the senator was immediately on his guard wondering how they knew about such a program. "Y-y-yes, I think I have heard of such a term," he replied hesitantly.

"Come on John, stop playing games with me, I know you know about this software because isn't it the software package marketed by Hirst-Bergan's company Management Information Systems of San Francisco?"

John H Frank nodded his head.

"I'm sorry; I didn't quite hear your reply. Is it or is it not the package that MIS purport to sell?"

"OK, OK," he replied, his anger and frustration beginning to show, "you're right and I was instrumental in getting him into Los Alamos so what?" he answered petulantly.

"What's this PROMIS got to do with all this Svetlana?"

"Could be nothing Ivan but just bear with me." She again turned to the senator. "So you introduced Hirst-Bergan into America's nuclear facility to do what exactly?"

"He wanted to sell PROMIS of course."

"What about NIR Corporation in Washington, don't they produce PROMIS?"

"I'm not sure...I think so."

"Hmm." Svetlana thought about his answer.

Now I wonder why Hirst-Bergan wanted to sell PROMIS to Los Alamos, more to the point, why did Los Alamos buy from Hirst-Bergan in preference to NIR?

"What is all this about Svetlana?"

"I'm not too sure myself," she answered, "but perhaps the senator can shed some light on what is going on. So senator, how come Hirst-Bergan's company was selected to supply PROMIS over NIR? "

John H Frank just shrugged his shoulders. "All I know is that he was keen to get a foot in the door at the Sandia facility and I helped him."

"OK," she said nodding her head, "let's leave that for now and concentrate on NIR. Who owns the NIR Corporation?"

"I think it is a guy called Weatherall, Mike Weatherall. So what's his connection in all this?" the senator asked.

"Never you mind," Svetlana answered curtly and once again the small group stood in silence whilst she considered what the senator had said. Eventually the silence was broken by Ivan.

"What are you thinking Svetlana, is he telling the truth or not?"

"Of course I'm telling the truth!" John H Frank protested vehemently, "I have no reason to lie about such things."

"Yes I think he is telling the truth Ivan, but I also think that the senator is way out of his depth, and he has got involved in some sort of deal that could have major repercussions one way or another."

Yes Mr Senator, I think you have some enemies within your camp and that you have been setup, not by Hirst-Bergan but by Weatherall, who I am sure, is either CIA or NSA. Now, more than ever before, I am convinced that Kristoff is Mr X or Oleg and to find him I need to get alongside Hirst-Bergan.

Svetlana's thoughts were rudely interrupted as the senator pushed her aside muttering

"Well if you are all done with me then I'll be getting along."

"Hold on there Mr Senator, we haven't quite finished with you yet. Besides you need these." Ivan jangled two keys that he held in his hand. John H Frank paused and turned with a look of puzzlement on his face. "Yes Mr Frank, you can't get far without these keys to override the default setting on the lift."

Slowly realisation dawned on the senator that his only means of escape was held in the hand of Ivan Pedrosky and he had little or no chance of getting them, so he reluctantly rejoined the three diplomats.

"Thank you senator for rejoining us," Ivan Pedrosky smiled benevolently. "I have been thinking about your cover story and I have an idea." He had taken into consideration the various traits of Hirst-Bergan's personality, his larger than life ego and his arrogance. He loved to rub shoulders with kings and queens the world over; this made him feel important and fed his egotistical nature. His main weakness was his love of the female sex; he was a womaniser and nothing pleased him more than the company of a beautiful young woman, unless it was to bed two such beauties. So using both these salient features of his personality the aim was to ultimately arrange an introduction for Svetlana. However the plan to achieve this by its very nature was complex and ambitious, but Ivan felt that with the senator's influence such a plan was achievable. His idea was that Svetlana was a relative of the tsars of Russia; her name was to be Svetlana Ilyinsky a direct descendant of Tsar Alexander II of Russia and his grandson the Grand Duke Dmitri Pavlovich Romanov, who was banished by his cousin Tsar Nicholas II for helping to plan the assassination of Grigori Rasputin in 1916.

"Very interesting indeed, but where do I fit into all of this?"

"A moment senator and I will explain further."

Having outlined the background cover story, Ivan then explained what he wanted from the senator. He told him that he needed naturalisation papers for Svetlana, to show her as a naturalised American citizen from New York, and an American passport. Although these things were a little tricky to organise, he felt it was not outside the realms of possibility, especially with the contacts that Senator John H Frank had.

"I know the story is a little sketchy, but I am sure senator that a man of your experience will have no difficulty in colouring in the details sufficiently for us to achieve the right result!"

"But I ..."

"No buts John that's the deal. American passport, showing Svetlana as a second generation American, papers proving her to be connected to the tsar of Russia and of course an American birth certificate confirming her name as Svetlana Ilyinsky." Ivan gave the senator a broad smile. "Ilyinsky is a good name you know, one that can certainly be linked to the Romanov family." Ivan smiled briefly then his face hardened as he said, "you have ten days senator that's all, ten days. Boris will see you out." Ivan handed the lift keys to Boris and dismissed the senator with a wave of his hand.

"But where shall I meet..."

"Boris will call your office the day before to arrange the details and senator...remember pictures!" Once more Ivan smiled at Frank. "Goodnight."

The Sheraton Towers Hotel in Manhattan - not too far from Central Park, Times Square and Broadway - offers the best of everything especially if you are Hirst-Bergan and occupying the Presidential suite on its twenty first floor.

Damn nuisance having to meet with Frank. If it wasn't for him I could have been out tonight. Ah well I suppose the one saving grace is this woman he's bringing, but there again his taste in women...

Just at that moment his private thoughts were interrupted by a gentle tap on the door.

"Yes." Hirst-Bergan called brusquely, "who's there?"

"Room service sir."

"Come in, come in."

There was a rattle of keys in the lock, the door swung open and a young lady pushing a hostess trolley entered the room. With the clinking of glasses and the rattle of the ice bucket the young lady pushed the trolley into the alcove near to the settee upon which Hirst-Bergan sprawled.

"Your favourite champagne Mr Hirst-Bergan chilled to your requirements and glasses for your guests. The caviar will be served at 7:30 in line with your instructions. Would you like the champagne opened now sir?"

"Why not?" He watched the young lady as she bent over, her uniform pulling tightly across her buttocks as she placed the ice bucket close to hand.

Hmm, very nice, very nice indeed perhaps you would join me later.

There was a resounding pop as the young lady removed the cork from the champagne bottle and poured a little into one of the glasses for him to try; she wanted to make sure that everything was as it should be on this, her first night of doing room service in the Presidential suite. She had been forewarned about the occupant and his taste for young women, but she knew if she got everything right then he was also renowned for tipping well.

"I'm sorry I don't know your name, but pour one for yourself and join me," he said.

"My name's Lisa sir and thank you for your kind offer but I must get back. Perhaps another time."

"What about after you've finished tonight?" She ignored his question and passed him his glass of champagne. "Thank you, so what time do you finish Lisa?" he asked again.

"Oh late; after midnight," she replied diplomatically, hoping he wouldn't pursue the invite, but she was out of luck.

"Well join me then." She smiled sweetly. "Thank you Mr Hirst-Bergan, but…" she had to think quickly and give a plausible excuse, "unfortunately I can't. It's my job you see. It's more than my job's worth."

"I haven't seen you before; you're new here aren't you?"

"Yes sir."

"Thought as much," he growled, "I bet that old dragon Jeannette has been giving you some tale about 'not to cavort with the guests, because if you're caught you will be dismissed'. "

"Yes sir," she blushed and looked down at the floor, "will that be all sir?"

"Yes, yes. That'll be all." He gave a dismissing wave of his hand. The young lady bobbed slightly and headed towards the door. "Err, there is one thing more."

She stopped and turned to face him. "Yes sir?"

"When the caviar is brought up would you please arrange for another two bottles of champagne and dinner menus?"

"Certainly sir."

That old bat Jeannette...

His thoughts were rudely interrupted by the telephone.

"Hello...Ah good. Would you arrange for someone to show them up?"

Hirst-Bergan picked up the bottle of champagne. "Another glass of bubbly Svetlana?"

"Yes please Andrew." She smiled sweetly at him, her green eyes full of mischief. She seemed to be saying 'flirt with me if you dare'.

Those lovely green eyes of yours are so alluring and that blonde hair...Andrew this is not doing you any good whatsoever. God you are beautiful. How I would love to...

"Thank you Andrew." Her dulcet voice brought him back to reality. "So tell me do you come to New York regularly, or just now and again?" she asked.

"Oh, I'm here frequently. You know, or perhaps you don't know, I have a number of business interests over here," he said trying to impress her.

"Oh really is that a fact now," Svetlana answered feigning great interest in what he was saying. She was a good actress and gave him the impression she was hanging on his every word as he went on and on about his wealth, power in the business fraternity and the number of companies he owned. She smiled to herself as he tried to impress her with his pretentious lifestyle that if he had only realised did nothing for her except to reinforce her dislike of him. She found him pompous, conceited and ostentatious, in fact everything she disliked in a man was here staring her in the face.

Good god, what a bore, what an egotistical old bore. But be careful Svetlana, he's no fool.

"So you say you have a number of companies in Bulgaria and Russia?"

"Yes that's right, you know I own over four hundred companies outright and have a similar number that I am the major shareholder in."

"My, my, how do you find time to eat? Oh, John your glass is empty…"

"Oh yes, sorry John please help yourself and pour another one for Svetlana and me there's a good chap," he said passing his glass to the Senator for a refill. This was Hirst-Bergan being his usual pompous and egotistical self, trying hard to impress this young beautiful woman who he learnt was directly related to the tsars of Russia.

Being that your family is from Russia perhaps you would come with me to Bulgaria. Yes that would be really nice…

"It has just occurred to me I have to make a trip to Bulgaria soon and I wondered if you would join me? No strings attached of course! I just thought with your connections and all that…"

"So what are your connections with Bulgaria Andrew?" she asked innocently.

"Ah, I have a number of connections there from owning a bank to computers, from nightclubs to friends in the government, from the head of the KGB to people in the secret service, need I go on?"

"No, I am impressed," she said convincingly.

And what about Kristoff, where does he fit into all of this. I wonder…do you know Oleg?

"So does that mean you will join me on my trip to Sofia?"

"Hmm, I'm not sure that I could…I mean I would love to but…well the truth is that even someone related to the tsar needs an income and I need to earn a living," she said convincingly.

"It never occurred to me that you would have to work."

"Well if you can call what I do work."

"So what do you do?"

"I work for a publishing company…you may even know them."

"Oh! Really? Who?"

"A company called *Andromeda Research*. I'm their Vice President and in charge of international marketing and publishing, which really means I get to travel all over the place." Suddenly Svetlana had an idea. "In fact… if you would allow me to do a profile on you and your companies in and around the Soviet Bloc, I could use it as an excuse to come with you to Bulgaria." Svetlana held her breath, hoping that the conceited Hirst-Bergan would see this as an opportunity to try his hand with her as well as getting additional publicity for himself.

Now Mr Media Tycoon let's see how that grabs you.

Hirst-Bergan didn't take too long to think about such a proposal, because just as Svetlana thought, here was his opportunity to bed this beautiful woman related to the tsars of Russia.

Although you're American and don't speak Russian I reckon that you really are a Russian princess and this could be my chance to say I've slept with royalty!

"Of course I don't mind. So how do I get in touch with you?"

"You can call me on this number," Svetlana said as she presented him with her latest business card for *Andromeda Research* which had been printed just for this very occasion. Like her previous card it stated that *Andromeda Research* was a freelance press and magazine publishing company interested in scientific and leading edge technology, with offices on Third Avenue New York. It stated that Svetlana Ilyinsky was the company's Vice President, Marketing and Publishing. She knew that what she was doing could well backfire on her, especially as Hirst-Bergan was involved in the world of news and newspapers, but she relied on the fact that he wouldn't know every single magazine or paper in this field, unless of course it was big enough to be regarded as serious competition.

"That's settled then." He looked at his watch, it was getting on for 9:00 and they still hadn't eaten. "I think we ought to dine, any preference?" he directed his question at Svetlana, totally ignoring the senator.

"I like the idea of China Town don't you John?" Svetlana looked questioningly at the senator who had been quiet all evening.

"Yes, that's fine by me."

"Good that's settled then. I'll just get them to call us a cab."

The sun streamed in through the windows of *Andromeda Research* and it had been nearly a week since Svetlana had spent the evening with Hirst-Bergan and John H Frank, drinking champagne and eating caviar at the Sheraton hotel before going out to dine in China Town. Later Svetlana had persuaded Hirst-Bergan to take them on to a nightclub, *The Silhouette Night Club,* the very same one that was raided by the FBI and owned by Hirst-Bergan. When he tried to talk her out of going to such a place in downtown New York, all she said was that with two strong male escorts she felt quite safe, so in the end he reluctantly agreed to her request. Little did he know that she had an ulterior motive, and that she already knew that the club was owned by him. Svetlana had pushed him into taking her there in the hope that he would admit to his interest in the place with his partner Seva, the head of the Rising Sun family in Moscow, but nothing was said nor did anything untoward happen. Since that night she had heard nothing further from Andrew Hirst-Bergan and she was beginning to think that maybe he had smelt a rat, or that the senator had betrayed her. However what was done was done and she couldn't undo it. Suddenly she was brought back to the present by Alexei the head of the KGB's New York station.

"Here Svetlana, we now have the electronics you asked for. We have also advised Trepashkin in Lubyanka about your forthcoming trip. He is going to arrange for someone he trusts to take a small team to Bulgaria to watch your back. He said they will not be visible to you but they will be there. They need to stay invisible but if you are at any time in trouble you need to call this number." He passed her a business card giving the name of a garage in Sofia. "If for any reason Hirst-Bergan is curious about the garage, your story is that the owner is a distant cousin of yours, and like your branch of the family his family escaped to Bulgaria and lived as peasants after the Bolsheviks deposed Nicholas II. Of course they lost everything and were very lucky to escape with their lives…"

"Svetlana - I'm sorry to interrupt Alexei," Natasha apologised for her interruption to the head of station.

"It's OK…"

"Yes Natasha what is it?" asked Svetlana.

"Andrew Hirst-Bergan is on the phone for you."

"Good, put him through." There was a click as Natasha put the call from Hirst-Bergan through to Svetlana. "Hello, Svetlana speaking…Andrew, I was beginning to think you had dumped me before we had started." She smiled and winked at Natasha and Alexei and with the mouthpiece covered by her hand she mouthed to them *need to make him think he's the greatest person I've ever met and that I'm desperate to see him again.* Natasha could all but contain herself as she sat there listening to Svetlana manipulating and soft-talking the media tycoon, making him think that she was absolutely infatuated by him and all that he stood for and how she couldn't wait to see him again. This was a game that Svetlana was a past master at. "OK. So there is no need for me to book a flight… Oooh that's something I hadn't bargained for, a private jet and you say you'll arrange a car to pick me up just after 12:00…yes of course. I'll see you then. Goodbye Andrew." She put the phone down and burst out laughing. "Do you know," she said, "I have never met such an egotistical and arrogant man! He is absolutely convinced that I am smitten by his charm…he has as much charm as…what can I say…as a…"

"As a pig!"

"No that is unfair to pigs! But you know what I mean. Anyway he's sending a car for me at midday tomorrow so I need to get everything packed.

Chapter 15

The weather in Sofia was grey, damp and cold with the temperature barely reaching eighteen degrees unlike that of New York where the average temperature was twenty-eight and brilliant sunshine. Apart from being buffeted by a tremendous electric storm en route, the flight in itself had proved uneventful. However because it was in Hirst-Bergan's nature to constantly boast about his wealth, his standing in society, the people he knew and where he was on the social scale, he had unwittingly told Svetlana some very important information about the man called Kristoff which proved of particular interest to her.

According to Hirst-Bergan, he had been introduced to Kim Kristoff by an old acquaintance who was none other than Mike Weatherall, to whose home Svetlana had paid an uninvited visit. In addition to this piece of information, he also let it slip that he had been told that Kristoff was not his proper name and he told Svetlana that the same person said 'I have it on good authority that Mr Kristoff is, or was, a KGB operator'. It was this latter piece of information that really grabbed her attention and, as such, she very gently and subtly quizzed him further about Mr Kristoff.

It was not long before Svetlana had Hirst-Bergan telling her all about Kristoff. How he had wanted to arrange another meeting and how, after they did meet, he fixed up a meeting with one of his 'good contacts' in Moscow, who turned out to be none other than a man called Seva.

"Seva, told me he had a lot of contacts around the world and he said he could help me get a lot of Russian Jews out of Russia and back to Israel."

"But what did he want in return?" Svetlana asked.

"Well, he said that he also had a number of business interests in Western Europe but was 'finding travelling outside of Russia more and more restrictive'. He asked me if I could help him get another passport, 'ideally an Israeli passport as that was widely accepted.' I said I would try."

"So were you able to get him one?" Svetlana asked and Hirst-Bergan immediately said "yes of course. I have many powerful friends in many countries." This comment, in his mind, only served to reinforce his position of power on the world stage. Perhaps in different company he would have been a little less forthcoming, which proved to Svetlana that he didn't regard her as a threat. It also showed that she could certainly manipulate this chauvinistic male without any real effort.

"So Andrew what was the main purpose for meeting this, this man called Seva?"

"Well to get the Jews out of Russia of course." But Svetlana was not fooled by his naïve attempt to cover up the main reason for his joining forces with Seva. After all she knew, and most of the western world knew, the man called Seva was a most dangerous criminal and as such he was the head of the Moscow mafia family known as the Rising Sun. Now there could only be one reason why the media tycoon Andrew Hirst-Bergan should team up with such a fraternity and that would be greed and wealth.

Also during the flight Hirst-Bergan boasted at length about his 60 metre yacht called *Lady Mona,* telling Svetlana how he had designed the very sophisticated security system and how he had purposely left a blind spot that only he knew about – "that way I can have some privacy away from the eyes of my own crew!" he added and winked at her. Svetlana immediately stored this piece of information away, ever mindful that this may well come in useful at some time should she or anyone else need to board his yacht in secret. She then made a mental note to speak to him further about the 'blind spot'.

As to Kristoff, now that information is very interesting indeed.

"Yes, you would like the yacht," he said. "It's got everything you could wish for, a jacuzzi, sauna and even a gymnasium on the top deck..." But Svetlana's thoughts were elsewhere as Hirst-Bergan prattled on about his beloved yacht and how it had everything. Hearing Hirst-Bergan's story about Kristoff and his first meeting with him, how he had been told that he was or had been an active member of the KGB, convinced Svetlana that Kristoff was none other than *Oleg!* How to flush him out into the open, although a significant problem, was not the be all and end all, for now the important thing was for her to stay focussed and to keep her mind on the job of making up to Hirst-Bergan.

Svetlana a little 'pillow talk' could reveal a lot more information, after all he is your main link to Kristoff and you know he would dearly love to bed you, so play the game, play the game!

There was a slight jolt as the Gulfstream landed. This was then followed by an instantaneous roar from its twin engines as the pilot applied reverse thrust to assist in slowing the aircraft down, a common practice that is normally used throughout the world of aviation.

"At last we are here," Andrew commented as the aircraft turned off the main runway onto the taxiway and headed slowly towards the remote apron and its parking area outside the private hangar.

Hirst-Bergan was always treated with great respect when he arrived at Sofia airport and today was no exception. It was a deference that was usually reserved for those persons in high authority who at the very least were high ranking officials from the Politburo. The red carpet was rolled out ready for him, a government chauffeur driven limousine was available for his own personal use, and motorcycle outriders were ready to escort the car and its occupants to their destination.

"My, my Andrew this is some reception committee indeed. I would never have imagined or expected such a welcome for two foreigners."

"This is nothing special; it's always like this when I arrive. I suppose it's the Bulgarians' way of showing respect for the person who, as one of their major investors, has made their economy what it is today," he said to Svetlana as they descended the aircraft steps.

"Good evening sir," the Bulgarian chauffeur stood smartly to attention and gave an unobtrusive nod of his head as he greeted Hirst-Bergan in Russian.

"Good evening. I believe we are to stay at the palace on Mount Vitoshi, is that correct?" Hirst-Bergan asked.

"Yes sir, that's correct."

"Come Svetlana, welcome to Sofia," he said rather pompously as he ushered her into the waiting car. "I am sure you will appreciate and enjoy the palace where we are to stay, the views from its balcony are absolutely stunning, but don't take my word for it, you see for yourself when we arrive."

Five minutes later their limousine, escorted by the motorcycle outriders, swept from the airport and out on to the highway that would take them to the palace set on the slope of Mount Vitoshi overlooking Sofia.

After lunch the rain stopped. Gradually the leaden sky started to clear and by late afternoon the heat from sun began to dry out the sodden ground. Svetlana really needed to make contact with her back-up team to let them know that she had arrived in Sofia and to advise them as to where she and Hirst-Bergan were staying. Another matter high on her list of priorities was that of Kristoff, and how she proposed to flush him out. As she stood on the balcony looking down on the town of Sofia deliberating about Kristoff and contacting her back-up team, fate took a hand. Somehow she needed to formulate a plan and it was whilst she was deep in thought the telephone rang.

"OK, I'll get it," Andrew Hirst-Bergan's voice floated to her as he called to the staff somewhere in the palace. From a distance she could hear the muffled voice of Andrew talking on the phone then, quite clearly, she heard the name Seva spoken. Hearing that immediately galvanised her into action and with her interest primed, Svetlana quickly and stealthily crept from the balcony through the open bedroom door and out onto the landing where she could now quite clearly hear the dulcet tones of Hirst-Bergan whilst he chatted on the phone. It didn't take her long to surmise, from what little she had heard, that there was some sort of meeting being arranged between Hirst-Bergan, Seva and another man called Ivo whose name she didn't recognise. Svetlana positioned herself far enough from the ornate landing balustrade so as to be as inconspicuous as possible should anyone inadvertently look up in her direction. From her vantage point she could hear quite clearly Hirst-Bergan's side of the telephone conversation.

"Don't worry Seva," he said, "we'll meet on my yacht the *Lady Mona*." He paused as he listened to the other party. It seemed to Svetlana that perhaps Seva was having some difficulty in coming to terms with leaving his safe haven of Moscow because Hirst-Bergan was trying to convince him that the yacht was far safer for all concerned.

"Listen Seva, I'll contact Kristoff..." he was cut short by Seva. Suddenly he lost patience and spoke curtly to his associate. "Seva, you're being paranoid. Now listen to me. I will anchor offshore away from any prying eyes. All you and Ivo have to do is get in a boat...No, no, no listen. I will arrange the boat, in fact I will hire it in my name and that way no one will be any the wiser. Now provided you follow my instructions to the letter you can get aboard without even my crew knowing. Of course there is blanket security on the yacht, but as I've told you before, I designed the sophisticated system with a blind spot, a window which only I know exists. After all if I take a woman on board I want some privacy on deck, I don't want my crew filming my exploits now do I?" Once again he listened to Seva who must have agreed to the plan. "So it's settled then, I'll let you know once I've made all the arrangements." At this point Svetlana had heard enough and, as quiet as quiet could be, she tiptoed back to the balcony where she thought about the conversation that she had just been privy to and wondered what exactly Hirst-Bergan and his friends were up to.

After his telephone conversation with Seva, Hirst-Bergan telephoned his friend Andrei, and arranged for him to meet up with them. However, so it would not look out of place for a person in Andrei's position, or seem strange for a person of Hirst-Bergan's standing to be seen together, Andrew thought it best for them to meet in a bar usually frequented by the KGB and other government officials. At 7:00 pm, dead on the dot, Svetlana and Andrew Hirst-Bergan entered the bar to meet up with Andrei and it was during this meeting that the subject of the telephone conversation with Seva came up. Andrew, believing that Svetlana was American and, as he thought, unable to understand or speak Russian continued to discuss, in Russian and in detail, the conversation he had had with Seva. Svetlana had quickly learnt from snippets of conversation around them that Andrei was none other than the head of the Bulgarian KGB and as such, she was quite taken aback by Andrew's disclosure and she was left wondering as to how far his criminal empire stretched.

Does this imply that the Bulgarian KGB are also implicated, if so then just how far does Seva and Hirst-Bergan's criminal empire stretch?

What she had just heard made it even more important to get a message to Mikhail but in order to do so she needed to contact her back-up team here in Sofia.

Perhaps they have a public telephone here, of course it will be tapped but if I'm careful...no that's no good because they will then know I can speak Russian.

No matter how much she poked and prodded at the problem there appeared to be only one way to deal with it, and that was to convince Hirst-Bergan to let her visit her *relative* at the garage as soon as possible, so with her mind made up she set about making a plan.

It was just after 6:00 am when Svetlana woke to another day of grey skies and rain but the weather forecast was that 'by mid-morning the cloud and rain would gradually clear from the west giving way to sun and blue skies with a temperature high of twenty four degrees'. For a moment or two she lay there gathering her thoughts on what she had to do. Next to her and still fast asleep lay the large frame of Andrew Hirst-Bergan. Getting him to allow her to take the car into Sofia had been far easier than she had anticipated. Once she had agreed to his sexual advances he became putty in her hands and readily agreed to her visit provided she was back before lunch. There was only one minor problem which stemmed from his belief that she did not understand a word of Russian, and in order to get around this it was necessary for him to know where her *cousin* worked so that he could tell the chauffeur where to go. A little dangerous maybe, but she could not see any way around it without blowing her cover.

Carefully, so as not to wake him, she slid from between the sheets and tiptoed across the master bedroom to the palatial en suite bathroom to take a shower and put the finishing touches to her carefully laid plan. Although Gorbachev was now General Secretary of the CPSU and his perestroika was gaining momentum, and even though the old school, the hardliners, in Russia had now gone, life in Bulgaria was still very difficult. This meant that Svetlana had to tread very carefully indeed. For this reason she felt that any subsequent visit to her back-up team would not only cause Hirst-Bergan to be suspicious but could also prove to be too dangerous unless she could devise another believable excuse. Whilst taking her shower she had an idea.

Perhaps her 'cousin' could telephone and say he had taken some time off work so he could pick her up and introduce her to her great-aunt and the rest of the ' family' she had never met.

The more she thought about it the more she felt Hirst-Bergan would accept it without question. Not only that, it would be less dangerous and give her more time to find out as much as she could about Hirst-Bergan's forthcoming meeting with Seva and hopefully Kristoff.

At just after 08:30 the chauffeur swung the limousine into a side road near to Botevgradsko shosse Boulevard and parked. He pointed to the Boulevard and said something in Russian. Svetlana shrugged and gave a puzzled look as if she hadn't understood. Again he pointed to the Boulevard.

"Garage, you hmm, you go garage," he said in guttural English.

Svetlana smiled and thanked him as she got out of the car. "You wait here?" she asked. He looked puzzled. So she pointed to the car, then to him and back to the car. "You stay?" He smiled and nodded his head.

This is hard work making him think I don't understand.

Svetlana smiled and thanked him in English knowing full well that everything she had said and done, her every move, was being mentally noted and would be reported back to his superiors as part of his job. After all this was life in Bulgaria and symptomatic of the 'old regime'.

On her return to the palace on Mount Vitoshi Hirst-Bergan immediately asked her how the visit to her cousin had gone.

"He was really nice," she replied, "and he said he would try and get some time off work so that he could take me to meet my great-aunt."

"That would be nice for you."

"Yes, I asked him to give me a call here as soon as he's arranged it. That'll be all right won't it?"

"Of course my dear but I hope it's soon."

"Why, is there a problem?"

"Oh no, it's just that I've got to meet some business associates which means our time together will have to be curtailed as I leave for Gibraltar at the end of the week, unless…"

"Unless what Andrew?"

"Unless you come with me…how do you fancy a trip on my yacht?"

"The *Lady Mona?*"

"Yes, the *Lady Mona* so what do you think?"

Brilliant! What a stroke of luck I couldn't have planned it better.

Her grin said it all. "Of course I would love to go."

"That's settled then, we fly from here down to Gibraltar where we'll be joined on the *Lady Mona* by Amir an Israeli friend of mine. Once we are all settled aboard then I plan to set sail along the coast to Barcelona where we will be joined by two other business associates. Now if all goes well, and I've no reason to believe otherwise, then I propose that once the business is dealt with and I have dropped Amir back in Gibraltar you and I continue our time together by nipping over to Africa – well Tunisia really – as I've arranged to meet an old contact of mine, a guy called Kim Kristoff, what do you think?"

My, my, it gets better and better.

Svetlana just couldn't believe her luck, he had played right into her hands and was about to deliver up to her, on a plate, Kim Kristoff the man she knew as *Oleg* and had been tasked by her masters to track down. Who could have foreseen such fortuitous luck and on the spur of the moment she threw her arms about his neck and squealed with delight. "There is one condition though..." he added.

"A condition, in what way?" She gave him a puzzled look wondering what he was going to say.

"Well, when we anchor off Barcelona..."

"Anchor off Barcelona?" Svetlana looked genuinely puzzled by this. "I thought you said you had two business associates joining us?"

"We have, but they will be coming aboard whilst we are at sea." She gave him a quizzical look. "Well it's easier for them to come out to us by launch rather than us having to find a berth just so they can come aboard," he quickly added in order to dispense with any further questions, and even though he knew it was a flimsy explanation it seemed to do the trick as Svetlana's look quickly turned from one of bewilderment to one of interest.

"You said there is one condition Andrew..."

"Yes," his tone was serious as he continued, "once we pick up my two associates from Barcelona then on no account must you enter, or even go anywhere near the stateroom. The stateroom is strictly off limits, is that understood?"

`So is that where you will hold your meeting? Perhaps I should take a look in there before hand.

"Of course Andrew," she replied demurely, her face the picture of innocence.

There was an air of expectancy in Lubyanka with rumours that Mikhail Gorbachev would eventually take over as President of the Soviet Union. Under his guidance, perestroika started to gain momentum, and Mikhail Trepashkin was deliberating on such a move when his thoughts were rudely interrupted by a knock at his office door.

"Come," he called and a young KGB clerk entered. "Yes comrade what is it?" he asked. The clerk gave an imperceptible nod of his head in acknowledgement. "This has arrived from our team in Sofia comrade Trepashkin," he said, handing him a folded sheet of paper. Trepashkin took the sheet, unfolded the paper, and read the decoded message which on first reading did not seem to offer much more than confirmation of the arrival of Svetlana and Hirst-Bergan in Sofia. Then a single paragraph jumped off the page.

> *Hirst-Bergan has strong links with Seva of the Rising Sun family and one other man known as Ivo. Also met with man called Andrei believed to be head of KGB here. HB spoke to him in detail about meeting Seva and Ivo. Seems as if Andrei and KGB here are implicated in criminal network. Can confirm HB making contact with Kristoff who believe is codename Oleg. Expect to contact Felix in next 24 hours for update. Grigory the mechanic*

He read and re-read the paragraph again and again, then carefully folded the sheet and placed it on the desk in front of him, looked up and smiled at the clerk who all this time had been patiently standing in front of him.

"Thank you comrade that will be all."

The clerk gave another obligatory nod of the head, turned smartly and left the office closing the door behind him.

Trepashkin, once again, picked up the sheet of paper and glanced down at its content.

So my Svetlana as I once said, 'you will do well and rise like a star through the KGB' and my love you have not let me down. God speed and may you be kept safe for me and your parents.

At just after 09:00 the telephone on the desk in front of Hirst-Bergan gave three rings.

"Yes."

"Is my cousin Svetlana there?" asked the voice at the other end.

"Yes, hold on and I will get her." Hirst-Bergan pushed back his chair and headed out into the large marbled hall where, in fluent Russian, he called to a member of the palace staff. A stern looking woman dressed all in black, with a face made to look even more severe by her black hair being scraped back and held in a tight bun, was ordered to find Svetlana and tell her that her cousin was on the phone. The woman immediately headed off in the direction of the drawing room where she had last seen Svetlana. In a short space of time the stout Bulgarian member of staff reappeared and ushered Svetlana into the study where Hirst-Bergan had resumed his work. As she entered he looked up.

"Ah Svetlana, your cousin is on the phone," Hirst-Bergan handed her the handset.

"Hello, Svetlana speaking and how is *Felix* your cat today?" she asked so he knew it was her. She smiled briefly at Hirst-Bergan and by way of an explanation told him that her cousin's cat had not been too well.

"Oh *Felix* is much better thank you," he replied. "I have managed to get some time off so I wondered if you would come with me to meet with the family?" he asked purely for the benefit of those government officials who were invariably listening to the phone call.

"Just a moment, I'll check with Andrew. I assume you mean today?"

"Yes of course, in about an hour if that's all right?"

Placing her hand over the mouthpiece Svetlana turned to Hirst-Bergan and told him what had been said, explaining that her cousin Grigory wanted to pick her up within the hour to take her to meet her 'great-aunt and the rest of the family'. Hirst-Bergan immediately gave a perfunctory wave of his hand to indicate his agreement.

"Yes that's fine."

"OK I will be there within the hour."

"OK, bye now." With that she replaced the handset.

Good, I can now update you on when we leave for Gibraltar and the latest news about Tunisia and Kristoff.

Nearly a week had passed since Mikhail had heard from Grigory his contact in Sofia and time was getting on.

What has happened Svetlana, what has gone wrong? Grigory said he was picking you up the following day and that was three days ago but still no word.

Abruptly he was brought back to the present by an unexpected knock on his office door.

"Come."

A young lady entered the office carrying a manila envelope reserved for inter-office communications. "Comrade Trepashkin I have just received this from our decoding section. They apologise that it is late but said that 'somehow it got overlooked.' "

Mikhail excitedly snatched the envelope from the clerk's hand, opened it with trembling fingers and read its contents.

Have news about meeting. We leave Sofia end of the week for Gibraltar. Join yacht Lady Mona. Hirst-Bergan's friend and associate an Israeli called Amir joins us there. We sail to Barcelona and anchor offshore Seva and Ivo arrive by boat and join yacht there in secret. Meeting must be short as they have to return by boat. Need to update you when on board so will call New York station, they will advise. Afterwards sail to Tunisia to meet Oleg do not know exactly where. Felix will advise as soon as known. Grigory the mechanic.

"Thank you comrade thank you," he inwardly sighed with relief as he read the contents. "That'll be all."
The clerk gave the obligatory imperceptible nod of his head, turned smartly and marched briskly from the room closing the door behind him. Mikhail now felt the warm glow of satisfaction spread from deep inside his belly and, at last, he allowed the trace of a smile to touch his lips. He leaned back in his chair and took out a pack of Nepti Russian cigarettes and lit one. He inhaled deeply the acrid smoke and pictured the image of Kristoff's face in his last moments of life and smiled sardonically.

Yes, it won't be long now. I can sense the sweet smell of victory. Oleg we are coming for you.
Slowly he exhaled and through half closed eyes watched the steady stream of blue smoke rise as a haze up towards the ceiling above him.

"Oh yes Oleg your time is up," he muttered to himself with smug satisfaction, "and it is my beloved *Felix* who will have redressed the balance, who will have tracked you down, ah such poetic justice indeed!" He picked up the message and slowly read it through again.

Who is this man Amir? Hmm, an Israeli; could he be the Amir who is my opposite number in Mossad?

The *Lady Mona* looked resplendent tied up alongside the other vessels in Marina Bay Gibraltar. The skipper, a young man in his thirties called Peter, was busy in the chart room plotting the proposed course along the coast to Barcelona whilst the crew, who were already on standby, busied themselves about the yacht whilst awaiting the arrival of Hirst-Bergan and his friends. The first that the crew knew about the proposed trip was when the skipper told them that he had just received a call from the boss who had said that he and two guests were arriving later in the day and that they were to be ready to leave for Spain soon afterwards. However, the skipper knew from past experience that this order could well be changed. In fact anything could happen as Hirst-Bergan and his moods were totally unpredictable. He changed his mind according to the weather. There had been many instances when they had set sail for a destination and then something would upset him so he would order a new course to be set only to question it a few hours later. Then when the skipper told him that he, Hirst-Bergan, had countermanded his orders to the crew he would immediately deny it and lose his temper, suggesting that the poor unfortunate crew member 'should listen to what he had been told'. Recently his unpredictability and mood swings had got worse, a lot worse, and the crew were beginning to talk among themselves about 'Hirst-Bergan losing it', or 'he's cracking up under the strain'. In fact the situation was so bad at one stage that he nearly faced open mutiny. Had it not been for the resourcefulness of his skipper telling the crew that 'the old man has been under lot of pressure recently,' all twelve crew would have walked off. Then for a short time it appeared as if he had turned the corner and everything in the garden was rosy. On such days he would be absolutely charming and you would be forgiven for thinking you couldn't wish to meet a nicer person, but these interludes were becoming less frequent.

Mikhail Trepashkin buzzed through to the overseas administration department.

"Hello," a young female's voice answered the phone.

"Hello, this is Trepashkin. I need the latest Mossad file containing information on their key people."

"Of course Colonel Trepashkin."

A few minutes later a young lady from the administration department holding a large bulging manila folder knocked at Mikhail's office door.

"Come."

"Here is the file you requested Colonel," she said laying it on the desk in front of him. Mikhail opened up the folder and quickly thumbed through its contents until he found what he was looking for, a photograph of an Israeli who, according to the file, was called Amir Peres, Deputy Controller Mossad. His biography read like a who's who of the world's Intelligence Services. He had spent time in Beirut and Greece where as a *kidon* operator he had removed many Israeli enemies. In America he had been seen attached to the Israeli embassy and often used as a liaison officer. He had, in recent years, spent time in London where he had worked closely with his counterparts in MI5, then according to the file he had returned to Tel Aviv in Israel where he took up the post as deputy to Uzi Ben-Gurion the head of Mossad had since developed close links with Britain and America. He had frequently been seen with the British media tycoon Hirst-Bergan who, had strong connections with Bulgaria and the Soviet Union. Beneath the typewritten script someone had added a pencilled in note about Hirst-Bergan being 'a personal friend of leader Andropov' and owning a number of companies within Bulgaria and the Soviet Union.

So I was right. The man meeting with Hirst-Bergan is Amir Peres.

Mikhail reflected on what he had just read and linking it with the recent communiqué he had received from Svetlana he began to wonder as to what exactly it all meant...

So what have Mossad, the Bulgarian KGB, Seva and Ivo got in common?

"Will that be all sir?" the administration officer asked.

"I'm sorry comrade, what did you say?"

"The file, will that be all sir?"

"Umm, yes I think...no...can you fetch me the file on Hirst-Bergan?"

"Certainly sir," she answered and with a slight nod of the head, turned smartly and marched from the room. Mikhail took out his packet of Nepti cigarettes and thought carefully about the implications of his discovery.

If Hirst-Bergan is working with Mossad, and is also working – as I believe he is – with us, then that has major implications. Yes Mr Hirst-Bergan we need to keep a very close eye on you.

It was two o'clock when Hirst-Bergan and Svetlana arrived on board the yacht. Having introduced Svetlana to Peter, he then ushered her aft to his private quarters where he promptly showed her around the suite of rooms including the staterooms. Once he had shown her the yacht's layout and where things were stowed he excused himself and went back on deck to check with Peter that, apart from Amir, they were ready for departure. Svetlana did not waste any time and as soon as Andrew left she headed off to check out the stateroom where she felt sure the meeting would take place. Her main task now was to find suitable places to secrete her electronic listening

198

devices so that she could eavesdrop on their meeting and pass the information back to Mikhail in Lubyanka. Having now successfully tested and hidden the devices there was little more she could do until their meeting. Once she knew exactly what their plans were, then in her role as Vice President of Marketing and Publishing of *Andromeda Research* she would call New York and pass them some form of coded message to pass to Lubyanka in Moscow.

"Come out here and enjoy the sun," the dulcet tones of Andrew Hirst-Bergan's voice drifted in through the open cabin door.

"What about your friend Amir, hasn't he arrived?" Svetlana called back to him as she dried her hair having just taken a quick shower.

"Not yet, but he isn't due to land for another half an hour."

"OK, just a moment and I'll be out," she called as she checked her appearance in the mirror before walking out into the Mediterranean sun. "There, will that do?" she asked.
Andrew looked up from his sun lounger and smiled appreciatively at the bikini clad figure standing in front of him. "Hmm, it certainly will. Come here Svetlana and let me rub some oil on you," he said as he made a grab for her. But she was much too quick for him as she nimbly sidestepped out of reach.

"Now, now Mr Hirst-Bergan we don't want the crew seeing what you're up to and getting the wrong idea do we?"

"Ahh but they won't, well not here anyway because this is a security blind spot."

"How do you mean blind spot?"

"Didn't I tell you? When I designed the security system I purposely left an area that was not covered by the camera system controlled from the bridge, that way I had an area of privacy where I could entertain my guests without the crew spying on me."

"So how big an area is it?"

"Come over here," he said as he struggled to get his bulk off the sun lounger, "and I'll show you. It runs from our cabin window over there," he waved in the general direction of his private quarters. "Now follow me." They both walked aft. "See this," he indicated a small brass plate affixed to the polished handrail, "from here right the way across to the aft entrance over there," he pointed to another cabin door that led to the stateroom. "So you see I can have quite an area for privacy and sunbathing. I'm not overlooked by any cabins or crew's quarters, in fact complete privacy."

"That is quite a large area. Aren't you afraid that someone could sneak aboard whilst you are asleep."

"What when I'm at sea!" his voice sounded incredulous. "You must be joking! From a boat over a ten to twelve foot side! Some hope!"

"No, it's more like six feet at the most."

"Well even then, six feet! From a boat bobbing about on the open sea...! You must be joking...! It would be impossible. Listen, to begin with you would need to be able to get in close enough and hold your small boat there..." he indicated a place alongside that would line up with the security blind spot. "That in itself would prove almost impossible, and then you would have to climb up a slippery, almost vertical structure..." he paused as if for a moment he thought it might be possible, then discounted it. "No not possible!" he said emphatically, shaking his head.

That's what you think Mr Hirst-Bergan. How little you know, with the right equipment and training I reckon anyone could be over the side in no time at all. I certainly know I could.

"What about when you're in harbour or in a marina, surely someone could board her then?"

"Ah, here's the clever bit. I have a camera installed that will cover that area, look up there," he pointed to a discreet camera situated just below the deck head and mounted on to the bulkhead at the corner of the cabin. "Now that camera covers this whole area and is linked into the video recording console up on the bridge. The other cameras are basically a sub system. With that camera included that is the master system and only I control the master system. So you see when she is in a marina or harbour I can make the choice as to whether or not we have full blanket security."

Thank you for that piece of information, that is very useful indeed.

"But...there is something I don't understand..."

"What's that?"

"Well how come only you can switch it on?"

At this Hirst-Bergan gave an exasperated sigh as much as to say 'how dumb can you be'. "Well the switch is in our cabin..."

"But that doesn't stop the skipper or anyone entering your cabin when you're not there and switching it on does it?"

"One small point my dear, come with me." He grabbed Svetlana by the hand and headed through the door into their cabin. "Now show me where the switch is."

Svetlana walked around the cabin and hunted high and low but drew a blank and with a shrug of her shoulders she said. "OK, I give in. Where is the switch?"

At this juncture he immediately went over to the bedside locker and gently pushed on the walnut panel above, which swung out to reveal a concealed key switch. At this point Hirst-Bergan with a theatrical flourish, produced a set of keys from his pocket from which he proceeded to select one and insert it into the key switch, turned it clockwise and withdrew it from the lock.

"Now we have full security coverage, not only out there, but also in here," he pointed up at the camera strategically placed to gain maximum coverage of the master cabin. "So there you are Svetlana, sound and vision, not only in here but also in the stateroom," he added proudly. Having shown her the full master system he then switched it back to the slave or sub-system and closed the panel.

"I'm impressed Andrew. You seem to have thought of everything and I agree it is a very sophisticated system and foolproof."

Thank you for showing me that. The camera in the stateroom, at some stage, may prove to be very useful if I can find a way of overriding the system.

The *Lady Mona* had made good time to Barcelona and they had arrived an hour ahead of schedule much to the frustration and annoyance of Hirst-Bergan. One thing he couldn't abide was sitting around waiting for other people, he felt that this was a desperate waste of time, but with Svetlana and Amir on board he had to keep his frustration in check.

"Now remember what I said; once their boat is spotted I expect you to disappear until we are inside the stateroom. On no account must they see you."

"What about Amir? He has seen me."

"Well he doesn't count. My other business associates, like me, are very private people and I promised them privacy out here on the yacht," he finished lamely.

He was like a cat on a hot tin roof, forever checking the time, in and out of the stateroom, up on the bridge and back down on the after deck; all the time he was on the go. Svetlana, on the other hand, lay on the sunbed drinking ice cold fruit juice and soaking up the sun whilst Amir was in his cabin reading.

At long last it was time and with binoculars pressed up against his eyes Hirst-Bergan scanned the expanse of blue sea that lay between them and the entrance to the Port of Barcelona. In the distance he could see the blurred outline of a small craft as it headed towards their position. Andrew adjusted the binoculars and suddenly the figure of Seva came into sharp focus as he steered the craft toward the *Lady Mona*. Andrew's mood visibly lightened as he quickly busied himself preparing for the craft's approach.

He had given them specific instructions to pass by the yacht, swing round and come in from the stern. As an additional safeguard of their 'secrecy' he had ordered the skipper to take the yacht's launch with the crew into the port of Barcelona so they could spend some time ashore. With them all out of the way there was little or no chance of discovery, and their meeting aboard the *Lady Mona* would go undiscovered, or so he thought! Very quickly Andrew had the steps over the side and in place ready for Seva and Ivo to come aboard. It was now time for Svetlana to disappear into the master suite and remain there until after the meeting had finished and Seva and Ivo had departed.

Outside on deck she could hear Andrew barking orders in Russian to the launch as it came alongside. There was a soft clang as Seva manoeuvred it close to the yacht's landing steps. Ivo threw a rope to Amir who quickly pulled it tight and tied it off. Hirst-Bergan held the launch against the landing platform by means of a boathook whilst Seva tossed a second rope to Amir which he quickly made fast. Once they were satisfied that the launch was securely tied alongside, both Seva and Ivo lost no time in transferring to the yacht and within minutes the whole operation had been completed. No time was lost on pleasantries as the four of them with Hirst-Bergan in the lead headed for the stateroom. Svetlana waited until she heard the stateroom door close, she gave them a further few minutes to get settled before she picked up the ship's satellite phone and put in a call to *Andromeda Research*.

"Hello Natasha. Please tell Alexei that I need him to pass messages through to Lubyanka and Trepashkin. Please tell him that I am now with Hirst-Bergan on the yacht *Lady Mona*. We have been joined by Ivo and Seva the mafia bosses from Moscow and very important – Amir Peres who I recognise as *Mossad*. Tell him I will call again as soon as I know why they are meeting. Bye Natasha." With that Svetlana replaced the satellite phone and listened carefully to what her 'bugs' were now picking up. She immediately recognised the strong stilted accent of a Russian who was unused to speaking English. She assumed this was Seva.

"We have a major problem, Gorbachev he is no good to us. He is keen to reform the Soviet Union which means trouble. Many people will rise up, much wealth will be lost. My family – the Rising Sun – will no longer have the power to help Israel and the Jews. We need Israel's help...in Ivo's country more problems. It is very poor region and people know no different..."

At this stage Ivo entered the conversation. "We in the KGB need to invest many millions outside of our country otherwise with Gorbachev's reforms we will lose and our wealth will go to other people. This will cause us and Israel a big problem. You see Amir the KGB holds much of the wealth, we own the big banks," he smiled at Hirst-Bergan, "that is most of them except for our partner here. Andrew, as you know, he owns a bank. Now all our funds go through his bank then through other banks including ones in Tel Aviv, then into Credit Suisse. This I think you are already familiar with, it is called money laundering. As you know the Bulgarian KGB in conjunction with the Rising Sun makes a lot of money through...what shall I say... re-homing people..."

"You mean trafficking people…" a soft voice without any accent filtered through.

"I wouldn't say that Amir," Ivo answered tersely. "We have already repatriated many Jews and you know it, and Andrew knows it."

"OK, I'll give you that," Amir stated in a businesslike manner. "So what is it you want?" he added quietly.

"Please hear me out," Ivo had now regained his composure. "If Gorbachev is not stopped Israel will lose out because the Jews are no longer coming home. Bulgaria will lose out because we cannot make money so our economy will fail. Russia will lose out because Seva and his family cannot operate as they should. There are many thousands in the Soviet Republic who think like this. Gorbachev must go," he said emphatically.

"So where does Israel fit in with all this?"

"Well we need some funding for a coup…"

The room fell silent as the Bulgarian and the Russian waited for Amir's reaction. He closed his eyes as if considering their proposal before addressing Hirst-Bergan with a question. "And where do you sit in all this Andrew?"

"I…" he started to speak, then paused as if to search for the right words. "I must admit that I think Israel would suffer if they did not take a stand. I think Seva and Ivo may well have a point. Look Amir, you know as well as I do that Israel, like many countries, has its little sidelines, its dirty money etc." Amir looked puzzled at this apparent support of Ivo and Seva, but Andrew pushed on with his point. "Let's look at PROMIS for example. I have sold your version of PROMIS to over forty governments, including those in the Soviet Bloc. Now if Gorbachev continues to push ahead with his perestroika at the present rate then we could all be in trouble. Perestroika is going too fast and Gorbachev is the one pushing it."

"I see, and that is what you honestly think Andrew?"

"Well to me it makes sense, after all we are all in the same boat together and whatever affects Israel affects me, also whatever affects the Soviet Union undoubtedly will affect all of us, including Israel."

Once more a heavy silence descended on the room. Amir considered what had been said and carefully weighed up the arguments put forward by all concerned. After some little while he slowly nodded his head.

"OK gentlemen. Israel will consider your request and I will put your arguments to the government and *Mossad* for their due discussion, but if we are to run with this then Israel must have something in return…"

"What is it she wants?" asked Seva.

"We need more Jews being repatriated from Russia. We need a percentage of your income, say ten percent, which you will pay through your bank accounts into our Credit Suisse account. Then *Mossad* will consider your request."

"OK then we do it. You will help us fund our coup?" Seva said, more as a statement than a question. "Good then that is settled." He looked around the table with a broad grin on his face, stood up and shook Amir's hand. "You make me a very happy man, now we drink some vodka?"

Svetlana, upon hearing what had just been said, was greatly concerned and it left her in no doubt as to the possible repercussions that this meeting could have not only for her country but for the world as a whole if such a coup were successful.

Ahh my oh my, this is dynamite, Lubyanka must be told straight away. So the Bulgarian KGB is in on this and the Israelis. Hirst-Bergan is a double agent, he is for Israel's Mossad and the Bulgarian KGB.

Without further thought Svetlana made a second call to New York station and relayed exactly what she had heard to Alexei for him to pass on to Lubyanka and Mikhail

Trepashkin. Her job here was almost done apart from one other matter and that was to flush out Kristoff. Once again fate was about to take a further hand in things.

It wasn't long after Svetlana had called Alexei that the meeting in the stateroom broke up. Seva and Ivo, pleased with the way things had progressed, persuaded Amir Peres to leave with them for Barcelona in order to catch an earlier flight back to Tel Aviv. In that way the *Mossad* deputy could put their request to his people with the least amount of time wasted. They were now convinced that Israel would assist them in their hour of need and as such their plot to overthrow Mikhail Gorbachev, would succeed.

Hirst-Bergan having seen his associates away safely returned to the relative calm of his cabin. He hadn't been back in there many minutes when the relative quiet was shattered by the strident ringing of his private satellite telephone.

"Hello…Why hello Kim and how are you?" He immediately covered the mouthpiece and whispered to Svetlana "leave me to talk to Kristoff in private." She smiled sweetly and went outside.

Well, well, well what good timing Mr Kristoff!
She had not been outside very long before Andrew appeared on deck.

"Well what do you know, Kim is flying down to Monastir airport in Tunisia in a couple of days' time so I've agreed for us to meet him at the Riu Imperial Marhaba hotel in Port El Kantaoui. In fact, I could book us into the same hotel and we could all spend a few days together sightseeing, what do you think?"

"Lovely," Svetlana said with enthusiasm. "I've never been to Tunisia before."

"Good that's settled then. As soon as Peter and the crew return we'll weigh anchor and set sail for Port El Kantaoui and in the meantime I'll call the hotel and book us in."

"There's only one thing, I will need to let *Andromeda Research* know in case they need to contact me so may I give them a call?"

"Of course you can."

"So when do you think we'll get there?"

"Umm, day after tomorrow."

Good then that will give department V chance to get someone down there for the wet job!

Chapter 16

Port El Kantaoui with its quintessential white and blue houses, cobbled streets, waterfront restaurants and chic boutiques made it very much a Mediterranean jet setters' paradise. So finding such a hotel as the Riu Imperial Marhaba, only a ten minute drive from the marina, tucked away in a quiet corner of town, was no great surprise. But even Hirst-Bergan with his experience of lavish indulgence and palatial surroundings had to admit that with its mind-blowing atrium, and polished marble and glass fronted elevators, the hotel took some beating. He paused in the entrance and looked around, his eyes taking in every small detail and it was obvious from his expression that he appreciated what he saw. Had he not been so absorbed in admiring his extravagant surroundings and the sheer opulence of it all, he may just have noticed the lean athletic man with piercing blue eyes slip something into Svetlana's hand as he walked by on his way to reception. But as usual, he was too wrapped up in his own little world, otherwise things may well have turned out differently. Svetlana casually slipped the small package into her bag as she took out her passport ready to register with reception.

"Andrew, I presume we need to book in?"

"Oh, yes of course," he answered her with a smile. "Well what do you think, is it suitable for royalty?" he asked good humouredly.

"Why sir, thank you," she replied mockingly.

"Then madam, after you." He gave an exaggerated flourish of his hand and stood aside as Svetlana made her way to the reception desk to register.

"Can I help madam?" the receptionist enquired.

"I believe you have a booking in the name of Ilyinsky, Svetlana Ilyinsky?"

"Err, I'm sorry madam there is no booking in that name…"

"Ah no, it's probably in the name of Hirst-Bergan," Andrew interrupted. "It was booked on my behalf…"

"Ah yes, there it is. Two single rooms I believe?"

"Yes thank you," answered Svetlana before Hirst-Bergan could argue.

"Thank you madam, then if you would both kindly fill out the cards with your name, address and passport details, I would be obliged." She passed Svetlana two registration cards for her and Andrew to fill out with their details. Having made sure all the details were correctly filled in she summoned a porter, who appeared as if from nowhere, picked up the keys and their two small bags and asked them in broken English to follow him. As they reached the glass fronted elevators he glanced at the keys in his hand and said. "You have room 422 and 423." Then stood aside as the glass door slid noiselessly back. "Thank you. sir and madam please," he indicated for them both to enter the lift..

Once inside her room Svetlana took out the small package that had been passed to her in the hotel foyer by her colleague Ivan Pedrosky, from the Washington station. Ivan had obviously been sent in by Moscow to oversee the operation to either 'remove' or 'eliminate' *Oleg* and as such had made contact with Svetlana to give her some instructions. She immediately took the package into the bathroom and locked the door. Carefully she undid the package to reveal a small container heavily sealed in plastic, a message and airline ticket from Tunis to Barcelona. The message, a hastily typewritten note, said:

> *Small container holds aconitine a natural substance*
> *that is untraceable within 18 hours of administration.*
> *Administer this evening, afterwards wash hands*
> *thoroughly and await further instructions. In envelope*

is single airline ticket from Tunis to Barcelona in the name of Natasha Yeltsin and a new passport in the same name. Once at Barcelona go to 'Airport Information' where you will get further instructions.

Svetlana read and re-read the note until she was happy that she could remember every single detail. Once she was certain that she had it firmly committed to memory she tore the note into tiny pieces then flushed it down the toilet. Picking up the rest of the items she returned to her bedroom and had just put them safely away in her handbag when there was a gentle tap on her door.

"Yes who is it?" she called as she glanced at her watch and noted it was already 3:00 pm.

"It's Andrew," the muffled voice of Hirst-Bergan answered. "Are you ready?" he called.

"OK I'm just coming." With that she opened the door and stepped into the corridor.

"I've just had a call from Kim to say that he'll meet us in the piano bar," Hirst-Bergan said as they walked along the corridor.

"OK fine. Then what shall we do about dinner?"

So shall I slip the powder into his drink now?

"Do you want to go down to one of the waterfront restaurants or somewhere else?" he asked as he pressed the lift call button. Svetlana grimaced. "Could, I mean, would you mind if we ate in the hotel tonight? It's just that I need to get on with some work and wire it over to New York plus I'm a little tired and I could do with an early night."

"OK," he said as they entered the lift. "I'll just tell Kim we're eating in and that he's welcome to join us if he would like to."

"Are you sure he won't mind."

"No it'll be fine and I'm sure he'll join us anyway."

I hope he agrees to eat with us because I can then spike his drink. Then at last my job here will be done and after all this time Oleg's debt will be paid!

She allowed herself an inward smile.

"Andrew!" A man in his fifties with a swarthy complexion and black curly hair, dressed in open necked shirt, shorts and leather flip-flops called to them as they entered the bar and headed over to meet them. Svetlana immediately recognised him as *Oleg*, the man whose photograph Mikhail Trepashkin had shown her. He was the man whom she had vowed to get even with all those years ago. He was the man she had witnessed rape her mother and beat her father. He was Kristoff. For many years she wondered how she would react should she ever come face to face with the perpetrator of the crimes and now here he was. She could reach out and touch him for that was how close he now stood to her as he shook hands with Hirst-Bergan.

"Kim, this is Svetlana," she heard Hirst-Bergan say as if from a distance.

Get control of yourself Svetlana, get control and smile sweetly.

"Pleased to meet you Svetlana," she heard him say.

"Oh, I'm sorry, I was miles away," she answered automatically and smiled as a myriad of pictures and thoughts tumbled through her head. "Pleased to meet you Kim." Momentarily the smile froze on her face as she thought about the past.

Come on Svetlana forget it, you have a job to do now so don't blow it. Soon you will have your revenge. Think of Mikhail. Think of Ivan. Think positive.

As they sat at the table Svetlana, only half listening to them both as they chatted about old times, quietly thought and planned her next move. Whilst they were deep in conversation she took the opportunity to take a good look around her surroundings, to see if she could spot anyone she remotely recognised. She already knew Ivan was somewhere in the vicinity, but try as she might she could not see his friendly face anywhere and this unsettled her.

"Andrew, Kim, if you'd both excuse me a moment," she said as she got up, "I just need to pop back to my room for something." She didn't wait for their reply but immediately set off in the direction of the foyer and the lifts. As she walked from the bar she caught a glimpse out of the corner of her eye, of someone as they got up from the table not too far away from where she had been sitting and start to follow her. On reaching the foyer she suddenly stopped dead turned and walked slap bang into a young man.

"Oops, careful Svetlana," the young man said quietly in Russian. Although he was heavily disguised she just couldn't fail to recognise Mikhail Trepashkin. He grabbed hold of her arm and said very quietly "shhh, don't say a word just walk to the lifts and I will follow. Go!"

Without saying a word she turned and did exactly what she was told, and on reaching the fourth floor Svetlana with Mikhail following, headed for her room. Once inside they could relax a little and talk openly.

"Mikhail what on earth are you doing here?" she asked.

"I am part of the wet team and now you have *Oleg* it is my duty to see that we finish the job we have started. I have also given my word to your father that I will look after you for him."

"Thank you Mikhail, it is so good to see you. I have missed you so much," she said as she took him in her arms and gave him a lingering kiss. "I, I'm sorry," she said, "I don't know what came over me comrade," she said putting on her professional KGB front. Mikhail allowed a fleeting smile at her obvious embarrassment.

"Listen Svetlana, once you have administered the poison leave a written message in an envelope for Mustapha at reception. The message will say 'my mother is ill so I have to go' that is all.

"Who is Mustapha?"

"He works for the embassy as our contact here in the hotel. We try to have someone placed in the reception at each hotel in Port El Kantaoui. That way we know who is coming and going which is especially important in a place where power and wealth go hand in hand. Once Mustapha receives your message he will make sure Hirst-Bergan knows that your mother is ill and you need to return to America urgently. Now, do you understand what to do?" She nodded. "Good. Then good luck my Russian doll and soon we'll meet again." With that he let himself out and disappeared back to the lifts.

It was mid-afternoon when the small select group sat down in what they called 'the conference room'. The room was situated in the Hadar Davna building, the Mossad headquarters in King Saul Boulevard Tel Aviv, and was generally reserved for the discussion of major projects, possible targets and problems with specific political overtones. The select committee had gathered specifically to discuss the meeting that Amir had attended on Hirst-Bergan's yacht three days previously and the ramifications of the meeting. It was at this meeting that Seva and Ivo had requested the help of Israel and, in particular *Mossad*, to fund a *coup* aimed at overthrowing Mikhail Gorbachev in order to stop his *perestroika* or restructuring of the Soviet Union. Whilst Amir had been on board the *Lady Mona* and listened patiently to their proposals, he had also asked Hirst-Bergan what his feelings were about such a *coup*, to which Hirst-Bergan had indicated that he had an empathy with such a move. This had both intrigued and interested Amir in so far as he wondered exactly why

214

Hirst-Bergan felt such a move would be beneficial to Mossad, Israel and in particular himself. Try as he might he could not see any major benefit but he could not help feeling that he had missed something obvious, and it was for that reason alone that he had indicated the possible interest of *Mossad*. The way he had said 'if we are to run with this then Israel must have something in return. We need more Jews to be repatriated from Russia, we need a percentage of your income say, ten percent,' had seemed encouraging from their point of view. And that was exactly how he had intended it to sound. If he was not mistaken and knowing Andrew Hirst-Bergan the way he did, he felt that he was up to something. All he could say was that he got the impression that Hirst-Bergan, because of his involvement with the other two, had already financed something with them and was now hoping that *Mossad* would bail him out.

"Why do you think that Amir?" asked Uzi. "After all he has been good for us and helped us in many ways."

"Agreed Uzi, but would you in his situation see it as a positive step forward?"

"That would depend whose viewpoint you were taking."

"I agree. Now if I were Hirst-Bergan I would only see it as a positive move if it was to be of benefit to me, and that's my point. Surely perestroika must be of more benefit than a *coup,* it will eventually open up the whole of the Soviet Union so making their life easier..."

"Unless by keeping a tight lid on things, which what happened before the start of perestroika, you as a criminal family hold on to money and power."

"Exactly and I suspect that Hirst-Bergan is more than just a broker between the two Russians and us, I think he has a link somewhere down the line. I think he is in partnership with them."

"But that fact wouldn't necessarily mean he was in favour unless he has already invested funds into some sort of..."

"And I tell you Uzi, I am convinced that either he has put in money or is on the point of doing so, that is why he is so keen to have us help, because without us going to the party he will lose his investment."

"Hmm. In that case perhaps we should hold back and see what develops, does everyone agree with that?" Uzi looked at each of those present in turn and each and every one gave a nod of their head signifying their agreement with his suggestion. So it was decided, that for the time being at least, *Mossad* would take no further active part in funding or conspiring to help with the hardliners in Russia with their proposed *coup* against Gorbachev and to let perestroika continue without hindrance from them. Had Hirst-Bergan known about the meeting then things may well have turned out differently, but the decision made in the conference room by that very select group of individuals was to seal his fate for the future.

Still with the image of Mikhail and what he said fresh in her memory, Svetlana thought carefully about how she was going to accomplish the job ahead of her. She went into the bathroom and took the small container from her handbag, then whilst she stood with the tin over the hand basin she very carefully peeled off the outer plastic coating to reveal what appeared to be a snuff tin duly labelled 'McChrystal's JIP snuff'. On the back of the tin it stated 'JIP snuff has a medicated and sweet flavour with a strong menthol kick that clears the nose, the scent lasts for a long time.'

Hmm, an interesting concept!

Very carefully Svetlana opened the tin to examine the contents, which appeared to be greyish-brown in colour not unlike the colour of horseradish root. She dampened her little finger, dabbed it onto the powder and touched her tongue with the resultant small dusting. The initial sensation was sweet but this sweetness was quickly replaced with a slight burning sensation, quickly followed by numbness of the tongue, not unlike that achieved from a local anaesthetic used by a dentist when one is having a tooth filled.

Very interesting sensation, it must act on the nervous system similar to that of Sarin or VX nerve agent but because it is a natural poison it is untraceable in the body. Very clever department V, very clever indeed.

Gradually the numbness in her mucous membrane started to subside and was slowly replaced with a slight tingling sensation as the peripheral sensory nerves in her mouth returned to normal. She carefully replaced the lid and made sure it was on tightly before wrapping the tin up in the plastic she had removed earlier, she then placed the item in her bag, making sure that it was upright to avoid any possible accidents or spillage. Having satisfied herself that the tin was safely and securely stowed in her bag, she then ran the taps in order to wash away any residue of the powder that may well have found its way into the basin. As a further precaution she tore off a handful of the soft toilet paper, dampened it under the tap and proceeded to thoroughly and carefully wipe the surfaces adjacent to the basin, thus making sure that none of the powder remained, not even the minutest trace. She then repeated the process for the hand basin itself. Once she had finished she disposed of the used toilet paper by flushing it away down the toilet. All she had to do now was thoroughly wash her hands to make sure that there was no trace of aconitine left on her fingers, after all the last thing she wanted was to absorb the poison through her skin.

At 7:30 pm Svetlana and Andrew headed off to the piano bar to meet up with Kim Kristoff for pre-dinner drinks. Svetlana had decided that she would lace Kristoff's drink during the meal. She already had a plan as to how she would actually achieve her aim, and having studied his drinking habits earlier in the afternoon she felt it would prove to be surprisingly simple to put it into operation. The idea was that during the meal she would excuse herself and go to the bar and order a good quality whisky for Kristoff, a glass of red wine for Hirst-Bergan and a white wine for herself. Whilst the bartender poured the wine she would slip the powder into *Oleg's* drink, the waiter would then deliver the drinks to the table escorted by her. The plan was foolproof provided she stuck close to the waiter and made sure that he took only the three drinks she had bought on his tray.

At 8:30 pm halfway through the main course, both Hirst-Bergan and Kristoff had finished their drinks.

Now's my chance.

She smiled at Kim Kristoff and asked, "Kim may I get you a drink?"

"No, I'll get them."

"No I insist. Anyway I need to pop to the ladies so I'll order them on the way. A whisky isn't it?"

"Well, if that's all right with you…"

"Of course it is, and for you Andrew a red wine?"

"Thank you my love, that'll be fine. In fact put them on my bill."

That couldn't be better. That way I am not implicated should anything go wrong!

"No I'll pay for them," she said knowing full well that his ego would never allow a woman to buy him drinks.

"No, I insist you put them on my bill," he repeated quite forcibly.

She smiled to herself.

OK Andrew, that's fine by me.

"OK then. So it's whisky for you Kim, red wine for Andrew and a white wine for me. I won't be too long boys," she said mischievously and winked at Kristoff.

Svetlana tried hard to appear interested as the two men chatted about different things that had happened since their last meeting, pausing every now and then to take a drink. It had been nearly fifteen minutes since she had laced Kristoff's drink with aconitine, but as of yet she had not seen any reaction, but there again he had not drunk much of it. She decided that she needed to gee him up a little so she threw down the gauntlet, picked up her glass of wine and finished it.

"Well gentlemen, may I suggest that as we have finished our meal that we ought to have a little fun." They both stopped talking and gave her a quizzical look.

"In what way?" asked Kristoff.

"Yes Svetlana in what way?" repeated Hirst-Bergan, intrigued by what she meant as fun.

"Well I bet that neither of you gentlemen can drink me under the table."

Both men looked at each other then at her and laughed out loud.

"What are you saying, of course we can," Hirst-Bergan stated in a matter of fact way.

"In that case, drink up your drinks and we'll go to the bar," she said standing up. That did the trick. Kristoff, always one to be up for a challenge, immediately downed his whisky in one and Hirst-Bergan not to be left out did likewise. Svetlana was already on the move to the bar safe in the knowledge that soon the poison would start to take effect and that the game will be suitably interrupted by Mustapha announcing that Svetlana's mother had been taken very ill and had been rushed to hospital.

"So what is the prize Svetlana?" asked Kristoff.

"Oh, didn't I say, if either of you men win, then I am the prize. The winner out of you two can have their way with me!"

Now that is some prize!

"Are you saying that if I beat you and Andrew I get to sleep with you tonight?" asked Kristoff.

"Yes, that's right, but if I beat you both then you have to buy me a diamond studded necklace, so are you still up for it?"

"Of course, what about you Andrew?"

"Definitely."

"One thing before we start, I need to pop to my room and make a quick call to my office back home, so if you'll excuse me for a few minutes I'll join you both in the piano bar on my return." With that she made her exit and left the two men to make their way to the bar.

Once inside her room she took one of the sheets of writing paper supplied by the hotel and hastily wrote on it 'my mother is ill so I have to go', neatly folded it and sealed it inside an envelope which she addressed with the name 'Mustapha'. The next thing she did was to take out the snuff tin and wrap it up in many layers of toilet paper before hiding it in her lightweight suitcase. She checked that she had everything already neatly packed in her case, hid the passport that stated her name as Svetlana Ilyinsky and made sure the new Russian passport stating her to be Natasha Yeltsin was placed in her handbag, along with her ticket for the flight to Barcelona. She made one last check around the room to make sure she had not left anything to chance, picked up the envelope for Mustapha and immediately left the room heading for the lift to take her down to the ground floor and reception. Upon arriving in the foyer she walked quickly to reception and handed the letter to the man behind the desk who glanced at the name and before she turned to leave asked her in a low whisper where she was going to be.

So you are Mustapha.

"I'm going to the piano bar," was all she said and left, heading straight for the bar to find the two men.

As she entered the bar she glanced at her watch and noted that she had been less than ten minutes, had a quick look around and immediately spotted them both at a table near a large tropical plant. They had already got the drinks in and were eager to start the drinking game. She chose the seat close to the plant, where if the worst came to the worst she could sneakily tip her drink away.

"Sorry about that, but I just needed to get a call into America, but would you believe it all the lines were busy so I'll just have to try again later," she lied. "OK let's start, one two three." All three picked up their drinks and downed them in one and it was Kristoff who summoned the waiter and ordered another round. In a matter of minutes three more drinks appeared. It was Hirst-Bergan who counted them in this time and once again they downed them in one. Andrew summoned the waiter and ordered three more drinks. Another few minutes and three more drinks appeared. It was now Kristoff's turn to count them in.

"One…twooo. Justa minute," he slurred. His brow showed signs of sweat. He tried hard to concentrate; it seemed as if his vision was blurred. He blinked his eyes as if he was seeing double. His speech became even more slurred and voices were echoing and distant. Through the fog in his brain he could hear Svetlana talking. He turned towards her, her face kept blurring and coming back into focus.

I feel terrible. I feel as if I'm going to pass out. My fingers are tingling and my lips are tingling. Concentrate Kim, it must be something you've eaten. It'll pass.

"Kim, Kim, can you hear me?" Svetlana's voice asked. "Kim are you feeling all right?"

"Hey come on Kim, what's wrong?" Hirst-Bergan asked as Kristoff swayed on the point of blacking out. "Quick Svetlana, he's not well get someone from reception to call an ambulance."

"OK Andrew. Hold on Kim I won't be long." Svetlana pushed back her chair and ran from the bar out into the foyer. As soon as she was out of sight she stopped running and took a casual stroll to reception where she beckoned to Mustapha.

"Yes madam, can I help you?" he asked in his best receptionist's voice.

Svetlana leaned forward and whispered, "it's time." Mustapha nodded, smiled at his fellow receptionist as he picked up the phone and dialled a number. Within a few seconds the call was answered.

"Ah yes, this is the Riu Imperial Marhaba hotel, we need an ambulance, a gentleman has been taken ill in the piano bar. Thank you." He replaced the receiver, turned to his fellow receptionist and said, "when the ambulance arrives would you send them through to the piano bar, I'm just going through with this young lady to see if there is anything I can do." With that both Mustapha and Svetlana returned to where Andrew Hirst-Bergan and Kim Kristoff were sitting. They had only been there a matter of minutes when the paramedics arrived. They checked Kristoff's temperature, took his blood pressure and asked him how he felt. He told them that he felt terrible and clammy. They asked him if he had any pain, he said he hadn't but that he felt sick. They asked him if he had any pins and needles in his hands to which he said he had. From what they saw and what he told them they diagnosed that Kristoff was having a heart attack and needed immediate hospitalisation. With that they placed him in a wheelchair and rushed him to the waiting ambulance. It was at this point Svetlana realised that they were no more paramedics than she was; in fact she recognised one of them as Grigory codename *the mechanic*, her so-called cousin from Sofia, and knew straightaway that Department V was about to take care of *Oleg*.

At last justice has been done.

With that thought she turned back through the main door into the foyer and back to the piano bar where she found a stunned Hirst-Bergan waiting for her.

"I'm sorry Andrew but I guess he's in safe hands now." Hirst-Bergan sat in silence, suddenly the silly drinking game had lost its charm, but things were about to get worse.

Within a couple of minutes of Svetlana's return a worried looking receptionist, in the shape of Mustapha, once more appeared in the bar. He was looking for Svetlana – he could have studied at RADA for his acting ability was second to none – and upon seeing her, rushed over to speak to her.

"I'm sorry madam, but may I ask if you are Ms Ilyinsky?"

"Yes why?"

"Well madam we have just received a telephone call from your company *Andromeda Research* saying that you need to return home immediately as your mother has been rushed into hospital and she is very ill."

Svetlana looked puzzled.

"Her mother you say?" Hirst-Bergan asked.

"Yes sir, I'm sorry sir but she must go immediately to the airport. Madam I am very sorry but as your company said it was vital you went home on the first available flight so I took the liberty of arranging a taxi for you. I hope you don't think it too presumptuous of me. May I help you with your baggage?"

"I'm sorry Andrew, but I must go…"

"Of course my dear, I hope everything turns out all right in the end, now go. Go on, go."

Svetlana gave him a weak smile, and a quick kiss and a hug.

"Please madam the taxi, he will be here in a minute…"

"OK, I'm coming," she turned and hurried towards the door of the bar, turned and looked back to Hirst-Bergan as he stood there watching her departure. "I'll call you in London," she called to him and blew him a kiss.

"You do, you do and good luck."

Both Mustapha and Svetlana rushed out of the piano bar toward the foyer and the glass fronted elevators that would whisk them to the fourth floor and her room. Once inside the elevator they both relaxed, looked at each other and burst out laughing.

"Mustapha, you are a born actor," she said to the Tunisian. "Thank you for that performance."

"Ahh, acting is second nature in this job."

At the airport Svetlana checked in under the name of Natasha Yeltsin, showed her new Russian passport and passed through to the departure lounge where she sat patiently waiting for her 23:40 Air Europe flight to Barcelona to be called. A lot had happened in the space of the last twelve hours, but the most important thing was she had achieved her main objective and that was to trap the rogue KGB operator codename *Oleg*. At last his debt to her family had been paid, now all she had to do was to get as far away from Tunisia in as short a time as possible. Suddenly she was brought back to reality as someone sat down beside her and whispered her name. At first she thought she was hearing things but there it was again. Fearing for the worst she glanced out of the corner of her eye to see who the person was sitting next to her and to her surprise she immediately recognised the tanned face with piercing blue eyes.

"Ivan Pedrosky, what are you doing here?" she asked in a low whisper.

"Come let's walk a little and talk a little," he answered in Russian.

So they walked and they talked. She asked him what had happened to Kristoff. He told her that unfortunately he was dead on arrival. So she asked him where they had taken him. He said 'Mr Kristoff must have died from a heart attack whilst walking on the beach'. This prompted her to ask him when he thought Kristoff's body would be found to which he replied, 'as it was a remote part of the beach not far from Port El Kantaoui it may be tomorrow or it may well take a couple of days or more'. She thought about his reply for a moment or two and then it occurred to her that he had not said anything about Mikhail Trepashkin or Grigory.

"What about Mikhail and Grigory?" She asked.

"Don't you worry about them, they are both safely out of Tunisia and on their way to Moscow by now," he glanced at his watch. "In fact they should arrive by the time we take off." She nodded her head in approval and Ivan slipped his arm around her shoulders as a father would to his daughter and they walked in silence for a short time. It was Ivan who broke the silence with his comment.

"So you see my Russian doll, Department V is very efficient when it comes to traitors." He gave her a comforting squeeze as they turned and retraced their footsteps. This time it was Svetlana who spoke first.

"Are you travelling back to New York with me?" she asked.

"No not this trip *Felix*." Then as if he was still considering his options he said. "I think I may go to London and talk to my friends about our 'other friend' Mr Hirst-Bergan..." but before he could finish what he was saying their flight was announced.

"Would all passengers for the 23:40 flight to Barcelona, the Air Europe flight number UX1088 please proceed to gate 6 where they are boarding."

"Well my *Felix*, that's our flight. The first leg of our journey is now underway Natasha Yeltsin."

"Yes, you're right Ivan Pedrosky and it will not be long before we start our next stage which for me is from Barcelona to New York."

Chapter 17

Sir James took a sip from his whisky. "So you see Brigadier, things were not looking too good for our Mr Hirst-Bergan."

"Damned right they weren't. So what happened after his return to London James?"

"Well as you know Svetlana had returned to America. Ivan Pedrosky came over here and Trepashkin returned to Moscow. Perestroika was gaining pace and Gorbachev was still very much in control. Russia was now on the point of entering a new chapter in her life."

Sir James continued with the story...

What with Kristoff being rushed off to hospital with a suspected heart attack, Svetlana receiving a message from *Andromeda Research* about her mother being critically ill in America, Hirst-Bergan suddenly felt very much alone and decided to return to London. However, had he looked behind the obvious and taken the trouble to check out which hospital they had taken Kristoff to or to make sure Svetlana had managed to get a flight at such short notice, then he would have realised all was not as it seemed. If he had just taken a little time to phone the airport he would have found that no one by the name of Svetlana Ilyinsky had purchased a ticket to America nor had anyone checked in by that name. Instead of showing a little compassion Hirst-Bergan, with his usual selfish attitude, decided to accept things as they were, checked out of the hotel and returned to his yacht whereupon he ordered the crew to immediately set sail for Gibraltar where his private jet was still waiting, his intention now was to return to London. Yes things could well have turned out differently if only...

He hadn't been in London long when he received a fax from his office in New York about a plane crash in Georgia. At first he was puzzled as to why they had sent him a copy of the article that had appeared in the New York Times, but as he read it puzzlement gave way to panic as the name Senator John H Frank jumped off the page at him. Alarm bells rang as he read the report in more detail and realised that one of his main assets John H Frank along with twenty two other people, including John's daughter, had perished in a plane crash in Georgia. The plane, a twin-engine turbo prop, was a commuter plane flying from Atlanta to the coast when it crashed just one and a half miles from its destination, killing everyone on board. To Hirst-Bergan this was a major setback to his plans and left him feeling more than just a little vulnerable to say the very least.

Slowly the enormity of what he had read sunk in and for a moment he sat in stunned silence, in total disbelief. He read and re-read the article but no matter how many times he read it nothing changed. His tame senator was dead. His key to hallowed places including the President's office and the Oval Room, in one foul stroke, had been lost!

Now what do I do?

Hirst-Bergan slowly laid the article down on his desk in front of him, picked up his private telephone and called Amir in Tel Aviv. With Kristoff being rushed into hospital, Svetlana's mother being taken ill and now this, it did rather seem as if his world was slowly disintegrating around him.

"Hello who's calling?" a lady's voice asked.

"It's Andrew from London, is Amir there?"

"Shalom Andrew, just a moment I will get him for you."

The phone went dead for a short time before being picked up by Amir.

"Shalom Andrew, Amir speaking."

"Shalom Amir. I don't know whether you've heard or not, but Frank is dead…"

"Frank?" he asked vaguely as if the name meant nothing to him.

"Yes our tame senator."

Suddenly realisation dawned as to who Hirst-Bergan was talking about "John Frank?" Amir asked incredulously as if he were hearing things.

"Yes…"

"Dead, when and how!" Amir exclaimed in disbelief.

"He was killed in a plane crash in Georgia; the plane he was on came down killing everyone on board." Hirst-Bergan picked up the article and read it out over the phone to Amir. "So we have lost our Presidential key Amir. Now what do we do?" he asked with a slight note of desperation in his voice and waited for Amir's response.

After a short silence Amir answered, "we do precisely nothing…"

Hirst-Bergan didn't give Amir a chance to finish before interrupting him. "Nothing! You say nothing, why nothing?"

"We have more pressing matters at moment …"

Again Hirst-Bergan didn't give Amir chance to finish what he was saying before rudely interrupting him. "Such as, such as?" Hirst-Bergan became agitated with Amir's laid-back response to what seemed to him a very important issue.

Amir gave an audible sigh of exasperation at Hirst-Bergan's animated tone, then he answered him in a quiet voice. "Well to begin with Andrew, what is currently happening in Moscow."

"In what way?"

"Well, after our meeting with Seva and Ivo, your Russian friends, I sense the distinct smell of a coup, a very dangerous smell if you ask me. Now Andrew, what do you know about that?"

Suddenly Hirst-Bergan sensed a trap closing about him and was now well out of his depth. He tried hard to shrug it off by pretending to know nothing but was even more worried when

Amir told him that Mossad had directed analysts to assess the continuing situation in Moscow.

"And what have they said Amir?" he asked trying hard not to convey any concern.

"They have reported that things are getting somewhat precarious there."

"In what way?"

"Different things such as Pavlov, the Prime Minister, suggesting that Gorbachev's health was suspect and because of that he should be relieved of a number of his presidential powers, also a *katsa* within the Russian Foreign Office has confirmed that Vladimir had been holding secret meetings late at night within the Lubyanka."

"Well, I can assure you Amir it has nothing to do with me," his voice conveying a confidence that he was far from feeling.

"In that case Andrew you have nothing to worry about but I need to go now as I have some pressing business to attend to. We will speak again soon."

"Amir, a moment."

"Yes Andrew?"

"Have you had any further thoughts about what was discussed on the yacht?"

"Hmm, I wondered when we would get round to that. Now let me see if I've got it right. Ivo and Seva want us, the state of Israel, to bring about the downfall of Gorbachev…"

"Well you did promise, through your connections, to bring about some form of logistical assistance…"

"No, no, no. That my friend is where you are wrong, I never promised anything. Now let's get this straight, your friends asked for Mossad's support in a plot to oust Gorbachev. I stated 'Israel will consider your request and I will put your arguments to the government and Mossad for their due discussion, but if we are to run with this then Israel must have something in return.' That was all I said."

"But the inference was that Israel would help..." Hirst-Bergan answered with more than just a little concern.

"Ahh, be that as it may; but to think that we would become involved in a political coup in such a volatile situation as exists in Russia shows naivety. After all such a thing is not like organising a takeover of some company." Amir admonished Hirst-Bergan for his stupidity. Suddenly Hirst-Bergan started to feel more than just a little isolated and he should have realised there and then that he was getting way out of his depth. His naivety in such things was now causing Amir grave concern.

With such a major error of judgement not only Amir's perception of Hirst-Bergan but also that of Mossad had now radically changed. Amir, Uzi and the other senior officers of Mossad began to see him as a loose canon, a man desperate enough to do anything in order to get his hands on vast sums of money, and that in Hirst-Bergan's case they were now dealing with an increasingly unbalanced and unpredictable individual. From now on Amir felt that as well as being an asset, Hirst-Bergan was becoming a threat and as such they needed to monitor him closely.

Too late Hirst-Bergan realised that he had committed the cardinal sin, that of making an assumption, and had already gone out on a limb and started to fund Seva and Ivo's plan, that in itself may not have been too bad, but it was the method by which he was funding them. He had taken it upon himself to surreptitiously use his employees' pension fund to prop up his various companies, against which he had taken out further loans, in the firm belief that this money would ultimately be repaid by funds he had assumed were coming from Israel. Assumptions in the business world may not be irretrievable, but on the world's stage at the very least they are, downright dangerous.

When he saw that the funds from Israel had now dissolved before his eyes he became desperate and made a further grave error of judgement in so far as he tried to raise additional money by deciding to sell his company in Tel Aviv. Unfortunately the chief executive who was also son of the Prime Minister was against such a move. This culminated in a very acrimonious telephone conversation between the two of them resulting in Hirst-Bergan slamming down the phone. This was yet another incident to add to all the other information that Uzi, the Mossad chief, was assembling about Hirst-Bergan for the record.

"So what did he do James?" asked the Brigadier.

"Well, a month later, finding himself in great difficulty, he turned to Amir his Mossad controller and friend to solicit Mossad's assistance."

"Ahh I see, but surely they wouldn't help, would they?"

"No you're right Brigadier, they didn't help. In fact Amir told him 'such help was outside the remit of Mossad'."

Sir James went on with the story…

In early October 1991, four members of Mossad met together. They were the four kiddon, the cell that removed traitors and enemies of the state of Israel. They were the group that carried out 'executive decisions' as MI6 call them or 'wet jobs' as Department V of the KGB call them. The four had completed their dossier on Hirst-Bergan and made their preparations. They had already assembled together video clips of his life, a breakdown of his financial holdings, the mounting debts, his mistresses, his connection to Seva and Ivo and the criminal underworld of Eastern Europe – all of this they had taken, studied and evaluated. They had thoroughly studied his way of life and routines. They had compiled a list of all the people who were important to him; the key people in his life, including family, friends and employees – even his lawyers were listed. They built a detailed profile of all these people including their individual addresses – both business and homes

- how accessible the addresses were and the surrounding area. They logged his movements in and around London, his telephone calls – especially those he made to Tel Aviv which had become increasingly more frequent. They even had a *katsa* log his movements in New York, so very gradually and slowly they built up a complete dossier on him. It was at this October meeting that the kiddon team was told to move to Condition Red, the penultimate stage!

Hirst-Bergan was now stumbling from one crisis to another and the city was baying for his blood. There was no doubt about it, life for the media tycoon was fast becoming intolerable. He was at his desk deep in thought, when out of the blue, his private telephone rang. The voice on the line said it was the Israeli embassy in Madrid calling.

"Huh I bet that made the bounder sit up!" exclaimed the Brigadier.

"Hmm, I expect it did Brigadier, anyway as I was saying…" Sir James continued, "there was a pause whilst the switchboard connected him."

"I bet that felt like a lifetime to him," interjected the Brigadier.

"No doubt it did, but I suppose if you were in his shoes it would be a small price to pay if you thought that you were going to be bailed out of the proverbial. Anyway, suddenly there was a click and the voice on the phone asked him to identify himself."

The Brigadier pursed his lips and then asked, "how in God's name did he do that?"

"Well he just gave his name and told whoever it was that he was a friend of Israel and a Jew."

"And they accepted that?"

"Well yes."

"Damned funny turn out if you ask me. Anyway sorry James, please continue."

"Thank you Brigadier, well as I was saying, he answered by telling them his name to which they greeted him in the traditional way and went on from there as follows."

"Shalom Mr Hirst-Bergan and thank you for that. I have received instructions from Tel Aviv for you and they wish you to fly to Gibraltar. Once there you need to take your yacht the *Lady Mona* and set sail for Madeira. On arrival you will be given further instructions. Oh and Tel Aviv says they have now carefully studied your situation and there is no need for panic. It will soon be sorted out."

"Hmm. More's the pity," growled the Brigadier under his breath. "I bet he felt relieved."

"From his point of view Mossad must have seemed like the United States cavalry, coming to his rescue at long last," answered Sir James who then took another sip of his whisky before continuing with the rest of the story as it had been told to him…

In Tel Aviv a quick phone call was made and the kidon's order was raised to that of Condition Green. They had the order to go. A further four separate telephone calls were made, two locally in Tel Aviv, one to America and one to London. The four persons in the team, who were all fluent in the French language, would travel on French passports. In addition, two of the team were also proficient in Spanish. As a cover they decided to go deep sea fishing and scuba diving, so as well as rods and tackle they took with them wetsuits and air bottles.

As a support team and independent of the kidon, a small group of people working in pairs travelled as tourists. Each pair carried a laptop computer and mobile phones. The equipment had been converted so that the laptop could act as a jamming device or call interceptor, whilst each mobile phone had been modified to allow the user to appear to be calling from different locations such as London, Cairo, Rome and so on.

On the day that Hirst-Bergan received the telephone call from Israel's embassy in Madrid the communications team and the kidon left for their respective destinations. The kidon would all meet in Zürich Switzerland, then would fly on to Las Palmas where they would pick up a high speed ocean going boat and wait. The support or communications teams left on a scheduled flight to Madrid and then went on to Morocco where they would pick up two boats, each one ocean going and fitted with a powerful engine. The overall control of the operation would be through the most senior officers within Mossad all working together from the building on King Saul Boulevard. They would at all times be linked by secure communications to the kidon team and at any one stage they could call off the operation.

"So tell me James, who actually made the call to Hirst-Bergan? Was it from Tel Aviv or Spain?"

"That's a good question Brigadier. I do believe that it was one of those senior officers who initiated the call by telephoning the Israeli embassy in Madrid."

"So are you saying the telephone call was definitely from the Israeli embassy and it was that phone call which then led to Hirst-Bergan making his own travel arrangements?"

"Almost certainly," Sir James said and took another sip of whisky before continuing with what he understood to be the events as they unfolded...

In Gibraltar, the captain of the *Lady Mona* supervised the preparation of the yacht in readiness for a trip to New York that had already been arranged by Hirst-Bergan upon his leaving Port El Kantaoui, the idea being that he would use it as a base for his Christmas holiday. As far as Peter the captain knew, that was where they were heading, until that evening that is. However that particular evening Peter had already left the yacht for Gibraltar's Main Street when Hirst-Bergan's senior secretary telephoned him. The call was taken by the second officer who immediately despatched one of the stewardesses to find the skipper. As soon as she located Peter, the stewardess, quite out of breath, announced 'London says we're not going to New York.' Peter was flabbergasted and just to make sure that what he had been told was correct he put a call in to Hirst-Bergan's pilot, who confirmed that he had received instructions to be ready to take Hirst-Bergan to Gibraltar early in the morning and that he had heard that Hirst-Bergan was 'intending to go to Madeira'. Still not totally satisfied the skipper telephoned Hirst-Bergan's secretary at his London newsgroup to ascertain whether or not she knew about the change of plan. She said she hadn't heard of anything, so he then decided to call the head office. The switchboard operator there put him through to the top floor but it was well after 10:30 at night and the security guard said everyone had gone home. So he then asked to be put through to Hirst-Bergan's penthouse, but the nightwatch said he was not there. As a last resort the skipper then tried the night news desk at the London Daily Record, Hirst-Bergan's newspaper, but according to them he had not been seen for hours and had not left a forwarding number.

"So Brigadier the plot thickens."

"Damn right it does, so what happened then?"

Sir James continued with the story…

One of the support teams – the communication team – was already out at sea off the Moroccan coast and decided to test their equipment. They quickly zoned in on to the *Lady Mona* tied up at Gibraltar. However as Gibraltar is a supplementary station specifically used by GCHQ and is regularly manned by MI5 and MI6 operators, the *kidon's* communications team had to be very careful not to cause any problems, so they only listened in to some of the skipper's conversation, just enough to know that Hirst-Bergan was going to Madeira.

"I suppose that whilst Hirst-Bergan was in Gibraltar on board the *Lady Mona* the city was spitting blood."

"Yes Brigadier. And whilst he headed off towards the sun and the Canaries, his son was left holding the fort."

At this point the Swiss Bank Corporation was taking a hard line with the media mogul's business empire and in a very terse call to his son, the financial director of the bank threatened that 'unless the bank was paid in full it would call in Scotland Yard's Fraud Squad'. This was the last straw and Kevin, Hirst-Bergan's son, decided to call his father on the yacht advising him that they were now in danger of collapse and owed in excess of £2 billion. He also said that he was unsure how much longer he would be able to stave off their creditors. Hirst-Bergan told him not to worry, 'just keep them at bay for a little while longer and I promise everything will be all right.'

At the time the *kidon* on Gran Canaria waited patiently, whilst out at sea the two boats of their back-up communication team cast an electronic net between the Canary Islands and Madeira intercepting anything and everything.

"So Brigadier, as all this was going on Hirst-Bergan, being the shrewd businessman he was, decided not to rely purely on Mossad for his salvation and turned to Dounev, his link-man to smooth talk Seva and Ivo his criminal partners, into arranging back-up funding for the £400 million he was expecting from Mossad. He knew that if anyone could do it Dounev could, but then there was a problem. Where was Dounev? Where was Mossad? More to the point where was the £400 million rescue package?"

Early in November 1991 the *Lady Mona* arrived at Funchal in Madeira and because it only had a small marina it was necessary for a yacht the size of *Lady Mona* to tie up in the harbour. Once they were safely tied up Hirst-Bergan, accompanied by his second officer, took a taxi to one of the local hotels at which point he ordered his second officer to remain in the taxi whilst he went inside. As Hirst-Bergan had never previously mentioned knowing anyone on the island, or that he had arranged to meet anyone at the local hotel, this proved to be somewhat strange. However he had received a mystery phone call on board the yacht the previous night, so had he arranged to meet whoever the caller was at the hotel? Was the mystery caller one of the back-up team from Mossad? Had he received new instructions concerning the payout he was expecting? Was that why the second officer had to remain outside the hotel whilst Hirst-Bergan entered? The conclusion must be that the mysterious phone call he received on board the yacht came from one of the senior Mossad officers in Tel Aviv who gave him instructions to go to the hotel, and that was the beginning of the sequence of events which was to follow.

Thirty minutes after entering the hotel Hirst-Bergan re-emerged, and without saying a word to the second officer he directed the taxi to take them to a bar where they drank a beer each before returning to the yacht. Once back on board Hirst-Bergan ordered Peter to slip the moorings and head off to the Canary Islands.

In the Gran Canaria port of Las Palmas, a small motorised yacht was prepared to go fishing, with crates of bottled water and food being stowed below decks in the cabin. On deck, wetsuits, air bottles and fishing tackle were already laid out in preparation. On deck there was a small dinghy lashed to the stern of the yacht with a small powerful outboard motor that had been fitted with baffles to reduce its sound. Sails furled and using its motor, the vessel made its way out of port. The day of the *kidon* had begun.

Over the horizon sat the two communication units who had now cast their electronic nets over the Canary Islands. One unit had isolated and locked on to the *Lady Mona's* radio frequency and the cell could tell which frequency was being used for international telephone calls, and that Peter was using the VHF channel 9 to call up the local coast station and for ship to shore communication. Through their laptop computer it had been a very simple matter for the two-man cell to establish the *Lady Mona's* precise position.

On the 4th November the *Lady Mona* had company as she cruised southwards from Santa Cruz in Tenerife towards Los Cristianos. The *kidon* yacht – flying no flag and displaying no name board was its constant companion and never far away. On board one of the team was crouched over a short wave radio listening for the next short burst of transmission from either of the two support craft. The last message the *kidon* cell had received was that the *Lady Mona* had filed a traffic report stating that she was setting 'a southerly course from Santa Cruz to Los Cristianos with an estimated cruising time of eleven hours that would take them through the night'. The communication cell advised the *kidon* cell that the *Lady Mona* would cruise 'through some of the most deserted and loneliest waters in the region and that boat traffic would not begin to increase until they were approaching Los Cristianos'. Just after 11:00 p.m. Hirst-Bergan called the bridge and spoke to Peter telling him to notify him before putting any further calls through. Approximately four hours later in the early hours of 5th November, the second officer checked the course and compass settings. All was as it should be with the *Lady Mona* still on her southerly course. Out on her starboard side, at this early hour, a few lights blinked ashore on the island Gran Canaria. The night was darker, as it always was in the pre-dawn. On the deck of the craft that was shadowing the *Lady Mona*, the crew had put aside any pretence that they were fishermen. Soon they would go to work.

At about 4:30 a.m., having checked all was running normally in the engine room, making sure the engines were maintaining a steady rate and the three generators were running at their correct output and not overheating, the second engineer came up onto the aft deck for a breath of fresh air. On reaching the deck he remembered seeing Hirst-Bergan standing only a few feet away in his favourite place – in the blind spot of the security cameras. He was looking out towards the lights of Gran Canaria. At 4:45 a.m. the bridge received a call from Hirst-Bergan telling the second officer that his cabin was too cold and ordered him to turn up the temperature by a 'degree or two'.

A short while after this two figures clad in black wetsuits boarded the *Lady Mona*. The first one aboard was a slim lithesome person, closely followed by a person somewhat thicker set, about five feet seven in height. Without a sound the first person moved quickly into the shadows and waited for the other to get into position beside the owner's cabin door.

Inside Hirst-Bergan's cabin the telephone rang and the bridge advised him that a Rabbi Zvi was on the line calling from Moscow. As the Rabbi was a great friend of his, Hirst-Bergan told the bridge to put him through. As soon as the two *kidon* heard the phone ring, they quietly and slowly opened the cabin door and stealthily crept in unnoticed. Before Hirst-Bergan could utter a sound they overpowered him and the slim lithesome member deftly administered an injection of VX nerve agent. The amount, albeit only 10 milligrams, was sufficient to induce death by asphyxiation.

"And the rest is history as they say."

"Hmm, a good story James, but surely that is pure supposition on your part."

"Well Brigadier, believe it or believe it not, I can assure you it is true."

"Yes, yes, yes. Very good," the Brigadier stated in a matter of fact way. "So if what you're telling me is true…"

"Excuse me for interrupting Brigadier," the steward said as he turned to Sir James and announced the arrival of his guests.

"Shall I direct the young lady and gentlemen through here or would you wish me to take them straight into the dining room Sir James?"

"Oh, through here I think," Sir James allowed a fleeting smile to touch his lips then it was gone. "So you want proof Brigadier?"

"Well you've got to admit it's a bit of a tall story now haven't you?" the Brigadier said as the steward left the room. A moment or two later the steward returned to the lounge accompanied by five people. "Your luncheon guests Sir James."

Sir James immediately stood up as the party of five entered the room, led by a stunningly attractive blonde lady with green eyes. "Now Brigadier allow me to introduce you to some very interesting people, this young lady is Mrs Trepashkin, Major General Svetlana Trepashkin of the Russian KGB, and this is Svetlana's husband Colonel Mikhail Trepashkin." Sir James introduced a man of average height and build with fair hair. "Before she married Mikhail, Svetlana's maiden name was Zaslavsky, although she has also been known as Svetlana Ilyinsky, Cheryl Brook, Sheri White, Natasha Yeltsin and various other names," Sir James allowed another smile to briefly touch his lips as he noted the expression on the Brigadier's face as the penny seemed to drop. Svetlana gave the elderly Brigadier a charming smile as he got up out of his chair. "Pleased to meet you Brigadier."

"No not at all, the honour is mine young lady."

"Pleased to meet you Brigadier," echoed Mikhail.

"And you too young man."

"Now allow me to introduce you to these gentlemen Brigadier," Sir James first of all indicated the two Jewish gentlemen from Mossad. "This is Amir and his colleague Uzi and finally Brigadier," he beckoned to the remaining individual, a man of about five feet seven and of average build, "this is our man. This is Richard James, a very talented young man indeed. Now if you would excuse us Brigadier our lunch is waiting."

"Oh yes, yes of course Sir James, enjoy your meal."

"Thank you Brigadier we will." Then in a low conspiratorial voice he added, "by the way, do you think Hirst-Bergan jumped or was he pushed?" Sir James winked and smiled at the wily old Brigadier as he and his guests took their leave of him and headed towards the dining room for their lunch.